A

SECRET

ASSIGNMENT

By

Leighton Harding

Copyright 2013

All rights reserved. No part of this publication may be reproduced or transmitted in any form or by any means, electronic or mechanical, including photocopying, recording, or any information storage system without either prior permission in writing from the author, publisher or a licence permitting and restricting copying.

The right of Leighton Harding to be identified as the author of this work has been asserted by him in accordance with the Copyright, Designs and Patents Act 1983.

> This is a work of fiction.
> Copyright 2015

Authors Note

Charts and Maps are provided at the end of the novel. It is suggested on Kindle that you use the Go to: Using the Menu button and then clicking down to End of Book to view.

CHARTS & MAPS

Boston

Boston to Camden

Penobscot Bay

Camden

Bermuda

North Coast of Spain

Battle of Vimeiro

Battle of Roliça

For details of Rigs, Uniforms, Instruments, Terms, etc Visit WWW.leightonharding.com

A Secret Assignment

Chapter 1

The merchant vessel *Mount Edgecome's* bowsprit and beak head rose into the air, hovered and then plunged into the Atlantic rollers. The sprit seemed to linger as if trying to collect as much seawater as possible to throw back across the deck. When it finally lifted, a great deluge of water and foam was thrown back, swirling around the legs of the gun's crew on the starboard side. The seaman paid no attention to the water around their feet as they worked the 12 lb cannon into its firing position. This was not the merchant ship's gun crew; this was a Royal Navy gun crew with their recoil-team. Because they were exercising, so not firing the gun, another gun-crew termed the recoil crew, hauled back the cannon on its carriage as fast as possible to simulate the recoil of a fired gun. The ship's merchant seaman watched from the shelter of *Mount Edgecome's* forecastle. The *Mount Edgecome* was carrying a Navy crew across the Atlantic for the newly built schooner *Hound*.

Up on the poop deck of the merchantman, Commodore Sir William Calvert Bart and the new ship's future captain Commander Craddock watched the crews exercise. The *Hound* had been ordered by the Commodore to be built by the North American boat builders who had constructed his first command, the schooner *Snipe*. The new schooner had been paid for with prize money won by the Commodore, as well as the quite considerable amount that he had been paid resulting from his successful secret capture of two Spanish bullion ships. The gold and jewels would otherwise have gone to help pay Napoleon's army and navy. King George had been so delighted that he had ennobled Will.

They were halfway across the Atlantic, which at this latitude should have been moderately calm. Neptune had decided that the storms to the north should continue to affect the seas to the south. There was only one gun crew on deck today. There were four gun crews; one for each of the four long barrelled 18lb cannons that Hound would mount when completed. The crews took it in turns to exercise against the clock. The fastest team, including the recoil team were awarded an extra tot of rum at the end of the week. It was not the only routine of the day. Everybody, including the officers had to run backwards and forwards along the deck as fast as they could to keep fit. The topmen had to climb the merchantman's rigging and down again against the clock. In the hold below, there rested four long barrelled 18lb cannons on specially designed carriages, eighteen 20 lb carronades, together with powder and shot for the guns. Added to the cargo were sheets of Welsh copper for the new schooner's bottom,

Will and Craddock descended to the upper deck and made their way to the passengers' lounge where the other officers were sitting about reading or writing. All had served with Will before, either on the schooner *Snipe* or aboard the frigate *Optimist*. Henri de Cornes, the French Aristocrat Surgeon looked up and smiled as his friend walked in. He had been with Will since they had both joined *Snipe*. Across from him, the massive frame of Chief Boatswain Tarrant seemed to swamp the chair he sat on, totally absorbed in scrimshaw work with a hot needle. Behind him Lieutenant Kemp, once a Merchant Master, and then a Navy Master's Mate before being promoted, was studying a thick work on tides. Through the far door, Lieutenant Thomas Tucker came in fresh from timing the gun crew. Thomas had been Will's servant aboard the Frigate *Artful,* and had been taught seamanship and navigation, by Will. This had helped him to become a Midshipman and then to be promoted to Lieutenant. The absent First Lieutenant was an ex *Optimist* officer, Oscar Cranfield, who was at that moment seeing to his crew forward. It was a close-knit team, who trusted each other implicitly. The crew up forward were all volunteers who had been handpicked by Will. There were no Midshipmen as Will had decided they were not necessary until the schooner returned to England.

The Admiralty had been instructed by Viscount Castlereagh, the Minister for War, to charter the new schooner to the Aliens Office. They in turn asked that Commodore Calvert to be able to use his own ship, under Instruction from the Admiralty, assigned to the dangerous shores of Northern Spain. The Aliens Office was the cover for Britain's spy network during the war against Napoleon. They had intelligence that Napoleon was going to march an army across north Spain to invade Portugal in order to deny Britain the use of the Portuguese ports and naval vessels.

The north coast of Spain faces the Bay of Biscay, with a fearsome reputation for its on-shore gales. Especially in winter, square-rigged ships would have immense problems trying to beat their way from a rugged lee shore. The schooner with her fore and aft rig and her speed would be ideally suited to the mission. Added to that, Commodore Calvert was already well respected for his secret missions on behalf of the nation.

Will went to his cabin and sat down to write up his

journal, something he had always done from a young boy of 12, when he first went to sea. The journal not only contained details of the position, and the sea state, but also had drawings of the essences (clouds) in the sky and estimations of wave height and wind force. Having written it up, he turned to adding to the epistle that was a letter to his wife Isabella and his child. Isabella had announced before he had left that she was expecting his second child. Will added each day to the letter, so that when they finally reached land, it would be up-to-date. Having completed his tasks, he joined the rest of his officers ready for their midday meal.

Chapter 2

The *Mount Edgecombe* would put into Boston to victual and take on water. Captain Grey had visited the port before and had charts from the War of Independence to help him. However, he had no up-to-date information on the tides to found around the entrance to the bay. His navigation skills had been excellent. When they sighted land, it was to confirm it was Cape Cod. Because of the tides, they had to luff up for the night and wait for dawn some ten miles off Point Allerton. Then it was a cautious approach across the Hunt Ledge to the narrow passages to the port.

Will with Craddock and Henri, stayed on the poop keeping out of the way. The on-shore breeze continued to blow for their benefit. About a cable and a half later, the helm was put up and they altered to a more northwesterly point, which would take them between Gallop Island and Lovell Island. The islands were rocky with scrubby trees and vegetation, as well as signs of gun emplacements. This channel was very narrow, and it was lucky that they had no need to beat. You felt as if you could almost reach out and touch either side. The *Mount Edgecombe* continued on this course heading towards Deer Island.

Captain Grey called up to them. "Entering the main channel to the harbour. We shall anchor off and wait and see what happens."

Straight ahead of them, they could see a Fort standing proud on an islet guarding the entrance to Boston itself. All around the land was verdant green with a cloudless blue sky reflected on the water. After about two and a half miles, they passed the Fort to starboard and a rocky island to larboard before starting to reduce sail and alter course slightly to starboard before dropping their anchor. Will was proud to see that members of his crew were helping the crew of the *Mount Edgecombe*.

So here they were lying off Boston Harbour. Will and all the officers of *Hound* were in civilian clothes. They had been forbidden by Will to wear their naval uniforms. The uniforms had all been stowed below decks. Their 'civvies' were allowed to be similar to those worn by merchant officers. At this point, only Tarrant was wearing anything resembling a nautical look. His was in a plain blue reefer jacket with plain buttons.

Since nothing seemed to be happening, although they were in plain sight of the harbour and other ships, the group on the poop went below to the passenger lounge. Here Will and Henri were joined by a strange member of the passengers. He was a Basque schoolteacher who had fled Spain accused of inciting his pupils to join the separatist movement. He hated the government of Madrid. He felt that with their own language and culture, the Basque people should rule themselves. He had fled to Portugal, and seeing an English ship had asked to be taken to that country. He spoke very little English, just Spanish, French and of course Euskera, the language of the Basque people. The Aliens Office had found him and was now paying him to teach Will and Henri the Spanish and Euskera languages. The latter was incredibly difficult. The language had no 'the' or 'a', nor adverbs. All the way across the Atlantic Will and Henri had spent four hours a day studying. Will had also set aside one hour a day, to teach Boatswain Tarrant the skills of navigation. He was determined to make it possible for his faithful boatswain to make the giant leap to 'upper deck'. He would make an ideal Master and this would mean that he could earn far more money. Such a promotion would make it possible for him to seek a wife at last.

It was a good four hours before there was any sign of anybody ashore coming out to enquire why the *Mount Edgecombe* was anchored off. Finally, a longboat appeared from behind the ships tied up to the quay and gradually made its way towards them. It was Lieutenant Tucker, who spied it from the windows of the lounge and drew the rest of the assembly's attention to its progress. Finally, it came clumsily alongside and a tall thin gaunt faced man climbed up the rope ladder and hauled himself over the bulwarks. There was no hint of a smile when he was met by *Mount Edgecombe's* First Mate.

"Welcome to America!" Said Will; pithily watching the proceedings.

"Bundle of fun!" Agreed Henri; watching beside Will through the open doorway.

The newcomer disappeared, obviously being escorted to Captain Grey's cabin.

Nothing happened, so bored with waiting, they returned to their places, and continued to do what they had been doing before. The lounge was quite small for the numbers present, but at least contained armchairs and low side tables as well as the dining table that took up the centre of the space. Off to either side were the small cabins for the passengers. Being a merchant ship each cabin had a window, so were light and airy. Will had long since forgotten to notice the terrible patterned covers to the seating. He had made sure though that there was adequate wine and spirits to keep his officers happy. Extra rum had been delivered at Plymouth, so that the merchant crew did not feel jealous of their naval passengers.

The *Mount Edgecombe* was anchored in 5 fathoms about a cable off the port. The town was on what was virtually an island joined by a causeway to the south. Two piers thrust out towards where the ship lay. Beyond the northern pier was a quay that disappeared around the corner. Beyond that across a strip of water was what appeared to be a new part of the town. Between the piers was a further quay with beyond to the south, a fort with its cannons poking out. Everywhere ships of various sizes and rigs were tied up. There would have been no room for *Mount Edgecome* alongside, even if they had wished to load. As it was, Captain Grey had informed Will that he would anchor and get the victuals brought out. That meant there was no chance of fraternization by the crew.

When the Boston official finally took his leave, he appeared to be slightly 'sailing close to the wind'. He had to be assisted over the side. Captain Grey entered the lounge to inform the assembled that he thought all had gone well, and that they could hope to be re-victualled within a few days. A few days meant in fact four days, before the flat-bottomed barges were towed out and loading could take place. Captain Grey had explained to the official that he was en-route to Canada and was dropping off a few passengers at Camden on the way. Camden was where the schooner *Snipe* had been built and was some a hundred and seventy miles to the North in the bay of Penobscot. They were further delayed when under a clear sky a white mist appeared to the east. Both Grey and Will knew what this meant. Fog - fog that rolled in from the sea, and could be so thick that it was difficult see the end of the bowsprit from the quarterdeck.

Chapter 3

Three days after re-victualling had been completed the fog finally lifted. The *Mount Edgecombe* hauled up her anchor and in a light breeze beat her way out to sea. After rounding the end of Deer Island, the ship was able to turn her bows to the north. Their course took them NE to clear Thatcher Island off Rockport and the Savages, a group of low-lying rocks that had seen a number of ships end their days upon their savage teeth. From here, it was a steady run NNE. Grey kept well clear of what was a lee shore in case the fog returned. You could just make out a smudge of land on the larboard side. Because of failing light, Captain Grey decided to turn and head out to sea and to wait for a new dawn.

This was a wise decision, because Penobscot Bay has some dangerous rocks just at the entrance. Captain Grey had decided to enter by the northern approach, which meant that when they picked out Matinicus Island, and then closer in, Seal Island; he knew where to proceed. To the north of them as they approached the entrance to the bay, they could clearly see the uninviting rocky foreshore. Once inside the bay, they could identify the islands off

Owl's Head. As they progressed, the low cliff of a headland came into view. The land behind was comparatively low lying with only low hills, covered in trees of all types. As they passed the headland, a small settlement came into view on the larboard bow, which Grey indentified as Rockland, from the map sent to Will by the boatyard. Straight ahead of them was Camden with a hill standing out slightly higher than those behind.

The future crew of the new schooner were clustered up in the bows, whilst the officers kept out of the way on the poop. There drawn up on the shore, clearly standing above everything else was a sleek black hull with three raked masts thrusting up towards the sky. Captain Grey, the Master of the *Mount Edgecombe* gave the order and the bower anchor was let go. Once satisfied that the anchor was holding and that everything was 'ship-shape' he ascended to the poop. He knew Will from old. He had been second mate on Will's father's ship when Will had first gone to sea. The *Mount Edgecome* by a strange chance had once belonged to the fleet of merchant vessels part owned by Will's father. Will had sold his holding to buy his estate overlooking the Dart.

"Well there she be!" Commented Grey; gesturing towards the shore.

"Aye." Replied Will; still admiring the graceful lines. The *Hound* was still up on the slipway. The copper sheets had still to be added before she could take to the water.

They were anchored some 1½ cables (approx. 300 yards) from both the north shore and south shore in 10 fathoms. You could see clearly into the narrow bay. The boatyard was right at the end of the bay on the southern side with a wooden jetty thrusting out. Up on the slips the schooner sat dominating everything around her. In contrast to Boston, here a skiff was on its way out from the pier, even as the anchor found the bottom. To the south of the yard low white painted lap-faced houses painted a refreshing white gave the whole scene a welcoming aspect. Behind the village, low hills covered in trees of every variety provided a green backdrop. To the north of the village, Mount Battie dominated the surroundings.

"Hi there!" Called a man sitting in the back of the two-oared skiff. He was still some way off, but he was smiling broadly. As the skiff turned and came smartly alongside, the man leapt for the rope ladder and was up it in no time.

"Mr. Calvert?" He asked.

Will walked forward arm outstretched to this welcoming figure.

"McKay." Said the man. He was of average height with sandy coloured hair and a square chin. His eyes were bright and intelligent.

"I am Calvert." Said Will; ignoring titles.

"Oh! Strike me! I clean forgot. Sir William Calvert. That's right isn't it?"

Will laughed. The man exuded such warmth, it was difficult not to.

Will turned towards his officers, and with a sweeping gesture introduced them. "Captain Grey the master of this ship, Mr. Craddock, who is my captain, his first mate Mr. Cranfield, My old friend Henri de Cornes, second mate Mr. Kemp, fourth mate Mr. Tucker, and the boatswain Mr. Tarrant."

"Delighted to meet you all! Welcome to Camden; home to the finest vessels afloat. Even if I do say so myself! Your schooner is all but ready. I take it you have brought those copper sheets you were so insistent were to be fitted. We don't usually do that here; not having the copper. I imagine you can't wait to see the little beauty?"

"She looks very fine from here!" Commented Will; looking out at his new investment.

"Biggest we have built, and though I say it myself, I think she is the best yet. Glad we settled on three masts. Much easier to handle, and you need less crew. Might I suggest you, Sir, come back with me, and that the good Captain...err, Grey, brings this fine vessel up alongside the pier. We are blessed with plenty of depth."

"Aye, I'll do that." Said Grey; immediately giving orders for the capstan to be manned, and the boats to be lowered and manned.

Will followed McKay over the side and joined him on the narrow seat at the stern of the skiff. It was obvious it could not hold any more.

As the two oarsmen lay to their oars, Will asked. "When did you come here?"

"My father settled here ages ago when he first came over from Scotland. He was a master shipwright who wanted to start his own business. He reasoned that he had to be where the timber was, and that is here. They float the lumber down from Bangor. They have an amazing assortment of trees to choose from up there. He laid down a vast supply to season. We used much of his original timber on yon *Hound* there. Each year we build up a bigger supply. You can see the woodpiles stacked behind the yard. My father still keeps an eye on it, and I now run it."

"It is certainly a beautiful area." Said Will; gazing about him. "Much game?"

"Oh aye; plenty of birds and fish to be had. Most of our schooners are for fishing in the Atlantic. They need to be fast to get their catch back first for the best prices. Ours are fast, so we have a nice line of orders. Yours tickled our fancy. Tell me, how did you get on with *Snipe* ?

"She was my first command....when I was in the Navy." Will added hastily. "I was instructed to arm her and use her against the invasion craft that the French were assembling on the North Coast of France. Being fore and aft rigged, I couldn't see how she could fare, her guns would be pointing at the sky or the bottom all the time. I decided to try fitting her with cannons mounted in the bows and stern, reckoning that they would always be, as near as possible, parallel with the surface. It worked brilliantly. *Snipe* was incredibly fast so we could out manoeuvre square-rigged ships. We even managed to outdo a French privateer frigate and bring it back for prize money."

"Wow! So what is *Hound* for? The same again?"

"Not if I can help it! Too valuable! No, I decided that I would go back to being an owner: However, I wanted a vessel that would handle the Bay of Biscay, so I could import Port Wine from Portugal and Brandy... illicitly...you understand, from France. We might be at war, but the rulers of our nation still demand their brandies!"

McKay shot a sideways glance at Will and laughed. "Got you!"

By now, they were close enough to study the lines of the schooner. She was stern first to the water, so her double bank of stern windows reflected the sunlight. The carving around the windows was of the highest quality.

"Who did the carving?" Asked Will.

"Frenchman – Philippe. Didn't want to serve under Napoleon. Preferred the old regime. More work, you understand. I pinched him on a visit to Boston. He was looking for employment and I heard about him...so!"

"Good thinking!"

The skiff's oarsmen threw their oars in time-honoured style and the skiff slid alongside the jetty close to the shore. A floating pontoon meant that you could exit the skiff easily before having to climb a ladder up the side of the jetty. Standing at the top, Will was able to take in the full beauty of the schooner. Sleek lines, slightly raked masts and a proud bowsprit all added to the impression of speed, even whilst she was supported by props ashore.

"Philippe is still working on the figure head, he

wasn't satisfied it conveyed enough 'esprit de corps'; McKay said."

They passed under the thrusting razor sharp bows to find a ladder propped up against the far side.

"Henry, this is Sir William, the owner." McKay said to the backside of a fellow crouched under the keel. The man backed out and straightened up. He was pencil thin with receding hair brushed across and bagged into a queue. He rubbed his hands on his overalls and put out a hand to shake Will's.

"Henry is my foreman. He is a perfectionist. Slows things down a bit, but the end result is worth it!" Added McKay.

Henry grinned sheepishly, and bowed his head.

"She looks very fine, thank you." Commented Will; to the man's obvious pleasure.

The black hull shone in the sunlight. Will had never seen such a glossy finish. When he remarked upon it, McKay roared with laughter.

"I was in Boston, and saw a rich merchant's coach. I thought what a fine finish it had, so I followed the thing back to where it dropped off the owner. Then I was able to ask the coachman if he knew who had built it. He told me the builder's name, and the address. I hurried round there and thought to enquire, when at the last moment I stopped myself. Instead, I waited until the workers started to go home. I asked if there was a painter amongst them. That was wrong for a start! A finisher was what I needed apparently. Anyway, I found a finisher and asked him how much he was paid. I then offered him twice the wage and the cost of moving his family up north. The man had to ask the wife, so we went back to his place. Twice the wage: a house of their own. No contest! She immediately started packing!" McKay chuckled at the memory.

Will ran his hand across the silky finish. Henry, the Foreman, went to the bottom of the ladder and held it steady for both Will and McKay to climb up safely. As Will's eyes passed the top of the highly varnished bulwarks, he was able to get his first glimpse of the deck. It looked as if it had been already 'holy-stoned' for years; it was pristine. The running rigging was neatly stowed. Everywhere the varnish shone, reflecting the brilliant sunlight. Three great booms lay in their cradles waiting to be lifted by new sails to the wind. Up forward the modest forecastle did not ruin the lines as Will had worried it might. He walked forward followed by both McKay and his Foreman.

Under the forecastle, there was just enough headroom for a gunner to operate his cannons. The low bulwark would just come to the lowest height of an elevated long barrelled 18lb cannon. Strolling aft Will touched and examined everything, from pintles to the capstan. He imagined where the belfry should be, but that would have given the whole game away. The double wheel had a generous binnacle in front of it. Two compasses were already installed. Further aft, they entered Will's private quarters.

"As instructed, we haven't put in any partitions." Commented McKay. Will had specially asked that they be left out. The reason was that when they reached Bermuda, the cannons would be off-loaded from the *Mount Edgecombe*. At that time, the two stern chasers would be hidden between double partitions. It would hide the fact that *Hound* was a warship. A bulkhead to the forecastle would also hide the bow chasers. The two large round hawser holes, normally capped, would disguise the two cannons' muzzles. The insignificant 12lbs lining the sides would be expected. No ship at that warlike time could be expected to go unarmed.

Will's private quarters were bright and filled with sunlight. The canvas flooring was painted in black and white squares. There were windows extending right across the stern and round to halfway back along the sides, except for where the quarter gallery doors were situated. The deck head was painted white to give it the feeling it was higher than it was in reality. Will was of average height so his head just passed below the beams. Henri would have to stoop in here. There was no furniture, nor any cushions on the window seat. They were all aboard the *Mount Edgecombe.*

They returned to the ladderway and descended to the deck below. Here looking forward, one could glimpse the essential stove for the cook, whilst down the centre were the tables and benches for the crew. Above them between the masts were generous skylights. Every beam had ample hooks for the crews' hammocks.

McKay noticed Will looking critically at the skylights.

"It's alright Sir William, we have provided wooden covers."

Will smiled. "Appreciated!"

Behind the ladderway, the bulkhead divided the wardroom from the rest of the crew's quarters. There were two doors, one either side of the mizzenmast. Will opened the larboard side door and found himself in a delightfully finished officers' area. To the stern was the wardroom with a window matching that above, except at the very quarter where there were doors to enclosed quarter galleries, or officers' heads. Forward of the wardroom on either side as far as the bulkhead, were cabins, each with a window. These windows could if necessary, be used as gun ports. Returning to the crews' quarters McKay lifted a long deck plank placed in the centre running fore and aft. Below, a narrow box came right up to the plank.

"Something extra for you: Sir William!" Said McKay; straightening up.

"A centre plate?"

"Aye; we have experimented with the idea and thought we would add it as a gift from us for ordering the largest schooner ever built around here."

"My thanks! But might I ask why?"

"It means you can sail straighter when close-hauled. It could give you an edge. My father and I built a small version to try. It works exceedingly well. I shall show you when you have settled in."

Will nodded his thanks as he gazed down at the metal plate that sat in the box. Square trunking rose from the back where the plank had been lifted. This obviously contained the tackle for raising and lowering the plate.

"Bit like a Schanke."

"I've heard of them, but never seen one".

"Very good for shallow water!"

Next McKay lifted a hatch in the deck to the side of the centre plate. He jumped down into the bilges. There was room for him to move about doubled up.

"See here; we have built in baffle boards to stop the ballast from moving about. It also helps with stowing anything down here. I can see you are surprised at how much more space there is down here. It is just that everything is on a much larger scale than you would have found on *Snipe*."

At 130 feet in length, the *Hound* was longer than most of the sixth rate frigates in the British Navy. She was though considerably slimmer, which would give her that extra speed, combined with the completely different hull design. Frigates were designed to be gun platforms as well as sailing vessels. The schooner was designed solely for speed.

They finished inspecting every corner of the new ship. There was very little that Will could find wrong. He decided to keep any small adjustments to later. They returned to the upper deck to witness the *Mount Edgecombe* being towed to the jetty. Will noticed that his crew was mixed with that of the *Mount Edgecombe* manning the cutters. A skiff from the yard was towing out a rope from the jetty, where a crowd of shipwrights waited to help warp the ship alongside. Will and McKay stood side by side watching the proceedings. When the ship was safely berthed, they could see a column of men leaving the ship and walking down the jetty. In the lead was Craddock followed by his officers and then the rest of the crew. All were smartly dressed. The crew, in their best rig of dark blue jersey over wide white canvas trousers strolled chatting to each other as if going to a party.

"Damned smart crew!" Remarked McKay.

Will felt a surge of pride. Every man was a volunteer and in the Royal Navy, that was something of a record in itself.

The column left the jetty and turned to walk around the bow of *Hound* as she sat propped ready for her copper bottom. Craddock's head emerged over the side of the bulwark. "Permission to come aboard?"

Both Will and McKay turned to each other expecting the other to agree. Then they both laughed.

"I haven't officially taken over the ship, so she is still technically yours." Said Will.

McKay turned back to the waiting Craddock.

"Permission granted for you and your crew."

"Many thanks!" Replied Craddock; straddling the bulwarks and dropping down to the deck. He moved aside to let Cranfield follow, but was already sweeping his eyes over the deck and up the masts. When the huge form of Tarrant appeared over the side, he knuckled his brow, then turned and gazed up; taking time to check each mast.

"Satisfied?" Asked McKay.

Tarrant turned towards him, a stern look on his rugged face. "Amazing!" was all he said, returning his gaze to the masts once more. Then he strode off forward, fingering the belaying pins, testing the halliards and plucking the ratlines.

"A perfectionist!" Commented Will.

"I can tell!" Responded McKay. "Your Boatswain? Been with you a long time?"

"Absolutely! The finest seaman I have ever come across. The crew worship him!"

By this time, a steady stream of *Hound's* crew had come aboard and were investigating everything.

"Mr. Tarrant!" Called Will. The big man turned immediately. "The crew are allowed anywhere today; that includes my quarters and the officers' quarters."

"Aye, Sir! Hear that boys. Sir William says you can even check out the officers' wardroom. But be warned, there are no spirits aboard!"

There were derisive catcalls, all in good fun, and the Boatswain beamed back.

Craddock came up to them as they stood by the wheel. "A fine job, if I may be so bold. A very pretty ship!"

"Think you can handle her?" Asked McKay; with a big smile.

"Rather!" Relied Craddock.

Tarrant came aft to join them, a huge grin on his face.

"Mr. McKay has given us an extra. She has a lifting plate in her keel, like a Shanke. It is so she won't fall off when sailing close to the wind." Will said. Tarrant looked dumbfounded.

Chapter 4

McKay insisted that *Hound's* officers joined him and his wife for dinner.

"But that will mean eight of us!" Cried Will; when asked.

"We know! That's nothing around here. My wife started preparing directly she saw your ship come into the bay."

"How did she know it was us?" Asked Will.

"Obvious! A strange ship making straight for Camden. That had to be you lot."

As they were leaving *Hound,* Allwood, Will's coxswain, sidled up to Craddock. "No boats!" He said quietly, but Will overheard and so did McKay.

"Never you threat. They are being built down at Rockport, next bay down the Sound. It is ...what? A mile and a half, only. They are finishing the paintwork. We don't make anything that small, so we leave it to them. They concentrate on turning out some of the finest small craft along the entire coast. You will be able to go over and pick them up in a few days." McKay said. Allwood knuckled his forehead and joined the queue to go over the side.

"My Coxswain." Explained Will.

"Also the senior quartermaster." Added Craddock.

"Very keen!" Commented McKay as he stood aside to let both Craddock and Will climb down the steps before him.

"I'll come and fetch you." Said McKay; as they parted company.

The birds were still singing in the trees, and various insects seemed to be trying to join the chorus as Will and his officers, including Henri de Cornes stepped down from the jetty to join Mr. McKay.

"Lovely afternoon!" Commented Craddock.

"Yes, great. This is a lovely time of year. We do have a problem with fog. It comes rolling in from the ocean and you can't see your own hand."

"Yes we were delayed in Boston because of fog." Replied Craddock.

"Captain Grey not joining us?" Asked McKay.

"No; he sent his apologises. He prefers to stay on

his ship at all times when possible in a foreign port. It is difficult to make absolutely sure you don't lose members of your crew otherwise."

"Ah! Very wise! Do you have that problem?"

"Sometimes when there are females ashore, who might take a shine to our lads, it has been known!"

"To be sure, all are safely locked up! Especially the daughters!" Laughed McKay.

McKay's house was an imposing wood fronted villa set back, but overlooking the harbour. There was a delightful porch running the whole width of the house, its roof supported by graceful pillars of wood. Wide steps led up to the porch and front door with its netted windows. A small front plot behind a white painted picket fence boasted an array of colourful flowers.

McKay led the way up the steps and on opening the door called out. "Florence, we're here."

A petite middle-aged women with light blonde hair tied back in a bun, came smiling to meet them.

"Do come in!" She cried, wiping her hands on a cloth, then pulling off the apron she wore over a flowered print dress.

They were in a room that spread either side to the

far walls with a staircase facing the front door. It was furnished with comfortable soft cushioned chairs. There was no pretence about the room; it was a family room.

"You get the drinks dear, will you? Do sit down gentlemen; we don't stand on ceremony here." Mrs. McKay cried with a little nervous laugh.

All the officers waited until Will had lowered himself into a Windsor rocker facing the fireplace. Then they found themselves a seat each. McKay came to stand in front of the mantelpiece.

"Right gentlemen, what's your poison. Here we have virtually everything. We, here in Maine are partial to a drink or two. We have rum, we have wine; we have Applejack, which is a brandy distilled from cider; very tasty. Beer, cider....". He petered out, looking hopefully around his guests.

Will knew he was expected speak first. "I think I might try a small glass of your Applejack."

"Coming up...any more takers?" At least half the company decided to follow Will's lead.

"We don't have much luck in wine making. The early settlers brought over vines, but they didn't take. More recently down south, they have tried with native vines. Quite palatable, though I say it myself. I propose to poison you with some, to go with the food." He gave a chuckle and disappeared. There was an awkward silence as each of them looked about.

McKay was soon back with tumblers of Applejack and rum for the others.

"A toast!" Said McKay; raising his glass. "*Hound*!"

"*Hound*!" Was the chorus.

The Applejack was surprisingly smooth, and Will decided to sip slowly. He did not want to disgrace himself in front of his crew.

Lieutenant Thomas Tucker nearly fell off his stool. His mouth was open and he had a silly expression. Will turned to see the cause. There just stepping of the bottom step of the stairs was a very attractive young lady. She had a sweet smile, which turned to laughter when she saw Thomas.

"This is my daughter Annabelle. These are the officers from *Hound*." Said McKay: pride written all over his face. "Sir William, will you do the honours?"

"Certainly!" Said Will; who was already standing, as were the others. May I introduce the Captain of my ship, Commander James Craddock, his First Lieutenant Oscar Cranfield, the second Lieutenant Anthony Kemp, the third Lieutenant Thomas Tucker, Mr. Tarrant, our Boatswain and last but by no means least Henri de Cornes our distinguished surgeon."

Annabelle McKay made a little courtesy. "Gentlemen."

"I hope my son will be able to join us shortly. He is away on an errand for the yard." Stated McKay.

At that moment, Mrs. McKay entered the room, smiled at her daughter, and accepted a glass of something from her husband. Will noticed that Annabelle did not drink.

"Do sit down, please." Mrs. McKay swept a generous smile around the company and they resumed their seats, except for Thomas who pushed his stool towards Annabelle. She gave him a ravishing smile and sat down with gentile poise. Thomas' flushed features told their own story. Will estimated that Annabelle must be aged around sixteen years or so. She had a good figure and a very lovely complexion. The officers were eyeing her with interest.

Neither McKay, nor Mrs. McKay seemed the slightest bit worried about the effect their daughter was having on sex-starved mariners.

"Are you married Sir William? Asked Florence McKay, but it was said without artifice.

"Aye Madam. Lady Calvert is expecting our second child."

"How wonderful!" Expressed Mrs. McKay: clapping her hands together. "And your officers?"

"As far as I am aware, Madam, none of my officers are married!"

Mrs. McKay raised an eyebrow and giggled. "Very droll, Sir!"

Chapter 5

Whether it was the drink, or the presence of Ladies, nobody would know, but the conversation began to become more animated as the officers grew more used to their surroundings. Both Annabelle and Mrs. McKay made their apologises; and disappeared. Then after a few minutes, the front door opened and in strode a tall well-built young man who had to be McKay's son. The resemblance was marked.

"Hi!" He said; which must be the usual greeting in those parts.

"My son Esmond." Said McKay; by way of introduction. "This is Sir William Calvert." Indicating Will, who rose to greet the newcomer. The young man was formerly introduced to each officer by way of them giving their name and their merchant rank.

Then a pair of doors to the side slid open. Will was intrigued; he had never seen doors that slid back into the wall before.

"Dinner is served Gentlemen!" Cried Mrs. McKay. McKay led the way indicating where each person should sit. Will was placed on Mrs. McKay's left with Henri opposite. At the far end, McKay had Craddock and Tarrant either side of him. In the centre on both sides facing each other were the siblings with Tucker next to Annabelle and Kemp next to Esmond. Two male servants entered with trays of soup to be distributed. The wine was poured from cut-glass decanters, with both red and white available.

Florence McKay was very intrigued to find that Henri was a Surgeon and French. He had remained very quiet as usual, but she soon drew him out. In the centre of the table, Tucker was telling the young McKays the story of *Snipe* under Will's command

and how they came to be prisoners of the French and how he and Henri had managed to escape with Will's most precious instruments and journals. At the far end of the table, the conversation seemed to centre on sailing techniques.

There was a fish course to follow which included locally caught lobster, then for the main course there was a succulent ham with local vegetables. It was very different from the fare at sea. To finish there was a tart of blueberries, which none of the English had ever tasted before. At the end of the meal, the Ladies retired and left the men to enjoy Applejack Brandy and cigars. It was a memorable introduction to American hospitality.

Later back aboard the *Mount Edgecombe,* Will suggested tactfully that Craddock had a word with Thomas. There could be no mileage in any flirtation or romance. They were at war, and expected to continue to serve their country. He did not want Thomas to be enticed away. He was too necessary to their future operations.

As it turned out, it was un-necessary. Annabelle did not appear again. The officers and crew remained on the *Mount Edgecombe* directing the ship's crew in unloading the copper sheets. These were hoisted up from the hold, placed on trolleys, and rolled down ramps that had been erected from the jetty to the shore. These trolleys were then manhandled around to either side of the schooner.

Hound's future carpenter, Mr. Money, supervised the fitting of the sheets by the yard workers. It was the first time they had handled the metal, but not Money's. It took a week for the sheets to be fitted. Whilst the final sheets were put in place, other yard workers under the eagle eye of Mr. McKay prepared the launching skids. This was a great cradle constructed to hold the vessel in position whilst the ship was launched. The cradle sat on greased timbers that ran down to the water. Where the high water mark ended, the slip continued into the water as flat smooth blocks of rock. The whole structure was held firmly in place by hawsers, which rested on wooden blocks.

Some of *Hound's* crew were detailed off to carry Will's furniture round and to hoist it aboard. It included a fine carpet that was a present from Isabella. Other members of the crew carried the cook's implements, as well as the extra items so necessary for sea. Just days before the launch, a group of workers arrived and erected scaffolding at the bows. Then a tall thin figure appeared with some others wheeling a trolley towards *Hound*. Esmond came to find Will and Craddock and invited them to inspect the new figurehead before it was mounted into position. The figure was covered by a canvas sheet when they found it. Philippe, the sculptor dragged the sheet aside with flourish. There, ready to pounce, was the crafted head of a hound, paws out as if in chase. To Will's, surprise it was painted very realistically.

"I hope you approve?" Came the voice of the Yard owner. Will turned to find McKay standing behind him; beside him his daughter.

"It is very fine!" Said Will, impressed.

"My daughter painted it." Said McKay quietly. Obviously proud of her.

"I can't believe how you managed to get the hair so right. The paint work and carving are brilliant." Said Craddock.

Indeed if you stepped back, it actually looked like the real thing. A hound in full chase, one front paw slightly bent, the other thrust out. A red tongue hung to the side of the open mouth. Ropes were lowered from the bowsprit and gently the animal was hoisted into place. Philippe climbed the scaffolding and drove the wooden pins into place that would hold it secure.

From behind her back, Annabelle produced a package that she handed to Will. "For you." She said.

"Thank you very much." Said Will intrigued. "May I open it?"

"Of course!" She said; with a sweet smile.

Will torn off the wrapping and there was a framed painting of a Hound at full speed. It conveyed the whole essence of the chase. Muscular power, bright eyes, flowing hair; all were there.

"It is brilliant!" Thank you so much!" He then turned to Philippe, who was climbing down the scaffold. "And to you my friend, a really brilliant carving; thank you."

It was obvious when you saw the painting and the figurehead, that the later was based on the painting. "Do you also paint landscapes?" Asked Will. Annabelle nodded her head. "Then I should like to commission you to do a painting of Camden. It would bring back such happy memories, and I can think of no better way of showing my wife where we have been."

Annabelle just inclined her head and gave him a beaming smile.

Finally, after two weeks, McKay declared that the schooner was ready for launching. Will, diplomatically asked Mrs. McKay, if she would stand–in for Isabella to break a bottle against the schooner's bow and name her. He also arranged to pay for refreshment for the yard workers after the launch aboard the schooner. Mrs. McKay insisted that the women folk baked cakes for the crew and the yard's men folk.

The launch was set to be at high tide. It being spring tides, the difference between high and low water was about 9ft. When Will rose early that morning, it was low tide. He stood aboard *Mount Edgecombe* watching as men from the yard applied even more grease to the slip. Seamen from *Hound* were helping men from the yard flake out warps that were secured to posts ashore driven deep into the ground. These would stop the ship from shooting across the small bay and ending up on the opposite shore. A skiff was pulling a line across the water to that shore, so that the stern could be controlled if it decided to wander. Heavy horses were dragging large round logs to positions in direct line with the bow on the shore. Tarrant's team were fixing warps round these so that when the cradle started to slide they would act as brakes, slowing down the rush. First, one would be dragged down, and then, as the loose few yards of warp paid out, the next would add its weight to the slowing down process.

High tide was estimated to be at 11 o'clock that morning. Craddock joined Will to watch the preparations. He and the crew would be aboard *Hound* as it slid down the slip, but only so there were enough bodies to man the capstan and to deal with the various warps needed. Craddock climbed aboard his new ship at nine o'clock, to be met by his officers and a side party to pipe him aboard, which wasn't strictly correct because the ship wasn't yet in the water. Will had given permission, when consulted by Cranfield. He reasoned that the natives would not be used to British Naval etiquette. By half past ten, it seemed the entire population of Camden and Rockport had turned out to watch the spectacle. *Hound's* new cutters and the jolly boat were safely tied to the *Mount Edgecombe* on the far side of the jetty. Craddock waved to Will, indicating that everything aboard was ready, so Will walked down the jetty to join McKay and his family near the bows of the schooner. McKay consulted with his foreman. Florence glanced nervously at Will, who nodded with a smile; then she climbed onto the little dais. She turned to the crowd and waited for silence.

"I stand here in place of Lady Calvert, who because she is expecting her second child, cannot be with us today." She paused as the crew aboard *Hound* gave an approving roar.

"So I name this ship *Hound*; I pray that she may have a long and successful life and that she may carry all who sail in her safely wherever needs be" Then she broke a bottle of Applejack on the solid oak bow. There was the sound of heavy mallets below being wheeled to strike out the wedges that held the cradle in place. McKay ushered the small party back away from the bows in case any warps should part and cause injury. Will stood with them as the sound of creaking could be heard. Then slowly and majestically picking up speed as she went, *Hound* slid into the calm waters of the harbour. A cheer went up from the watchers on the shore as well as from the deck of the moving ship. The logs worked their magic and there was no headlong rush. *Hound* just parted the waters and took to them as of right. The flaked restraining hawsers unfolded and then checked her backward movement to bring her to a halt exactly in the middle of the harbour. The heavy horses were goaded into hauling out the cradle, from which the ship had now parted company.

Once *Hound* was settled in the water, Mr. Tarrant's voice came clearly across the water. "Let go starboard forward on land!" A party of *Hound's* crew who had been positioned ashore to carry out that task, unhitched the starboard warp, and dragged it round to the jetty head, where they secured it. The leading hand in charge of the shore party waved to the ship that it was secure, and a fiddle could be heard starting up on the deck of the schooner. Beside Will, Mrs. McKay and her daughter were both weeping, overcome by the whole affair. Slowly *Hound* crept forward and turned towards the jetty. Astern, the original warp that had been taken across to the far shore was now being lifted from the skiff to the end of the jetty, where it was secured. It took a lot of heaving, but finally *Hound's* new crew managed to bring their charge safely alongside the jetty.

Will regarded his new ship critically. She would need more ballast, but that was to be expected. He was standing facing the bows on the shore. He could see that she sat true upon the water.

"Well at least she doesn't have a list!" Comment McKay, with a chuckle as he stood just behind Will.

"She's beautiful!" Commented Annabelle; and Mrs. McKay gave a loud sniff.

Chapter 6

The party for the yard workers and their family aboard *Hound* passed off fairly well. A couple of the men got very drunk on the free Applejack, but otherwise there was much merriment and good will shown by the people of Camden and the ship's crew.

Hound had not officially been handed over. The next morning McKay supervised the addition of more ballast until both he and Craddock were satisfied. Will kept out of it. Isabella had given him strict instructions that he must let Craddock do his job. "It would not be fair to keep interfering in front of his crew!" She had said.

Two days later, Craddock took *Hound* out into the Bay and tried her at every point of sailing. The weather had been kind and there was a stiff breeze to power her through the water. Will keeping a keen watch on the proceedings with McKay on the poop, was thrilled by her speed and ease of handling. Mr. Tarrant was everywhere, joking but also goading his crew into adjusting the sails to get the ultimate performance from this racer.

They cruised out past a sandy cove to their larboard and then after passing between a rocky point and some small low islands, they turned to run up the bay. Even though this was her first outing, she was as taut as if she had been doing this for years. The wind was from the SW, which was ideal; so they turned onto a broad reach.

"Certainly understands Schooners!" Commented McKay; watching Tarrant's efforts with professional interest.

They shot up between the mainland and Warren Island and on past Islesboro Island, with its narrow isthmus joining the north and south parts together. It was exhilarating! With Belfast Bay to their larboard they came round to shoot round Turtle Head before beginning to do short tacks down the east side of the islands. This was a much greater test for the crew. The men handling the sheets for the sails were easing and tightening them to try to achieve the ultimate performance from the new sails. The local pilot standing beside Craddock told them where it was safe to go. After leaving the islands to the south of Cape Rosier on their larboard quarter, they came round to a close-hauled run to the SE of the Bay and Deer Island. Here they went about. to pass between The Porcupines and Bald Island.

All the way, the bay's water had reflected a cloudless blue sky. After passing Oak Island, it was a fetch to leave Goose Island to larboard and then head home to Camden, passing Curtis Island as they shortened sail. Craddock made a masterful display of seamanship as he brought his charge neatly up the inlet, dropping a stern kedge anchor and turning to come alongside the jetty.

For the next week, they took *Hound* out each day to work her up. The second day they tried the drop keel and sailed as close to the wind as possible. Another day they ventured out into the Atlantic, to test her in rougher sea conditions. At the end of the week, it was time for the hand over. It was at this point that the crew moved their belongings into their new home. Up to that time, they had spent each night back aboard *Mount Edgecombe*. Now both officers and crew were safely installed, it was time for the final payment to be authorised. The crew manhandled the water barrels up to the creek that ran into the inlet. It was extraordinary because there was a natural weir, so the water above the weir was completely fresh within feet of the seawater. The water barrels were stowed in the bulges as near the centre line as possible. Other members of the crew carried the victuals that had been ordered, along the jetty to be loaded aboard.

On the last day before leaving, the McKays and their foreman were invited to dine aboard *Hound*. This was a test for the cook, who was still getting used to his new stove. Will was worried that Tucker might get too distracted by Miss Annabelle, so the two were put at either end of the table. This then led to him worrying that Commander Craddock seemed a little too attracted to her charms.

Early the following morning, on a bright summer's day, *Hound* let go her mooring lines for the last time in Camden and turned her bow to the Atlantic. The *Mount Edgecombe* would travel in company with them. As they slipped out, a small crowd lined the waterside and waved their good-byes. Will had been worried in case there might have been any antipathy between the Americans and their former colonial masters. As it had turned out the people of Camden seemed completely oblivious to any former aggression. Will felt that he could have handled things better between the young people, but Britain was at war, and both Craddock and Tucker were in the Royal Navy. Perhaps if the war with France ever ended Tucker might try to get back to Camden, if he felt strongly enough.

It would have been much more convenient to have trans-shipped the guns at Camden, then they would not have had to go out of their way to Bermuda, just to transfer the weapons.

Once they were out in the Atlantic and the mainland had dropped over the horizon, it was a long fetch down to Bermuda, with the currents trying to force them to the north. Craddock had never visited Bermuda, and it was a very long time ago that Will as a young man aboard his father's ship had called at the island. Luckily, Captain Grey had visited a number of times and had explained how to approach in case the two ships were separated. The problem for those aboard *Hound* was to make sure they did not go too fast and leave the merchantman far behind. It was exasperating to have to rein in *Hound*, so Will suggested to Craddock that they made fast runs to the limit of visibility. That way they could get to know her capabilities in an ocean, whilst at the same time never losing sight of their companion. The voyage to Bermuda took a good six days because of the *Mount Edgecombe.* They sailed past the Island twelve miles to the north before following the *Mount Edgecombe,* as she turned south.

The *Mount Edgecombe* turned at 32degerees 30'3 North; 64 degrees 44'23 West. The north coast of Bermuda could be clearly seen, set in an azure sea. *Hound* dutifully followed her as they altered to sail SW.

"She's sailing straight towards Little Head according to my chart." Said Craddock as Will joined him by the wheel. Will took a look at the chart, and then the binnacle.

"That must be Paget Island on the starboard bow. Should be able to see a fort on the southern tip soon." Said Will. He took a scope from the rack and focused it on the point where the land seemed to drop into the sea.

"I'd forgotten how verdant the islands are! The humidity seems very high, is it me?"

"No Sir. Even in just my shirt, I feel sticky." Replied Craddock; with a chuckle.

Agonisingly slowly, they followed in the wake of their companion. Then, as if they were about to run straight into St David's head, the *Mount Edgecombe* turned to starboard, and a moment later all aboard *Hound* could see the channel open up.

"By the lead five!" Called the leadsman; leaning out from the foremast shrouds. The channel turned back upon itself to pass between Paget Island and Smith Island. A few minutes later and the harbour of St. Georges opened up for them to see. Pastel painted houses with white roofs, almost jumped out of the canvas. The sand at the edge of the water was pink! The crew were excited commenting amongst themselves as they glided towards the small town. All around there seemed to be forts guarding the whole harbour.

The *Mount Edgecombe* signalled it was dropping its

anchor. *Hound* slid past to drop hers about fifty yards away in a depth of five fathoms. *Hound* had flown the American flag when she had left Camden. Now she wore the red ensign, and at the peak of the main mast a broad red pennant, signifying that the Commodore aboard was directly responsible to the Admiralty and on Admiralty business. For the first time the officers wore naval uniform. Will had changed into his dress uniform because he would have to go ashore to meet the Governor. At his side, hung the dress sword, that Isabella had given him. As befitted a Commodore, Lieutenant Tucker had been assigned by Craddock to attend him.

Allwood still stood beside the wheel; even though the anchor was down, and holding. He waited until Craddock nodded to him and then he called out. "Jolly boat's crew to your station!"

There was the sound of bare feet on bare boards as the boat's crew scampered across the deck and up to the poop deck to where the jolly boat was suspended by davits over the stern. Two of the lightest members of the crew climbed over and into the boat. Then the boat was carefully lowered to the water. The men in the boat cast off the tackle, and the boat was hauled round to the ship's side by its painter. Once alongside the crew slid down ropes to their seats in the boat, ready for their distinguished owner to descend. The Jollyboat had the same black hull as its mistress, but the gunwales were painted white and there was gold carving across the transom. It was an exceedingly smart outfit. The blades of the oars were also painted white and the crew all wore horizontally striped jerkins and black lacquered hats, with jaunty red ribbons.

Allwood was the last into the boat, casting a critical eye over his crew and their kit. Tucker used the ladder as befitted an officer, then Will climbed down and took his seat in the stern. At a word from Allwood, the bowman pushed off, the oars were raised to the vertical and then on another order, slowly all together lowered so their blades rested on the water. Allwood nodded his head to the stroke oarsman; the blades rose, moved forward, bit the water and in an impressively smooth action, the oarsmen pulled together.

When they reached the quay, there was a small crowd watching them. Allwood turned the tiller hard over at the same time as a sharp command stopped the oarsmen, then their oars were tossed into the air to remain rigidly upright, as the bowman stowed his and picked up a boathook. They glided smoothly up to the side of the quay and the bowman caught hold of a warp hanging down and held fast. The oars were lowered and Allwood used the second boathook to pull down another warp. Very gently, the jollyboat was worked forward until the steps were exactly opposite Will's position. Tucker climbed out first and stood ready to give Will a hand if necessary. It was only form; Tucker knew very well how agile Will could be. They mounted the steps and Tucker asked a nearby lounger where they could find the Governor. The fellow did not bother to stand upright; he remained lounging against a pile of crates that were stacked on the quay. The fellow pointed to his right where a street ran parallel to the water. "The big white one on de' right." Said the fellow laconically .

In fact there was a row of white houses, but the nearest was certainly the biggest and smartest. Together Will and Tucker strolled to the front door of the building. Tucker raised and slapped down the knocker. Almost immediately, a black servant opened the door.

"Sir William Calvert to see the Governor." Exclaimed Tucker; very formally.

The black man bowed and moved back to let them pass and then indicated a room to the left of the door. He then left them without a word. A couple of minutes later a man of middle height and about thirty plus years came into the room. He was well dressed, his coat of silk, even though it was rather out of the mode.

"Good day to you gentlemen, I fear that you have

been ill informed. I was the Governor for a short period last year until Mr. Hodgson arrived. I take it, you Sir, are from the splendid schooner anchored in our harbour?"

"Sir William Calvert." Will said; taking the man's hand. "And this is my aid, Lieutenant Tucker."

The Gentleman's eyebrows were raised. He looked searchingly at Thomas. "Are we related by any chance?"

Thomas looked dumfounded.

"I Sir, am Henry Tucker, President of the Island Council. Are your family from Devon or Kent per chance?"

"No Sir, they are from Derbyshire."

"Ah well, still a pleasure. Might I ask why such a senior officer arrives here in such a fine craft?" He said; turning back to Will.

"I am on Admiralty business Sir. We are here to transfer cargo from the merchant vessel to our schooner."

"Are you fresh out from England?"

"No we had to pay a visit to America first. We are on our way back to Britain and to war."

The Gentleman's manner was friendly and courteous. Will felt an affinity to the fellow.

"I am sorry we have troubled you. Perhaps you would be good enough to put us right."

"I shall do more than that, I shall take you there myself." With that, he went to the door and shouted out. "I'm off my love with two Naval Officers to visit the Governor."

"Right you are!" Could be heard from afar.

"This way Gentlemen." Mr. Tucker held the front door open for Will and Lieutenant Tucker.

They retraced their steps to the town square and then turned left for a short distance to a house, where Mr. Tucker stopped. "This is what you were looking for. I hope that you will return after you have seen the Governor and take a glass with me Sir William/"

"That is extremely kind of you, thank you."

A flunkey opened the door to them and after taking their names left them to wait for a good quarter of an hour, which did not please Will very much. Thomas paced up and down annoyed by what he considered a slight, to his senior officer.

Finally the Governor appeared and was effusive

with his apologises. He had been in conference and nobody had had enough intelligence to interrupt. He accepted Will's compliments on behalf of the Admiralty and did not seem remotely interested in the fact that the two ships were here just to transload guns and other cargo. All that seemed to interest him was how Will was a Commodore at such a young age. Will explained that it was always a temporary rank, and just meant that the occupier of the rank was on Admiralty business at the time, or that a Captain, such as the late Lord Nelson, could be appointed one when he was to lead a squadron on detached duty.

After leaving the Governor, they returned to the Mr. Tucker's house, where they enjoyed a glass of wine with the Gentleman. Back at the jolly boat there was a small crowd of young women chatting to the crew. They seemed very disappointed when the jollyboat pushed off to return to *Hound*. Craddock had already had *Hound* warped alongside the *Mount Edgecombe.* The hatches were open and Mr. Tarrant was supervising the hoisting out of the first of the specially designed carriages for the long barrelled 18 pounders. Will joined Craddock to watch, as the first of the guns appeared through the open hatch, and was gently settled on its carriage. Once the trunnions were in place, the metal hoops were shut and the retaining pins driven home. Then the crew hauled the carriage and its gun aft on rollers. The special carriages did not have wheels, as they were more like carronade carriages. The bulkhead to Will's cabin had been removed in the middle and the gun was positioned in the centre of the cabin to be joined by its fellow. They were secured to the deck with one barrel resting on the other to take up as little space as possible. Whilst the next two cannons were transferred, the carpenter and his crew replaced the bulkhead and fitted the partitioning to hide the guns. Where they were positioned between Will's and Craddock's cabins, the partitioning at the lower half looked as if it contained locked drawers. Above was a space for hanging clothes. To the aft of the guns, Will's servant, Millward's pantry filled the void. This was constructed as a series of boxes which when shut could be stowed below. With their fronts open, they looked as if it was a fitment within the pantry.

Up forward, the two bow chasers were rolled beneath the forecastle and the bulkhead replaced. Then the shot was hoisted out of *Mount Edgecome's* hold, swung across, and stowed, followed by the gunpowder, which went straight into the two magazines. By the time that was completed it was time to finish for the day.

The next morning *Hound* was walked aft, still secured to the *Mount Edgecome* and the twelve pounders were installed. By midday, the whole enterprise had been completed. They would, weather permitting; start their journey to Britain early next morning.

It took two and a half weeks to reach Plymouth, where *Hound* left the *Mount Edgecombe.* The trouble was that the merchantman being so much slower, *Hound* had to ease her sheets to slow herself down. They had a comparatively trouble free crossing, only encountering one near gale. *Hound* showed her metal. Just like *Snipe* before her, she just nonchalantly brushed the seas aside.

Hound then continued up Channel and as morning was breaking turned to slide almost un-noticed up the Dart past Dartmouth, to drop anchor above Dittisham, where *Snipe* had first had her base.

Directly the anchor was pronounced to be holding, the jollyboat was lowered; Allwood and his crew rowed Will over to the landing stage for Calvert House, which overlooked this wide stretch of the Dart. Will climbed up the steep path followed by his servant Millward who carried a light bag. Will entered by the Kitchen entrance, as he had years before. The staff were just finishing their breakfast, and were surprised by their Lord poking his head round the door and saying good morning. Isabella's lady's maid immediately rose and ran over to him.

Her face showed that something was wrong, and Will felt a cold shiver wash over him.

"Lady Isabella is not very well at the moment. She is resting in her room." She said.

"Is it serious?" Asked Will.

"We had the doctor round, and he said she should stay in bed."

"How is the baby?"

"The doctor didn't rightly know, Sir William."

Will raced up the stairs. Isabella had been so fit before. He burst into the room to find a wan Isabella propped up against the pillows. She turned her head to see who had come so precipitously into her room. A weak smile made Will's heart sink.

"Oh, how lovely to have you back. I am sorry about this." Isabella said; in a weak voice.

Will crossed to the bed and took her hand in his.

"What has happened to you? Is it to do with the pregnancy or what?"

"I don't know. I just felt terrible about five days ago. They called the doctor, but he seemed to be pretty useless. Mama is in London so they couldn't call on her. Oh, but I shall feel so much better now,

I am sure, with you by my side."

Will let go her hand and strode to the door.

"Millward!" He called at the top of his voice. A few seconds later the trusty servant was racing up the stairs, ignoring the fact that they were the main stairs.

"Get a signal to *Hound* as quickly as possible for the surgeon to come here."

Millward didn't say a word; he turned and fled down the stairs in remarkably quick time. He would go to the flagstaff and hoist the imperative flag, which would summon the jollyboat back to the landing stage.

Will returned to his wife. "We'll get Henri to take a look at you."

"Thank you. Have you seen our daughter yet?"

"No; I came up directly I learnt that you were not well."

"She will be in the nursery. Go and comfort her will you?"

Speechless, Will left his wife and went to the nursery. His little daughter was sitting on the floor nursing a rag doll, a look of absolute misery on her little face.

"And how is my Mary Elizabeth!" Will said, as he got down to her level. The child looked at him, but there was no sign of recognition. Will looked up to where the nursery maid was standing watching them. There was a gurgled chuckle from beside him and he looked down to see his daughter laughing up at him. He bent down and picked her up.

"Recognise me?" He asked.

A beaming smile and a frantic nodding of the head told him that she did.

"Mary Elizabeth, loves to tease!" Commented the Maid.

Will still holding his daughter, said. "I am taking her to see her mother."

"But the doctor said...."

"Bugger the doctor!" Cried Will; and then apologised. He carried the dark haired little beauty along the corridor and into the darkened room, where Isabella lay.

"Your daughter to see you." Said Will. Mary Elizabeth tried to wriggle out of his arms to reach her mother.

"No, Mummy is not feeling very strong at the moment. You sit with me beside her and we can have a talk."

Chapter 7

Will and his daughter sat on the bed next to a propped up Isabella, as Will recounted everything that had happened since he had last seen them. Then there was a knock at the door and Henri de Cornes, came in.

"Hello Isabella, Oh and Miss Mary Elizabeth. Now what seems to be the trouble/" His cheerful manner was almost a tonic in itself. Isabella was used to the wringing hands and mutterings of the elderly doctor who attended her.

Henri had trained in Paris as a doctor and surgeon before joining the French Navy. When the revolution came, being an aristocrat he had fled to England and after a bad time working with a doctor in London, offered his services to the British Navy. He had been officially an Assistant Surgeon aboard *Snipe,* Will's first command. They had become great friends. Will made sure he had the Frenchman in his crew whenever possible.

"I think we had better call your maid, Isabella. Will, I suggest you leave us for the moment."

He placed his bag on the end of the bed. Will went over to the new bell pull that had been installed the year before. As he left the room, Isabella's lady's maid was hurrying from the servants' stairs towards him.

"Doctor de Cornes is here. He is going examine my wife. He requires that you be there."

The Maid curtsied; then rushed into the room.

"Right my girl; let's get you back to the nursery. I promise to come and see you as soon as Doctor de Cornes has finished with Mama."

Having deposited Mary Elizabeth, he went to his dressing room, where Millward had laid out a civilian suit. He washed and changed. Then he went back to Isabella's room only to find the door open. Peeping in, he discovered a relaxed Henri standing at the end of the bed, with both Isabella and her Maid in fits of laughter.

"Ah Will. Come in. Your wife is a fine physical specimen. She is just having a little problem balancing the needs of the baby with her own. It is very common in pregnant women. I have made a note of what she needs. I am surprised that your doctor didn't seem to realise what was happening."

"Thank God!" Cried Will. He ran forward and embraced Isabella.

"You'll stay for dinner?" Asked Isabella; after Will had relaxed his grip.

"Thank you! But, you madam are staying right where you are until I give you permission to get up. In the meantime, please make sure that a window is open at all times. This extraordinary English medical idea, that air is bad for one, has a lot to answer for."

Isabella's Maid went straight over to one window and opened it slightly.

"Not very generous!" Remarked Henri; but it was said with a smile. The Maid blushed, but opened the window even wider. "Your Mistress is wrapped up under the bedclothes. Only we will feel the chill, if there is one. I'll be in that fine library of yours when you want me." Henri turned, picked up his bag, and left the room. Will stayed to talk with his wife, much relieved.

Two days later Will left for London, taking with him Millward and Allwood to carry messages. They stayed at his London house, Calvert House, in Highgate, where the housekeeper seemed to take

Will's unexpected arrival in her stride. A late cold collation was arranged although there was no cook. Beds were hastily made and aired. Early the following day Will had himself driven to the Admiralty, where he discovered that being the equivalent rank to a Rear Admiral, really did have its benefits. There was a problem though. He discovered that William Marsden had retired. Will had known that he had wanted to, but was shocked to find that he had done so. His place had been taken by an Honourable William Wellesley Pole. This meant that he would have to deal with somebody he knew nothing about. Lord Mulgrave, who had been a distinguished Army General, was now First Lord. All was change; how were they going to react to the ideas of their predecessors? What was a General doing in charge of the Navy? Will wished that he had stopped off at one of his clubs; he might have been able, perhaps, to find out about the character of these individuals. It was too late now, he thought, as he was shown into the First Secretary's office.

A tall thin man with a long nose, arched black eyebrows and a pointed chin, stood up to greet him.

"Sir William, delighted to meet you. I have read up on you, though there are areas that I understand, are so secret that even here in the Admiralty we are not allowed knowledge of. I gather though that it was decided that you were to purchase a schooner in America and bring her back for use on the North Spanish Coast. Is that correct?"

"That is correct."

Wellesley Pole, smiled for the first time. "I had the honour of dining with My Lord St. Vincent the other night. Lord Castlereagh and he were discussing you. Apparently you are thought of very highly."

Will smiled, but refrained from speaking.

"So I read Marsden's notes. I served in the Navy for a short time, so I can appreciate the soundness of the idea of a schooner for those waters. So how was your trip Sir William?" He asked.

"Very exhilarating! *Hound* is incredibly fast and agile!"

"All everybody hoped for?"

"More so, I do believe."

"Excellent". Wellesley Pole rang a bell and asked the attending clerk to fetch the *Hound* file.

Once he had this on his desk, he got down to business.

"I have here your secret orders; your commission,

and all the other paperwork you need, just in case a Navy ship stops you." He paused for a moment, then smiled and said. "But of course it would have to be a very senior Admiral to be able to order you to stop, By the way, next door has been asking after you."

Will knew, full well, that this meant the Aliens Office which was the cover for the spy network that had been set up in Europe. Unfortunately, it did not cover Northern Spain, which was the whole point of Will's secret commission.

"The Board have appointed a Captain Caspar of the Marines as your military advisor. I understand that he is an expert on explosives. He is to have twelve marines with him. Have you thought of whom you are taking as Midshipmen?" Wellesley Pole added.

"I thought to take two. Do you have any ideas? I have nobody tugging at my coat tails at the moment."

"In that case I shall consult. It would be best if they were near taking their Lieutenants exams, as they will be of more use to you."

"I am not sure who I should consult; but is it possible for a Warrant Officer to be promoted to Lieutenant, without him having to become a midshipman first?"

Wellesley Pole leant back and gave it some thought. "My dear Sir William, I should have thought that since an Admiral may promote within his command. As a Commodore, you have that right. But let us check on this." He rang the hand bell.

Will blinked at the unexpected turn of events.

"You obviously have someone in mind?" Continued Wellesley Pole

"I have; Sydney Tarrant our Boatswain. He has studied navigation so could pass any exam. He took the sights all the way across the Atlantic and was as accurate as any of us. His seamanship skills go without saying. I consider him to be wasted as a mere Boatswain. The Navy needs such men in command of its ships. I know he is not of the aristocracy, but he is respected wherever he goes."

The door opened behind the First Secretary and a clerk entered.

"Find the rules about Admirals promoting within their jurisdiction." Demanded the First Secretary.

Surprisingly the fellow held his ground.

"An Admiral may promote or demote any officer he considers suitable for such promotion; or the reverse. He must though inform the Admiralty immediately. The Board have the right to countermand if they see fit."

Wellesley Pole nodded, waved a hand in dismissal, and said. "I suggest you write down the fellow's name, and I shall have it added to the Navy List. I take it you are promoting him to Lieutenant, so not forcing him to go through the agonies of being a midshipman!"

"Exactly!" Replied Will.

"Very good, consider it done."

"Thank you. It will make my life easier, as I hope to have my ship's Captain made Post as soon as possible. He has already given up at least a year or more seniority by volunteering to come with me to America. He is an experienced Schooner man you see."

"Ah, quite so. I suggest you leave his name with us, and we could look into it for you. By-the-by; I understand that you are a personal friend of Castlereagh's?"

"I have that honour."

"Mmm. He has been talking to my younger brother, Arthur. He is in Denmark at present, having some success I understand. Castlereagh asked if he would consider taking charge of an expeditionary force to Portugal, to help the Portuguese against any French invasion. Know anything of this?"

"No Sir, I have come straight here from *Hound*. I have not yet had time to visit Lord Castlereagh."

"I know the First Lord would like to see you, but he is at the House at the moment."

"I am on my way there immediately to see Lord Castlereagh." Replied Will.

The Palace of Westminster was quieter than Will remembered. He was shown straight up to Lord Castlereagh's rooms. He was greeted like a long lost brother by his friend; the noble lord embraced him.

"My Dear Will; so good to see you! How are you and Isabella, is she well?"

"Isabella has been poorly. Something to do with being pregnant. Fortunately, Henri de Cornes, our Surgeon was able to give her some magic elixir, which put her back on the road to recovery. This second child seems to be more difficult than Mary Elizabeth."

"I am so sorry to hear that. Pity she isn't in town. Emily could have popped round to see her."

"Isabella misses her company!"

"Give her our love when you see her. Now down to business. How is the new ship?"

Will proceeded to tell him all about *Hound* and her capabilities.

"So we chose well! By God, we need you down there as soon as possible. Gambier keeps sending signals to say that he cannot keep a frigate down there if the weather changes. Of course, he doesn't have anything suitable to hand. Mark you, he also asked for you to take command of a ship-of-the-line when we ordered him to the Baltic. We fear that Napoleon has his sights set on the Danish Fleet. It has a large number of useful ships that could give us immense problems if they fell into his hands. The bloody Danes keep insisting that they are neutral, which is fine if Napoleon was to take any notice. We have to keep the Baltic open for essential supplies for the Navy. Now that the Americans are getting stroppy about us boarding ships under the American flag and searching for deserters; it is even more important. We have sent troops to Germany under Arthur Wellesley. I had some problem with my colleagues in choosing him, but I admire what he achieved in India. So, you see we are having to look both ways at once. The Corsican keeps changing his mind. We desperately need to know what he is planning to do. We have reports that he has put Junot in command of a new army in the southwest of France. There can be only one reason for doing that; he obviously plans to cross the border and march on Portugal. We have definite intelligence that Napoleon and King Charles of Spain demanded that Portugal declare war on us by the 12th August. It is obvious that he wants to take Portugal out of the equation, so we will have no bases there. He could then bring round his Mediterranean fleet to join up with what is left of his Atlantic fleet. We must find out what is happening down there."

"I am due to see Mr. Granger at the Aliens Office, and then I shall be on my way as soon as possible after that. Unfortunately I have to pick up marines from Plymouth on my way south."

After words of encouragement, Will left to go back to Whitehall and the Aliens Office. He was shown straight up to the office of the mysterious Mr. Granger. Here he was met with much warmth and as much information as they had, which amounted to very little. Next Will called at the Admiralty and picked up the papers that were waiting for him. Collecting Millward and Allwood, he had the coach start out immediately for Devon.

It was after midnight when they finally crawled up

the drive to Calvert House. The Dart below shimmered in the moonlight. Will was prepared to sleep in his dressing room so as not to disturb Isabella, but she had obviously heard their arrival and was waiting for him, much restored to health. Will was in part relieved and in part annoyed when a message from *Hound* informed him that essential supplies had yet to be loaded, as they had not arrived at Dartmouth. He was therefore able to spend an extra day with Isabella.

Early, on an ebb tide, *Hound's* jollyboat left the Calvert landing to be rowed down to an anchored *Hound* off Dartmouth quay. Will was met by Craddock who informed him that the supplies had at last arrived and were about to be brought out. An hour later *Hound* upped her anchor and sailed for Plymouth.

They anchored in the Hamoaze and Will sent Lieutenant Tucker ashore to the Port Admiral to ask about the extra members of the crew. When he got back, Will mentioned the extra Lieutenant to Craddock, who nodded agreement. The entire crew was called on deck. Craddock then addressed them, first reminding them they were on a secret mission as far as anybody here about was concerned. The schooner was American. She would support a large flag hanging at the staff at the stern to indicate when at sea or in foreign ports that fact. He then announced that they had more Lieutenants aboard than the crew might think. He called Tarrant forward and then read the official paper that stated that Sydney Tarrant was officially a lieutenant in the Royal Navy and that his name had been added to the Navy List. There was a great cheer. Tarrant was almost overcome. He had not expected this and he turned to Will for confirmation.

"And not a moment too soon; old friend." Said Will. He could see that the big man's eyes were watering. "Luckily we won't need a uniform where we are going, so you will have plenty of time to kit yourself out when we get back." He added.

The new semaphore telegraph system to London must have worked this time. A wherry set out towards them carrying the marines, and their officer commanding, Captain Caspar, together with two midshipmen, the extra crew, including boys to act as powder monkeys and servants. As a result, *Hound* was able to turn immediately about and set sail for Spain.

Captain Caspar was a red-faced jolly fellow with a barrel chest and a wide smile. The first of the midshipmen introduced himself as Roland Manning. He was in his early twenties, but had previously been a Master's Mate, so was experienced. The second midshipman was much younger. He was seventeen with the unusual name of Christain Surprise. He was an athletically built young fellow with obvious charm. He observed everything with intelligent interest.

They left Plymouth Sound as the sun was setting, close hauled in a moderately stiff south-westerly breeze, which raised the odd white horse. *Hound* seemed to relish this point of sailing; though Craddock refrained from setting the topsails, as he did not want to arrive off Ushant until there was enough light. Soon after first light, the lookouts reported land fine on the larboard bow. Very soon, it was possible to identify it as the low-lying island with its threatening rocky outcrops that projected well out to sea beyond the most westerly point. The wind had remained from the south-west so they remained on course until well past the island and rocks, then they came round to a south-south-easterly course on what was a moderately broad reach. The topsails were hoisted and trimmed and the schooner lent to the wind as if racing.

Hound arrived off the northern coast of Spain the next day. She had powered through the water under full sail, her scuppers creaming the water into white foam. They had met only one other ship, a British frigate which had sailed to challenge them, but on seeing the large red ensign and the broad red pennant had come about and dipped her flag, before sailing off. Craddock had a chart of sorts for the north coast of Spain, but he was wise enough to luff-up and await the dawn before closing land. When they did approach the coast they realised why it was so feared by seamen. Rugged cliffs seemed to rise straight out of the sea. They managed to fix their position by the obvious San Sebastian Bay. The two mounts on either side with the island in the middle protecting the arc of sand behind, could be no other. They turned and followed the coast in an easterly direction, before they found what they were looking for. Two high hills either side of a narrow entrance, with the cliffs steeply thrusting out of the sea. Craddock had a cutter lowered and with a leadsman up in the bows: it entered the harbour under the command of Lieutenant Tucker. *Hound* waited for an hour sailing back and forth before the cutter re-emerged. Tucker stood up in the stern and signed for *Hound* to follow them into the entrance. Under foresails alone, with leadsmen on either side, *Hound* picked her way between the high cliffs. The wind played games by backing off the cliff on the eastern side once they were between the two headlands. Tucker kept the cutter close to the bow to be able to take a line if necessary. Craddock stood calmly by the wheel, with Allwood at his place as Quartermaster. Lieutenant Tarrant stood by the foremast quietly giving his orders to make sure that the sails did not back. To starboard, a small spit jutted out into the channel, but not enough to cause any worries. Then a remarkable sight opened up for them. A village hung to the mountainside on the larboard side. Some of the houses actually built out over the water. A larger number of vessels than expected were anchored further in. There was no sign of anything approaching a naval ship; they all seemed to be fishing smacks. Craddock had the bower anchor dropped on an extended hawser so that he had a way of controlling the ship when they wanted to leave. The wind was from the west, but it was moderate. In water that was far deeper than indicated on their chart, their snuffed the hawser and *Hound* slowed to turn and face the sea. The cutter came alongside and its crew returned aboard.

Will had watched the whole proceedings from beside Craddock, but had not said a word. Once they were certain they were securely anchored; the cutter was manned by a fresh crew, and a kedge anchor laid out astern.

A high prowed boat came out from the quay and a dark haired man stood up in the stern and greeted them in English. "Signor's, welcome to our fine port. Where are you from?"

"America!" Replied Lieutenant Kemp; who happened to hold the watch.

"I know that! I mean which port are you from?"

"Camden." Replied Kemp.

"I know New York, I know Boston, I know Novia Scotia; but I no know this Camden!"

Kemp looked perplexed. He might be a good navigator and seaman, but he was not good at subterfuge.

Lieutenant Tucker joined him at the rail and helped him out.

"North of Boston: Penobscot Bay".

The man still looked confused.

"Halfway from Boston and the Bay of Fundy" Added Tucker. The man nodded his head.

"And what are here for?"

Without any hesitation, Tucker said. "We are looking to trade. The British Navy would not let us anywhere near the French Ports. Threatened to sink us: so we came south. Got any wine here abouts?"

"Ah! Si Signor. Very good wine, very good food, very, very good cider and very pretty women"! He laughed.

"Is there anybody we should report to?" Asked Kemp.

"You could pay a call on the Mayor; but really nobody here worries. If there is an official from Madrid, perhaps we have to appear to take more interest. Otherwise you come to me, I very important sea captain. I travel all way to your country many times. I fix everything. Just ask for El Captán Gora Etzanoi". With that, he sat down; flicked his wrist to indicate to the oarsmen that they should start rowing and waved goodbye.

"Well that was a turn up for the books"! Commented Tucker to Kemp. Together they strolled aft to Craddock's cabin and told him what had transpired. He was buckling his sword to his belt. Tucker looked pointedly at the naval officer's weapon. Craddock noticed, gave a rueful smile, and took it off to replace it with a cutlass.

Chapter 8

Craddock knocked on Will's day cabin door and Millward immediately opened it. Will sat on the window seat gazing out at the harbour. "Strange how the hills are so high by the entrance and yet here the west side is so flat inland".

"Must get a lot of rain. It is so green and yet we are

in the middle of September". Commented Craddock. Will nodded. "Going ashore to make your mark?"

"Aye. Kemp and Thomas had a conversation in English with a so-called Captain, who claimed to have visited America a number of times. Didn't know Camden though".

"Not a trading port, I shouldn't have thought".

"No. I am to see the Mayor, although the Captain didn't think it absolutely necessary. I think it should be a matter of form though, don't you?"

"Absolutely. Good luck"!

As Craddock left, Will called for Patxi Mendiluze, the Basque schoolteacher to join him. He had volunteered to stay with *Hound* on her journey to his homeland, so that he could provide any assistance that might be needed. This Will had realised was going to make his life a lot easier. Will and the schoolteacher were now on christain name terms, they had spent so much time together.

Henri de Cornes knocked and entered. "May I?"

"Of course! I have just asked Patxi to join me. So what is your first impression of the Basque country?"

"Evil looking coastline! I can quite see why Gambier has found it almost impossible to patrol this part of his remit. Intriguing place this though. I like the painted houses and the way some of them are built out over the water. Make a great sketch, Will".

At that moment, Millward announced the schoolmaster. Will indicated for him to take a seat.

"So we made it".

"Very quickly! Exhilarating, I think is the word".

"Too right"! Commented Henri.

"So who do you know around here who might help us?"

"There is a man who has much influence in these parts. He was a priest, but he offended the Inquisition. He was forced out. He objected to the fact that his flock could not understand the Latin of the Mass. He translated it into Euskera. He had to hide. Now he has a band of followers who help those who object to the rule of our country from Madrid. The trouble is that he moves about a lot. He has to! If you were to ask for him, I don't think you would last long. They would consider you a spy and 'Bang'. That would be the end of your life! I suggest that I travel inland, I am known around there. The village of Henani which is about your four miles as the bird flies, is where there are people who could get a message to him".

"How old is this priest?" Asked Henri.

"He must be in his fifties, but he was very fit when he helped me. He does a lot of walking!" Patxi smiled at some memory.

"How long will that take?" Asked Will.

"To get to Henani. If I could be taken by boat to the southern end of this bay, there is a farm about a mile inland. I know the farmer well. I shall borrow a mount. Then it is only about an hour and a bit's ride to the village."

"Good, that sounds feasible. I suggest you leave it until the morrow. We don't want people to start talking. What we shall do, is to make many boat trips here and there. That should confuse people and make your being put ashore less noticeable. What we must do is for you to arrange a meeting, so that I can find out more about the situation before we go any further. If this priest is still operating, then he might very well have up-to-date information. Thank you Patxi, you are a very brave man".

"I have changed my appearance. I was always

clean-shaven when I was last here. Now I sport beard and mustachios!"

"Where is this place on the map?" Asked Will; pulling out the only map they had that was not a chart.

Patxi pointed to the area. "Here is the road from France, which passes just to the south of us, before it turns inland". He pointed out of the window. "You see those hills over there; well the road goes behind those. Henani is the other side of those hills. The main route to the south goes through Burgos. The road here continues to near Deba before turning south. Most of the traffic from Madrid comes up that road".

"So if the French were to invade, to get to Portugal, they would take that road?"

"I imagine so. The road follows the river. It passes through narrow valleys before it reaches the plain."

The next morning, *Hound* was a mass of activity. The two cutters kept going to various corners of the harbour as if taking soundings. The jollyboat was ready on the larboard side, so that it was not visible from the village. At ten o'clock, when the fishing boats had come back from their early morning sortie to the fishing grounds, the jollyboat drifted away from *Hound* and made its way to the southern shore of the harbour. Patxi went ashore with three of the oarsmen. Once hidden from view, the sailors helped Patxi to remove his outer garments. Whilst he put on different clothes, the sailors packed his previous attire with old clothes and then made their way back with the stuffed version between them.

Will spent the morning sketching the harbour and the village from the poop. Although he had brought paints, he was not used to them, so he kept to pen and ink. On the edges of his sketches, he wrote the colour he thought would be correct when he made a painted copy. In the afternoon, when the sun had come round to the south and the light within the village would be better, he was taken ashore and set up his easel in the village. Four marines in civilian dress lounged around watching him. Beneath their lightweight overcoats, they bristled with weapons.

Patxi did not return that night, which concerned Will. 'What if he had been taken?' An anxious Henri and Will eat supper together in silence. Craddock joined them halfway through, but the silence continued. They all missed the Basque, who had proved an amusing and gracious companion. Late in the evening as darkness descended the jollyboat made one last trip to the drop off point, but returned without the passenger.

It wasn't until late the next morning that Midshipman Surprise alerted everybody with wild un-officer like whoop. He had a scope to his eye and it was trained on the far shore. Cranfield joined him and took the scope.

"Jollyboat's crew away!"

Craddock and Will emerged almost together.

"Mr. Surprise was keeping a close watch. Mr. Patxi is on the shore waving." Said Cranfield.

It was Allwood himself who slid down the rope to the jollyboat to coxswain it.

When Patxi had been welcomed back aboard, he was taken into Will's day cabin.

"Well what happened?" Asked a relieved Will.

"I am sorry my friend, but I think you will approve of my actions. I was told where I could find father Joseba – that is our version of the name Joseph. He was not too far away, so I went straight to him. He listened attentively to what I had to say. In return, he told me that French soldiers are already mapping the road. They are not wearing uniform, you understand, but our people are sure they are French. You see what this means! The French are going to invade Spain!"

"You acted absolutely correctly, but we have to make certain that the French are in the country. Can you get hold of horses?"

"Si! Yes! Of course. When do you want them?"

"We need to think this out. I suggest that we consult with the gallant Captain Caspar. Would you be able to arrange mounts by tomorrow first thing?"

"Of course!"

"Good! Now show us where they said the mapping party were last seen."

At that moment, Caspar entered; Millward had acted promptly without being told.

"What's up?" He asked as he joined the group around the table and the map.

"Patxi here has spoken to Father Joseph – our priest. The French are already here mapping their route."

Patxi had a finger on the map at a point south of Deba.

"Father Joseph said that they were between Mendarozabel and Elgoibar, here."

"How far is that from here?" Asked Caspar.

"I suppose about 40 of your miles."

"And the terrain- the road?"

"The first part is fairly flat. The area they are surveying is a narrow valley with a river running along the bottom. It is quite a difficult part of the route."

"So the survey party will have to take their time!" Commented Will.

"Who do you want to take?" Asked Craddock.

Will straightened up from stooping over the map. "We don't want too big a group; difficult to mount them. I suggest Caspar, Henri, Patxi, and say three marines. They have to be marines who can ride. Do any of your marines ride?" Will asked; turning to Caspar.

"Haven't the slightest idea, but I shall ask." He left the cabin.

"Patxi, can you organise the horses for tomorrow. I suggest that we mount them out of sight of the village here."

"I shall see to it immediately. That is if Commander Craddock will lend me the jollyboat and a crew of course."

Craddock put an arm on Patxi's shoulder and guided him out.

"What do we take in the way of weapons?" Asked Henri.

"Pistols, cutlasses, and a lot of luck!" Will replied; smiling at his old friend.

Chapter 9

Very early next morning two cutters left *Hound* and silently made their way to the point where Patxi had been landed. They were met by the man himself, wearing dark brown clothes. He led them a short way to a small copse where a group of men stood holding horses by their bridles. Patxi had with him a large bundle that turned out to be filled with the local drab brown garments. These the team put on over their normal clothes. Now each member of the party wore similarly weaves of various muted browns. This was the colour of the local sheep, so most of the locals dressed this way. Captain Caspar immediately checked each horse in turn, feeling their flanks, running his hands down their legs and picking up the hooves to check their shoes. Satisfied he turned to Will.

"All correct!"

"Where on earth were you able to get hold of such specimens at such short notice?" Asked Will; turning to Patxi. In the semi darkness, all he could see was a mouth full of white teeth grinning back at him.

Each man selected a mount and on being seated, adjusted their stirrup leathers. Patxi had managed to provide two mules as pack animals to make their progress look more peaceful. Blanket rolls were strapped to the front of the saddles, a pair of leather holsters hung by the riders' knees. On the pack mules, the travelling canteen and food was divided between the panniers, together with the rum and brandy.

By the time they set off at a steady trot, the sun was beginning to make its presence felt, although the 'essences' to the west, held the omen of rain to come.

The horses lived up to their looks. They kept up an effortless easy trot. The problem was that half the riders had not been on a horse for some time. As a result, they had to slow to a walk to ease the strain. It was not until after midday, that Patxi held up his hand and they reined in.

"We are now about to enter the area where the French were last seen."

They were moving slowly south. They had joined the river that ran to the sea at Deba. From the road, which was on higher ground, they had been able to see clearly the harbour and the winding river heading their way. Here the hills around seemed to close in so they were riding down a narrow valley with the river to their right. Between two steep and heavily wooded sides to the valley, the road crossed a narrow arched bridge over the river. Now they were on the west side of the river, riding along its bank, which was only wide enough to allow two riders to ride side by side.

Will called a halt and they tethered the horses to trees, which had plenty of grass under them and broke out the food and drink. After half an hour, they were on their way again, at a slow trot. At the village of Mendarozabel, they slowed to a walk. Valleys spread out either side, with tracks going off in different directions. As they continued, the valley narrowed again, with steep heavily wooded sides.

"Just the place for an ambush!" Commented Caspar, who was riding just behind Will. Will turned in his saddle. "Hopefully not on us!" He retorted. They walked on for another quarter of an hour or so, then Patxi, who was riding beside Will at the head of the column said. "We are being watched over!"

"How do you mean?" Asked Will.

A Secret Assignment

"No self respecting Basque would cut timber this far from home!" Will turned and caught a glimpse of a figure amongst the trees to his right.

They came to a place where the sides of the valley were too steep for a road on this side of the river and they had to cross to the east bank by another humped back bridge. They now rode amongst trees with the river slightly below them on their right. The river curved sharply round a bend and they followed it. Another track joined theirs at this flatter part of the bank.

"That is the long route to San Sebastian." Patxi said, eyes concentrating on the road ahead.

They crossed another bridge so they were back on the west side of the river.

"Very soon now!" Stated Patxi.

Will looked about him, but could not see any signs of anything that might give Patxi that idea.

A mile or so further on and they came to a small village on the banks of the river.

"Elgoibar." Explained Patxi. A moment later he stopped his mount to speak with a local.

"There is a party of men, just beyond the bend!" Said Patxi, falling in beside Will. The road was now very close to the edge of the river, with a steep side to the hills rising immediately from the road.

As they rounded a corner, there ahead of them was a cart blocking the narrow road. A number of men were crowded around it. They turned to see who was approaching.

Will had briefed them for such as this moment. He would do the talking. The others would make sure they could reach their weapons instantly.

"We are still being watched over, my friend; have no fear." Whispered Patxi. They reined to a stop, as there was no way around the cart.

Will quickly rehearsed his lies to himself. "Arratsalde on." He said in Euskera.(Good afternoon)

The man who was so obviously in charge starred up at him, brows furrowed.

Will tried in Spanish. Still the man appeared to be confused, because he looked around as if to see if any of the other eight men understood what Will was talking about. Now Will played his trump card.

"Vous êtes Français?"

"Oui Monsieur."

"Ah! Qu'est-que vous faites?"

"Nous preparons une carte, Monsieur."

"Bon! Nous avons besoins d'une nouvelle carte!"

The Frenchman gave a wan smile.

"Est-il possible de déplacer votre chariot, Monsieur?"

The Frenchman shrugged his shoulders and then turned to his unfortunate colleagues. At that moment, one of them gave a stifled shriek and the men crowded round the wagon pulling out muskets. It was an awkward moment; all Wills companions drew their pistols, but Will realised that the men were looking up to the trees above them, not at him or his companions.

"Quel est le problème?" Asked Will; pretending to search the tree line above.

"Bandits!" Retorted the Frenchman.

"Je vous assure que, Monsieur, il n'a pas aucun bandits autour ici. Pourquoi il y aurait ?" (I assure you, Monsieur, there are no bandits around here. Why would there be?")

The Frenchman turned and starred at Will. Then he turned and gazed up at the wooded area immediately above.

"C'est rein!" He shouted; and his men put away their weapons reluctantly.

Finally the French managed to get the bullocks to move forward to where the road was slightly wider, and Will's team was able to trot past in single file, waving their thanks as they passed.

Caspar rode up to beside Will directly there was room. "That was a near thing!" He said. "You know there were men up there in the trees."

"Yes, they have been with us for the last five miles or more. Patxi, here, says they are looking after us."

Caspar turned to Patxi, who gave him a broad grin.

About three-quarters of a mile further on the river divided into two: so did the roads. The one to the left continued through an equally high-sided valley, whilst the one to the right followed a wider valley with gentler slopes. Patxi turned his horse's head towards the road to the right. Shortly afterwards a small valley joined them again from the right.

Three long, piercing whistles echoed around them. Patxi placed two fingers in his mouth and made the same three loud whistles.

"We turn up here." He said and led the way up a

winding track into the woods above. From behind the trees, a brown figure emerged, with a dark green cloak thrown back from his shoulders. In his hand, he carried a musket. The man had a full black beard, over which his moustache was waxed into points. A beak of a nose divided two dark hooded eyes. The smile though was wide and welcoming. He put out his arms wide, and Patxi slid from his horse and embraced him.

"This is Basa-Juan, not his real name, you understand, but his err, err, code name. It means in Euskera Lord of the Forest."

"How suitable!" Commented Will; dismounting and going to shake the man's hand.

"This is the American." Said Patxi; as a way of introduction. "Basa-Juan's men have been tracking us to make sure we don't run into any trouble."

"Tight moment back there." Commented Henri; from his saddle.

The man looked up and in rapid Euskera, explained that it was a deer, which had startled the French. His men had accidently got a little too close to the animal.

"So what do you want us to do now, that you have positive proof the French are already on our land?"

The Basque asked.

"Ideally, I would like to make sure their maps are destroyed. However that would mean following them, and we are supposed to be ahead of them."

Basa-Juan grinned. "I assure you, if that is what you want, that is what you will get. We will burn the wagon, with everything in it."

"Exactly who are we dealing with here, Patxi?" Asked Will.

"We are Basque, we are not Spaniards. We demand that we continue to live our lives the way we have always lived our lives, without interference from Madrid or the Inquisition. Now it seems we shall have to fight the French as well."

"And what does Father...." Patxi put his hand on Will's lips.

"Elazar, that is what we call him. In our language and customs, names have meanings. Elazar means in whose help is God. You understand? From now on, we use only that name whilst here in Euskadi"

Will nodded his assent. "And how can we repay you for this service?"

Basa-Juan, looked at Patxi. "This American speaks our language; that is unusual. Have you been teaching him? I thought so; it is a very formal form of our language. You need to spend some time with us to learn to speak like a peasant!" He roared with laughter at Patxi's expression.

"Still, how can we be of assistance to you, and your band?" Asked Will.

"You have muskets and powder?"

"We can certainly let you have a number of such weapons, the powder and the shot; plus spare flints."

"When?"

Will turned to Patxi. "Where can we off load such things without the whole world watching?"

Patxi stood thinking. He turned to Basa-Juan. "Ogella: could you collect from there?"

Basa-Juan considered for a moment and then smiled and nodded. "When/" He asked.

"Is this place Ogella overlooked?" Asked Will.

"No! Nobody lives near there, but there is a track, so it would make transporting the weapons easier. It is a fairly sheltered bay. However, like most of our coast not when the wind is blowing from the north-west. From the west, then it is good." Patxi explained.

"Probably best at night. There is a quarter-moon for the next few nights. How will we get in touch?" Continued Will.

Patxi consulted with Basa-Juan. "In two days time, there will be a constant presence there until you arrive."

Chapter 10

Basa-Juan took them to a 'Baserri', a remote farm set overlooking a south facing pasture, itself hidden in the woods. The ancient farmer led them round to the back where an unexpectedly large barn was able to provide them with cover, both for themselves and their horses. The rain had returned, but that did not stop a number of men arriving with homemade food for the party. The straw gave them a moderately comfortable bed for the night. Very early Basa-Juan collected them, riding a muscular 'Cabalo Galego' a working pony of the region. He led them across their original road and into the hills to the east. They followed winding mountain tracks, past remote farms and through thick woods. The rain came in waves. Not heavy rain, just light, but penetrating rain that seemed intent on getting down their collars, even though they wore wide brimmed local hats.

At a broken down shepherd's hut they reined in. A tall white haired man emerged dressed in plain black robes. There was no sign of any religious order, but it looked uncommonly like a priest's garb. The man's face was heavy lined and sun burnt. His eyes were bright over his snow-white beard. Patxi dismounted and dropped to one knee to kiss the proffered hand. This then was Elazar the priest.

Since the rain had stopped for the priest, Will and his companions were able to join the fellow in a glass of local cider, whilst Will discussed with him the aims of the group. Will explained that they knew that the French had an army on the border. The priest already knew this and was even able to give numbers and their regiments. What the French called an Observation Corps.

They discussed at length what would be the best course of action if the French crossed the border into their land. They agreed that there was no possibility of stopping such an army, but they did agree that they could make life difficult for them, but they had to have the weapons and utensils to affect anything. Will suggested that the best course of action was to hit the supply train, after the main body had passed. It would mean that the French would have to divert troops to protect their supply routes. This could mean that a much smaller army took to the field of any battle. Caspar ruled out any ambushes on other than the supply chain, as being too likely to have the dire effect of retribution on the local inhabitants.

Elazar finished their meeting with a profound homily. "It is sad that man must seek glory to such an extent that he loses sight of his fellow man. It happens everywhere. Certainly, in the Clergy it is prevalent. Bishops forget their flock, and seek self-aggrandisement. Kings forget their people, and usurpers such as Napoleon, well their ambitions defy logic. We must do everything in our power to try to keep this land for the people. The people who till the land: who fish the sea. These are God's people."

Hound's lookouts were on the ball, because Will's party, having made their way to the water's edge, found the cutters were already on their way to collect them. Back aboard a relieved Craddock welcomed them. Will recounted what had occurred whilst towelling himself down and then changing into dry and more comfortable clothes. The kedge anchor was retrieved by means of its marker buoy: then they waited for the tide to turn and manned the capstan, with sails hoisted but not sheeted in. Once the anchor had been hauled up to the hawser pipe, the sheets were adjusted so that they could slowly make their way out through the narrow entrance to the harbour.

Once free of the land, *Hound* turned her bow to the west. It only took them a couple hours before they were passing the bay, pointed out by Patxi. The bay of Ogella was protected from the westerly wind by a rocky cliff that ran right back to a sandy bay. It being low tide they were able to make out the sharp rocky outcrops just off the cliffs to the west. There were breakers on the shore, but they did not appear, from where they were, to be a great problem. *Hound* continued to sail west; then turned to run north to escape the coast. Craddock had plotted exactly how they would approach the bay. They spent that night luffed up, riding the waves. In the morning, they were out of sight of land. Craddock had the helm put up and they slowly made their way south until they could clearly make out the landmarks previous chosen as guides. Craddock had decided to take a risk and approach whilst there was still light. He was aided in his decision by the fact that there was a light mist, which would make it difficult for observers onshore to see what they were doing.

The shore dives so steeply into the sea, that there was too great a depth for them to use the anchor, other than close in. The cutters were swung out on either side. The muskets with their powder and shot had already been loaded aboard the cutters. As the light faded, the two cutters were manned and then rowed to the beach. As they approached, men emerged from seemingly nowhere to help pull the boats up onto the stony beach and unloaded as quickly as possible. A bray, gave away the fact that they must have donkeys or mules up the track. Not a word was spoken; there was no point, since neither side spoke the other's language. As quickly as they had arrived, the Basques disappeared into the gloom. The cutters returned to *Hound* to be lifted aboard. Immediately all sail was set, and *Hound* turned for home.

They had disposed of all but the marines' supply of muskets and powder. Added to which they had handed over pistols. That night Captain Caspar joined Will, Henri and Craddock. He sat on the window seat and produced a lead ball. "Interesting; this is a Spanish musket ball. It is the same size as a French ball. However, what we have given the Basques were English balls, and they are a different size. If we are to provide more weapons, I suggest we try to get hold of captured French Muskets and their shot. Trouble being, the British haven't fought the French on the ground for some considerable time."

It was a point Will stored away to put to the Aliens Office when he next had the chance.

Biscay decided that it might as well bring a little winter to the bay before it was really necessary. As they raced north, the winds veered to the north-west, and increased. The wave tops became white with foam and the height built. They were forced to take down the topsails, and later to reef the courses. Still *Hound* managed to cut through the waves, but the motion became rather uncomfortable, as the waves were on the bow. She still managed a respectable time to Plymouth Sound, now flying the red ensign and the broad pennant. Even as the anchor was dropped, the jollyboat crew were lowering their charge to the water. Lieutenant Tucker was given the task of carrying the signals to the Admiralty Telegraph Station. Here he had to brow beat the Officer in charge to send the signal immediately without the local Admiral's approval.

"You see that schooner at anchor out there. Now look to see what ensign she is flying and the pennant at her masthead." He told the reluctant officer. Once the fellow had taken in the red ensign and the broad pennant, he accepted that *Hound* was on Admiralty business. The shutters clacked as the message was relayed to London that the French already had troops in Northern Spain. One of the cutters, with Lieutenant Kemp, carried coded messages to the Port Admiral, with the request that a fast Admiralty rider take then immediately to London.

Immediately the boats returned to *Hound,* she upped her anchor and sailed out into the Channel again. It was better not to stay and have too many questions asked. It was dusk as they majestically coasted up the Dart to their home anchorage.

Will discovered that Isabella was restored to her usual health. She was positively blooming, so he asked if she would like to accompany him to London, so that they could spend time together. She was enthusiastic, and immediately started to plan their journey for the next day. She insisted that they took Mary Elizabeth with them so that the child could see more of her father. They would be travelling in a Landau, so that the child and her nurse could travel with them in the same carriage. Isabella's lady's maid, their cook, plus two extra housemaids would travel in a second coach. Allwood and Millward would ride beside the carriages, together with the extra footmen and grooms.

As far as London was concerned, it was already out of season. There were very few elegant carriages on the streets. The Calvert closed landau drew hardly any glances as it was covered in mud from the fast journey from Devon to London. Will reported straight away to the Admiralty to be immediately shown up to the First Lord's Rooms. Lord Mulgrave, whom Will had not met before, greeted him.

"Sir William! How nice to meet you at last. Grenville told me all about you. Do take a seat. Now what's all this about the French already being in Spain?"

Will explained what they had seen.

"But they could have been acting on behalf of the Spanish. They are allies after all."

"With an army poised on the border. I hardly think so, my Lord."

"Oh well; I suppose you are off to see Castlereagh, or have you seen him already."

Will realised the dangers that lay here. "No my Lord, I came straight here. I am after all a Naval Officer, first and foremost!"

Mulgrave looked placated.

Castlereagh greeted his friend with great warmth. "William! Great to see you. Got the message from the Admiralty, though Mulgrave said he expected the facts to be checked."

"Yes, he is a doubter at this moment. He suggested that the mapping party could be working for the Spanish. I myself doubt that, especially as they were so nervy. If they were working for the Spanish, they would have had a liaison officer with them."

"Quite!"

"We managed to make contact with a group that could be of help to us, if the French do invade. Their leader is a disenfranchised priest. Only a small band, but we gave them as many muskets as we could spare to get their loyalty. Given the training, and the powder, they could cause the French a great deal of trouble. Captain Caspar was right in my opinion, to counsel against assaults on the Army. He was all for attacking their supply lines: blocking roads, diverting rivers; those sorts of things."

Castlereagh sat and listened as Will expounded the ideas they had thrown about on the trip back to

England.

As Will was finishing, the mysterious Mr. Granger joined them. Will had no idea how he knew he was there, but he came.

"We need to have somebody on the ground organising the resistance." Stated Granger. Will's stomach churned. 'Oh God! Not again!' He thought.

"How did your little yacht fare with that coast?" Asked Granger; changing the subject in an instant.

"Well when we left it was still summer. The shores are lethal. I quite understand why Gambier finds it difficult to patrol them. *Hound* is fore and aft rigged. She can sail out of places where square-riggers would not stand a chance. There is a limit though, because it is a very exposed coast, and we have no safe bases there."

"Could we land troops there?" Asked Castlereagh.

"You would not stand a chance. Now that it is winter, you would lose at least half your men, before you began. I know it is tempting, because the main artery into Spain on that side runs so close to the coast for the first twenty-five miles or so. If the coast was kinder, the Navy could sit off the coast and blast away. Trouble is we are nearly into October, and the weather has already turned for the

worse. No fleet could survive so close to the land."
He paused for effect.

"I do have a present for you, which I think proves that the French are about to invade!"

He picked up his leather bag that lay beside him on the floor and pulled out a rolled up map.

"Courtesy of our bandit friends. They managed to 'retrieve' this before they set fire to the wagon which contained all the work the mapping party had achieved; or so we are lead to believe."

Both of the gentlemen stared at the map, as Will unrolled it. There were whoops of laughter.

"Did you show this to Mulgrave?" Asked Granger.

"No, I felt it better to save it for more believing eyes." Commented Will.

They stood gazing down at the map of northern Spain. Will explained where the road ran, and where it turned inland to head for Burgos and then on to Portugal.

"That is where we must inflict our barbs. It would be easy to close that main road - just there. Very close to where we came upon the French mapping party. It would take days to clear. Everything would have to be sent by alternative country tracks, which will be virtually impassable come the heavy rains."

The discussions went on into the night.

Will learnt that Rear Admiral Sir Sydney Smith was being sent to Lisbon, to add extra weight, but also so that the Portuguese Royal Family could be extracted if necessary.

It was after midnight that an exhausted Will reached his London House.

Chapter 11

Will spent the next few days, either at the Aliens Office, or with Castlereagh. Each decision was made after much discussion. Finally, it was agreed that Will should take *Hound* back with supplies for the Basques. Captain Caspar would be sent to be the liaison officer, much to Will's relief, to co-ordinate and train the Basque group.

Intelligence arrived from Paris that Napoleon was ordering General Junot to take his troops across Spain to invade Portugal, so denying the British the use of their ports.

At one of the meetings, General Wellesley was

announced. He was fairly similar in appearance to his older brother, but with a more pronounced beak to the nose. He seemed to Will, to be rather distant and self absorbed. He did not particularly take to the man.

When informed that Will had brought back proof of Napoleon's intentions, he seemed to dismiss the information as not being of much note. When Castlereagh explained that they intended to impede Junot's supplies, once the main force had passed, he remarked that it would not help that much in defeating the French. He needed a larger army.

Will left them arguing the case.

By the time Will was able to get away from London, with all the relevant paperwork, it had taken a fortnight. This meant that Will had been able to spend all his free time with Isabella, visiting their friends who were still in town, going to the theatre or to concerts. Now they had to travel back to Devon. Because of Isabella's condition, they took it gently, stopping on the way, so as not to tire her too much.

Will did not go straight back to *Hound*; he was taken into Totnes where he paid a visit to the Blacksmith. He showed the man the sketches he had made for a system to allow the stove aboard *Hound* to be used when the ship was heeling. It consisted of a weight to be hung under the stove, which would be supported by a series of gimbals. The Blacksmith contemplated the drawing for some time, before saying in his broad Devon accent.

"Cause bloody mayhem below!"

Will realised the man was right. In his enthusiasm for the idea, he had forgotten about the effect the heavy weight would have down below in the bilges.

"I could make you up the gimbals. The sheer weight of the stove would keep it pretty level. I would need to measure up the stove though. I gather from your drawing it is quite big."

"You are right. Unfortunately I am off, so I shall have to leave it for my return, but thank you."

Isabella was very worried about Will going back to the inhospitable coast of Northern Spain. She tried as usual to disguise her fears, but they were evident to Will. He had to drag himself away reluctantly, to be rowed back to *Hound*.

It was now October; the winds were getting up, and the waves were steeper and breaking. It took them a whole day to just make it round to Plymouth and the Hamoaze, because of the near gale conditions, which meant entering past the Ho was tricky. Next day they loaded all the weapons and powder, etc., from the Armoury. Whilst they were in the middle of transferring, a signal came for Commander Craddock to report to the Port Admiral. When he came back, he was in a sombre mood. He went straight to Will's day Cabin.

"I don't know quite what to say. I have been given command of a frigate at Chatham. I am to report soonest. This means I have got to leave you."

"I am delighted for you, James. You have given up much to support me, and I am very conscious of the sacrifice you have made. It is far too late really; you should have made Post years ago. I have been incredibly selfish to allow you to stay. For that I owe you an apology."

"Will, No! I have learnt so much from you. I shall make a far better Captain now, than I would have done if I had been promoted earlier. I am afraid I leave you in the lurch. What will you do? Have they appointed a new Commander?"

"No, I shall act both as Captain, and when necessary as Commodore. I should by rights, still be a Captain. It is only for the convenience of the Admiralty that they have kept me in the Commodore's rank."

"Did you know about this when you left London?" Asked Craddock; brows furrowed.

Will looked sheepish. "I have to own that I did speak of this matter to Wellesley Pole."

"Well I don't know whether to thank you or not. On the one hand of course it is a great leap forward, but on the other I shall miss you and the ship."

Craddock was 'dined' by the wardroom with Will as an invited guest. Then the jollyboat, suitably decorated, with Allwood in charge, carried their Commander to the steps after a rousing three cheers from the crew. All honours due had been carried out with enthusiasm. He had been a first-rate 'Captain'. Will had lost a good friend and he felt the loss acutely. He was grateful that he still had Henri de Cornes still aboard. He made Oscar Cranfield acting Skipper, with Lieutenant Kemp moving up to acting First Lieutenant.

They had to wait for the gale to blow itself out, before they could leave. Two days later, they left behind Penlee Point. The wind in the Western Approaches was from the southwest, so *Hound* was close hauled. This had just the effect that Will had been worrying about. The stove could not be used at the angle of heel, so there was no hot food for the crew. Luckily, at this stage all the food was fresh, so cold ham with fresh bread would have to do. They had the centre plate down, but they were so close hauled, that there was a danger of being backed by a wave at any moment. By six o'clock that evening they were some ten miles to the west of Ushant as the wind veered and allowed them to run down into the Bay of Biscay. *Hound* had to contend with high breaking waves and deep troughs. Millward came into Will's day cabin and much to Will's surprise pulled down the top of each window, which opened inwards and slid in a board that completely covered the glass on the outside, before shutting and bolting the window frame. It was the first time this had been necessary, and Will asked how Millward knew about this little extra protection.

"Shipwright at Camden thought it out and was very pleased with the idea. Showed me how it worked." Replied Millward; still busy with his endeavours.

The further south they ran, the worse the weather became. They were soon running on triple reefed courses and only two small foresails. Lifelines were rigged, and Lieutenant Kemp, now the First Lieutenant, checked that everybody was suitably secured as they came on deck. To make matters worse it came on to rain. Heavy, driving rain; penetrating everywhere and everything.

Bargeboards stopped the worst of the water heading straight down the ladderways, or running aft and through Will's quarters. Every time *Hound* drove her bows through a tall wave, it came flooding back, braking against the bargeboards, and slopping over. Millward had removed the carpet as a precaution, but Will working at his desk had to lift his feet up each time the water flooded aft. Below the crew's hammocks felt damp, and the pumps operated full time to keep the bilges dry.

No longer a onlooker, but back in charge, Will spent much of his time on deck through the night. In the morning, he decided that it was far too risky to approach the coast, so they turned to face the waves under virtually bare poles. It was during the morning watch, with Lieutenant Tarrant, officer of the watch, that he asked what the ex-boatswain thought of the idea of hoisting spare foresails, back to front, in place of the courses. Tarrant mulled the idea over.

"Give us steerage, without the weight up aloft. Yes, I like the idea. May we try it out?"

Will grinned at his old colleague. "Carry on Lieutenant!"

Tarrant gave a bark of a laugh. "Bring up the two spare Fore Staysails and a spare Inner jib." He commanded.

Once they had been hauled onto the deck, Tarrant

went forward and supervised the fitting of the three sails in there unusual positions. The new Boatswain Mr. Frobisher, who had been boatswain's mate, took over once he realised what was required. On a pitching deck, with waves constantly trying to wash you off your feet, it was no mean feat. Once hoisted though they gave *Hound* a forward drive, which helped control the ship. If they had hoisted the gaffs, there would have been a great weight of wood thrashing about up aloft threatening the top masts and all below.

After two days of suffering bruises and one broken arm, *Hound* met a new day to a blue sky and the wind rapidly reducing in force. At midday, they were able to take sights and then set a course for the north coast of Spain. Will decided to investigate Santona, which was nearly ninety miles further west than their previous port of call. It was unlikely that anybody there would know about the three masted American schooner, so there was less likelihood of questions being asked as to how they could cross the Atlantic and get back in such a short time.

Santona was well protected from Westerlies or even North Westerlies with a depth of six fathoms between the sand spit and the headland of Monte Ganzo, which rose to over 1,200 feet. When they had anchored off the small town, which is on the west bank, they were sheltered behind the mountain; Will had himself rowed to the town quay. Here in formal civilian dress of a plain brown silk outer coat over a handsome waistcoat, he asked for the mayor in haltering Spanish. On his way to the Town Hall, he passed several Spanish soldiers, which obviously meant there was a military presence here. At the Town Hall, he explained that his 'yacht' had been blown off course in an Atlantic gale and that they needed to do some repairs aboard and to dry out. Asked where his intended port might be he unhesitatingly replied Corunna. Just in case, he asked if there was anything that the town would like brought over from America, the next time they made the trip. He suggested that the Mayor might like to join him aboard for a drink, but the Mayor was obviously frightened of something or someone, because he became very unsure of himself. He then blurted out that the town was now under military control. Will decided to ignore this, saying that as a private American merchant ship, he did not need to check with the military. However, the Mayor politely turned the offer down, and suggested that *Hound* leave as soon as possible. Will promised they would leave the next morning.

Back aboard, Cranfield had the cutters lying alongside, with crewmembers pretending to bail them out. It would mean that the cutters would remain in the water as darkness fell.

As soon as it was dark, and before any moon could rise and floodlight the area, the cutter on the far side from the town was manned and Patxi, together with Captain Caspar and three marines were taken to the sand spit on the far side. By the time the moon rose, all was quiet around the schooner.

Patxi had contacts in Limpias, a village about six miles upstream. He hoped to be able to borrow horses to get him to Turtzioz, a small village right in the middle of the mountains.

Here there would be members of Elazar's *Partidas* band. They were patriotic Basque's who hated Spanish rule from Madrid. If he could get to them, he was convinced he could organise mules and their attendants to get to the beach at Sonabia, which was just round the coast from Santona and was fairly protected from Westerlies. If it were safe to land, they would wave flags on the beach. If it proved to be under the scrutiny of the Spanish military, they would then make their way to join another band near to the original landing site at Ogella. The problem that faced Will was that now they were well into October, the weather was not likely to stay as beneficent as it was at that moment.

Early the next morning *Hound* raised her anchor and coasted out of the estuary to be seen turning westwards. Once well out of sight of any lookouts she turned North. This was so she was out of sight of land; and to give her plenty of sea room, if the weather changed. Two days later and approaching from the east, flags were seen being waved on the Sonabia beach. As night fell, *Hound* settled to a long anchor half a mile off the beach. The cutters ran in and many hands helped them to be beached. The Spanish and French muskets were unloaded together with the powder and shot, especially cast by the Plymouth Armoury. Patxi and Caspar; together with their marines returned after the final shipment had been loaded onto the mules, and were being hauled off.

Patxi was very excitable as he climbed aboard. He could not wait to tell Will that the first elements of the French army had crossed the border on the 18th October. This first part of the Army was bivouacked on pastureland just south of Deba. When Will measured this out on the chart, he realised that the French Army was just eleven miles as the crow flies from where they lay at anchor.

"I think we should go and see for ourselves." Said Captain Caspar. "There is nothing better than first hand intelligence."

"But for whose use?" Questioned Will.

"Why ours of course!" Replied Caspar; a smile playing at his lips.

"I can get you up onto the mountains above the road. You know where we met the map makers the first time." Added Patxi.

"Lieutenant Cranfield, do you feel up to keeping *Hound* out of trouble, whatever the weather for the next few days?" Asked Will.

"Aye, Sir." Came the confident reply.

"We can be there easily before sunrise." Added Patxi.

Will studied the chart, then the map. He looked up at Cranfield. "There must be no margin of error. The ship comes first. If you feel that the weather is about to change; don't hesitate. Go right out to sea and sit it out. If necessary, we shall get Patxi to cook us a meal and find a roof." Patxi smiled. He was used to gentle teasing.

"I should like to join you, if I may?" Henri de Cornes said quietly from the window seat.

"I should be honoured to have you my friend. Just like old times." He was referring to the time when he and Henri had landed on the shores of hostile France and carried out a close-up survey of St. Valerie-sur-Somme, before they decimated part of the French landing fleet.

As the cutters left *Hound*, Cranfield already had the

capstan manned and was shortening the anchor warp.

Chapter 12

Patxi and Caspar must have conspired together, because horses were waiting for them as they landed in pale moonlight on the beach. As they left, men were pulling branches over the sand to disguise the fact that there had ever been animals on it. How the lead riders knew where they were going or the horses could be so calm about being ridden in the dark surprised Will. It was a gentle pace, as they zigzagged along narrow tracks between heavily wooded sides to the hills. They skirted villages, keeping mostly to the high ground. At one stop, Patxi informed Will that they were following a smuggling route. Will was not surprised.

One moment they were climbing steeply, the next they were heading down a precipitous path, which appeared to have no bottom. They crossed streams and up over more hills. It was a quarter moon, which flitted in and out behind speeding clouds. The scent of the trees seemed far more intense at nighttime. Having ridden up the side of a steep mountain, Will was grateful that the descent into a long valley that appeared to run southwest was exactly on their route. They traversed a valley that ran at right angles to their track and plunged into another long valley before winding their way down a steep path to ford a river and then follow it northwards until another valley opened up on their right. At the end of this valley they had to slowly plod their way up a narrow track single file; over the top of a high area until finally the leading rider reigned in. The fellow dismounted and took their reins from them. One of the partisans stayed to hold the horses and they set off on foot through a dense forest of trees. One had to walk with an arm on the shoulder of the man in front, with the other arm up in front of your face to make sure the fellow ahead had not pushed aside a branch and it was about to swipe you across the face. They walked for about half an hour, and then rested for ten minutes before setting off again.

Quite suddenly, they all had to stop. Patxi whispered to Will and Caspar the instruction that had been passed back. They had to crawl on their stomachs. One by one they crawled after each other until the lead stopped again. When finally the moon came out again, Will could see that they were on the edge of the mountain, in thick undergrowth looking down on the very road they had travelled a couple of months earlier.

Caspar had wriggled up to be beside Will. Patxi did the same his other side.

"The French will send out "travailleurs", what we would call in layman's terms scouts. They work ahead of the column on both sides to keep a sharp lookout for any opposition."

"Won't they come up here?" Asked Will.

"Na! This is too dense scrub for them. They will probably ride the high ground behind us. No self-respecting Frenchman would crawl on his belly to look in this stuff. They are generally under a sergeant or even only a corporal. I understand that this army is composed of raw recruits."

"Really?" Whispered Will. "How do you know that?"

"Patxi's lot have had the Corps of Observation of the Gironde, which are about 25,000 strong, by the way, under observation for well over a year." He chuckled. "Smugglers, half of them, and everything is reported back. Originally to secure safe routes into France."

The first hint of dawn appeared in the west. Will pulled his faithful leather bag, which had been his father's before him, round and extracted his telescope and his flask. He took a sip of brandy mixed with water. Beside him, he could just make out that Patxi was eating a biscuit and had his flask on the ground in front of him. It was definitely getting lighter. A couple of hours passed, and nothing happened, then all of a sudden, they heard a voice calling in French behind them.

"Hope they don't fucking well find the horses." Muttered Caspar.

There was an answering call, then vaguely what sounded like laughter. Everybody kept stock-still; you could only hear gentle breathing. Further off now, Will heard a voice call to someone else.

"Merde! C'est impossible pour une souris, encore moins un homme!" (This is impossible for a mouse, let alone a man.)

Then all went quiet. The dust was the first sign of the advancing army. Then round the corner came a couple of officers on horseback, looking closely at the forest above them. Then the bulk of the troops followed. It was no orderly progress. Soldiers with packs on their backs shuffled forward, mixed in with the ox-drawn carts, piled high with boxes. There seemed almost a festive spirit amongst the troops. On and on they came, occasionally the line being broken by a team of horses pulling a limber and gun behind them.

Beside Will, Caspar was writing everything down in a kind of shorthand. Will focused his scope on the officers; who appeared not much smarter than their troops.

Suddenly Caspar thrust Will's scope to the ground. Annoyed Will turned to Caspar. Caspar mouthed "The reflection of the sun, be careful!" Will nodded his understanding. It was something that had never occurred to him. It did not matter at sea. Either you could be seen, or you were out of sight. It took all day for the French Corpse to pass where they were hidden. Then came the stragglers. Carts drawn by emaciated horses or mules. Amongst the later lot were quite a few women, and a few soldiers limping from bad feet or boots.

As the sun went down, they had to crawl back they way they had come. Checking every few yards that there was no one about. The odd small animal was disturbed, but strangely, the fact that they were crawling did not seem to put them to panic flight. At last, they made the more open ground. Finally able to stand they made their way at a jog through the trees to a point where the leader stopped. He stood listening, then raised both hands to his lips, and made a loud bird call. Another bird replied, then a third. A few minutes later, the horses were led up from all directions. It was apparent that they had been dispersed.

It was another laborious night ride back to the beach at Ogella. Partisans rode off ahead as they neared the water. There are cliffs overlooking the bay, with trees growing virtually to the edge. It was amongst these trees that they rested, eat their hard rations, and waited. Will was not too hopeful of being taken off. There were breakers on the beach below. Any boat attempting to ride the waves onto the sand would be in danger of being tipped over.

As the sun went down, so the wind dropped and the sea in the bay became calmer. Out at sea it still looked rather rough.

Then the sight to gladden their hearts, a three masted schooner came round the point from the west. It swung round into the bay, still with all sails set. A good six cables (1,200 yards) off, a cutter was left in the wake as the schooner came about to head out to sea. Will was impressed by the manner in which his own oarsmen handled the situation. They pulled hard, then let the waves work for them before pulling again. Will thought 'Allwood', and trained his scope on the boat. There standing in the stern was his faithful coxswain.

From all directions, partisans appeared on the beach to wade waist deep into the sea to help the boat as it rode in on the crests of the waves. To everybody's surprise, the oarsmen downed their oars; leapt out leaving Allwood all alone in the boat. Then with hand gestures and pushing they indicated that the cutter should be turned about to face the waves. Eager hands helped to lift the boat and turn it. Will, Patxi, Henri and Caspar all waded out and climbed aboard. At that moment, a horseman came galloping onto the beach. He rode straight into the water and up to the boat, thrusting a rolled paper at them.

"Signor Calvert!" He cried, and Will grabbed the paper.

"Is there a lantern aboard?" He asked.

Allwood lent down and said in his ear. "No Sir."

"I'll have to read this once we are aboard."

The oarsmen patted the partisans on the back, handed them a couple of kegs of, what looked suspiciously like rum, and climbed back aboard as the partisans ran the boat into the waves. They were soaked but seemed to be laughing and joking as they waved goodbye.

Hound came in to make another turn around the bay. She was still moving through the water when a line was thrown, and the cutter taken in tow. Gradually the line was hauled in until the cutter was alongside. Will was the first up the rope ladder, closely followed by the others.

"Well done Cranfield." Will said as he met his number one at the gunwale. Cranfield admitted that it was Tarrant's idea to keep moving, so the schooner could not be taken by a surprise wave and turned whilst lingering.

Will unfolded the rolled paper as he made his way to his cabin. Millward was pouring a brandy for him. Will crossed to where there was a light to read by.

The message was from Elazar. He wrote that one of the most influential noblemen of the region, Señor Alphonso Ekain de Hondarribia, had been so upset by the invasion of his land that he had sought out Elazar and offered to lead any Partisans who wished to defend their ancient nation, from the marauding French. Elazar added that the French Army's soldiers were already pillaging and raping the women folk. The nobleman was part of the family that had once ruled the entire Doniblane area. His family hated the French, because their castle that overlooked the Bidasoa River, had in 1792 been demolished by the invading French Army. Señor de Hondarriba now wanted to meet Signor Calvert. He knew that Signor Calvert had a ship, so he would like to meet up at sea. He would rendezvous off San Sebastian in two days time, so long as he was still free and the schooner was still able to sail those waters.

This man could be very influential. Will decided that for the sake of a few extra days it would be worth hanging around. There could be a problem though. What would happen if the French decided to use ships to land soldiers along the coast? *Hound* was still flying the American flag. Would that be recognised by French naval officers? In the end, he decided to stay, so informed Cranfield of his decision.

In a moderate sea, but with long rolling troughs, *Hound* cruised off the coast of San Sebastian two days later. They were a mile out keeping more to the eastern side of the entrance to the horseshoe bay. At four bells of the forenoon watch, a larger than usual fishing boat was seen to be heading in their direction from Pasaia. Pasaia was a small fishing village at the mouth of a narrow estuary just a few miles to the east of San Sebastian. It was a harbour that Will had considered as a possible haven for *Hound*, but it was too near to the road from France to Burgos. Half an hour later, it was obvious that the vessel was making straight for *Hound*. Approximately two cables off, it was clear to see that the ship sported a huge ensign that was neither the Spanish nor the French flag. As a precaution, the gun crews were closed up, with the tompions out of the gun muzzles. As the vessel got steadily closer, Cranfield had rope fenders placed all down the leeward side of *Hound.* As the ship drew alongside a finely dressed man stood out from the rest. He wore a wide brimmed hat, held by one hand to the top of his head. His coat was of silk and there was evidence even at that distance that there was lace at the cuffs and neck.

Once the Basque vessel had been made fast alongside, the Gentleman was lifted bodily across the two gunwales, by the Basque sailors. The man swept off his hat as he made an elaborate bow, with one leg brought back behind the other.

"Alphonso Ekain Ybarra de Hondarribia." He stated; looking about.

Will dressed in his plain dark blue serge sailing jacket stepped forward. The Gentleman had very dark black hair, which was his own; a goatee beard and waxed moustaches. Bright dark eyes above an aquiline nose radiated intelligence.

"Signor Calvert?" Asked the Gentleman.

"Yes." Replied Will in Euskera.

Ybarra's eyebrows showed his surprise. "Gure hizkuntza hitz egiten duzu." (You speak our language.)

Will smiled to acknowledge the fellows surprise and indicated that he should pass ahead into his quarters. Millward was there with a tray in hand, which he placed on the table. It contained a cut glass decanter full of Claret and two cut glass wine goblets.

"Father,...errr..., Elaxar tells me that you have provided us with weapons. For that, we are truly grateful. I, myself, will be very active from now on. However, I have a problem. I am known around here, and that means that my wife and daughter will not be safe. Nowhere in Spain will be safe. I therefore ask you Sir, if you could possibly take my wife and daughter back to America. I fear they will be raped and then killed otherwise." The fellow looked distraught.

"I am afraid that there might be some misconception. We fly the American flag, so that we can operate here. In fact, I am Sir William Calvert, a Commodore in the British Navy. If I was to take aboard your wife and daughter, they would not be transported to America, but rather to England."

"English! Then perhaps you can get your Government to send us an army to fight the French. Once they know what is happening here, surely they will want to help?"

"I assure you Sir, my Government would indeed like to help, but I doubt if it would be possible to land an army on this part of the coast in winter and then to supply it."

Ybarra nodded his head sadly. "Of course, you are right. I still ask you Sir, if you would be prepared to save my family?"

"It would be an honour Sir."

"Really? Sir, you are without doubt an English Gentleman!"

"Where are your wife and daughter at this moment?" Asked Will.

"They here. The French have already started to ransack Pasaia. It is terrible."

"Then I suggest you have them transferred immediately. Millward, tell Number One to have the Ladies aboard the ship alongside transferred immediately, and then sling my cot in Commander Craddock's old cabin alongside his cot."

"Aye aye Sir!" Millward came out of his pantry and disappeared.

"Let us go and greet them." Said Will.

Ybarra with perfect manners indicated that Will should leave the cabin first. They waited on the quarterdeck as a well-dressed elegant Lady was hoisted across in the same manner as her husband, to be deposited on deck in front of them. Then a much younger Lady was similarly handled across. Both looked flustered at their treatment.

"Sir William Calvert, at your service madam." Said Will; making an elegant sweeping bow after the manner of their husband and father.

Once the Lady had shaken herself, she put out a hand as if it should be kissed. Will lowered his head over it, but refrained from actually kissing it. This he understood was what happened at Court. The Lady had a pale skin with dark black hair, which fell in ringlets, framing a handsome face. Her dress was of silk. Behind her, a much younger woman, judged by Will, to be about fifteen to sixteen, was looking about. She had similar black ringlets, which framed a soft complexioned face with startlingly black flashing eyes under enormous lashes. This young woman was already flowering into a beauty. Both had well proportioned figures, though the younger one's was more boyish.

Will introduced his officers in turn. The young Lady was introduced as Antonia. He noted that the young woman showed most interest in Lieutenant Tucker. He realised that Thomas had grown into a handsome young man.

Will showed the Ladies into what had been

Craddock's Cabin. Millward was just finishing hanging Will's cot beside that of the Commander's. Helping him was Midshipman Surprise.

"I hope you will find it comfortable in here. You shall of course be invited to take food with me in my day cabin through there." They did not say a word, nor show any surprise that Will spoke in their language. Both looked scared stiff. When her husband embraced her, the wife burst into floods of tears.

"Will I ever see you again, my love?" She cried. The daughter stood mutely taking everything in, but there were tears in her eyes. Ybarra then embraced his daughter and they left the Ladies to settle down in their unfamiliar surroundings.

"Will you be coming back?" Asked Ybarra.

"It will depend on the weather, and what our masters at the British Admiralty decide. We shall be leaving you an expert in demolition, a Captain Caspar, who had best travel back with you." Will had yet to find out if Patxi wanted to stay, or return.

"What we do need to do, is for you to set up a watch from various points along the coast. When they see a three masted schooner, they will know we are back. The beach we have been using is I understand called Ogella. Do you know of it?"

"Yes, I know it vaguely."

"Good! If you could send messengers there, when we appear, we can get in contact with you. I expect that you will want as many muskets, powder and shot as we can get hold of for your enterprise. The last ones we brought were Spanish and French, because the British musket uses a different size of ball. Is there anything else you can think of at such short notice?"

"I have yet to muster my thoughts. My first concern was for my wife and daughter. You say a Captain Caspar is returning with me. Does he speak our language?"

"He is learning. He is a Marine Captain. A sort of sailor cum soldier. Excuse me." Will turned to Midshipman Surprise. "Pass the word for Captain Caspar." Will ordered.

They were now on the quarterdeck once more, with *Hound's* officers watching everything that was going on. Cranfield stood to one side, ready to join Will if required. Caspar came bounding up the ladderway from the wardroom, a leather bag over one shoulder, and a Baker rifle in his hand. At either side pistols rested in holsters. Around his chest was hung a canvas strap with a number of pouches attached. He was dressed in a sombre brown tweed coat over lighter brown riding breeches with leather riding boots. He grinned at Will.

"All present and correct Sir William."

"Is Patxi going with you?"

"Of course, how would I get along without the old bugger?" It was said with a wide grin.

"Where is he then?" Asked Will.

"I am here!" Came the reply; as Patxi walked aft and bowed to Ybarra. Patxi was dressed also in dark brown, but had a couple of green cloaks over one arm. He carried a couple of Baker rifles in his hands. A Sailor planted a large bag at Patxi's feet. He turned and thanked the man.

"I shall offer you all the luck in the world. I shall endeavour to push your case at as higher a level as I can."

Ybarra bowed low. Caspar saluted Will and Patxi just smiled.

Chapter 13

An hour later *Hound* was sailing on a northerly course and the fishing boat had disappeared. Will sat at his desk writing up his Journal. When he heard somebody being sick next door, he leapt up and opened the door to the Ladies quarters. On her knees, the mother had her head over a chamber pot. At the far side, the door was opening and Thomas was in the process of entering.

"Give us a hand Thomas to get this lady into a cot. And send for the surgeon... oh there you are Henri."

Thomas helped Will to lift the lady up and place her gently in a cot. At the same time, Henri asked Millward for a glass of brandy. When this was produced, he added a few drops of something from a small glass bottle that he had taken from his bag. He swilled the contents around and then handed them to the Madam Ybarra.

"Drink this down, it will do you good." He said in Spanish.

Madam Ybarra froze with a look of extreme alarm. Will realised the reason.

"It is alright Madam, he is an English Surgeon. Yes,

he was a French aristocrat but he has served with me in the British Navy for years. You have no need to worry about Señor de Cornes."

Madam Ybarra looked searchingly into Will's face, before relaxing back onto her pillows and allowing Henri to gently place the glass to her lips, for her to sip.

Will suddenly realised that Thomas was still there standing beside Antonia. "Are you on duty, Thomas?" He asked.

Thomas smiled. "No Sir, Lieutenant Kemp has just taken over the watch. I was just leaving the quarterdeck when I heard this lady call for help."

"Good! I suggest we leave the Ladies to settle down." Said Will.

"It is a case of mal du mar, Madam. It is not unusual, especially when one is not used to the sea." Commented Henri; taking the glass from Madam Ybarra, then handing it back to Millward.

They all filed out. Thomas and Henri left through the quarterdeck access. Will and Millward exited to the day cabin.

"Did you provide the chamber-pot?" Asked Will; once the door was shut behind them.

"Aye Sir. I thought they might need one." Replied Millward.

"Very thoughtful of you Millward. Well done!"

Back at his desk, Will pondered over the eating arrangements. He doubted if Madam would want any food, but her daughter did not seem to be affected by the motion. He called for Millward to ask the 'Skipper' to join him. When Cranfield entered, Will said. "Been mulling over the dining etiquette: I don't think it would be suitable for me to entertain Mademoiselle Antonia alone. I should like you to join me, together with Henri, and I thought perhaps Tucker. He is more her age. What do you think?"

"I can't fault your reasoning Sir."

"Good, would you be so good as to pass the word. I shall dine the other officers in turn."

"Very good Sir." Cranfield replied; and left.

"Millward, lay for five will you?"

"Very good Sir William."

It struck Will how much more confident Millward had become over the years. He had turned into a first class servant.

Antonia was delighted to join the four officers at Dinner. Will thought it was probably the first time she had been alone in the company solely of men. Thomas was practicing his Spanish. He had been getting Henri to teach him the language at every opportunity as they crossed the Atlantic and back. Now he had to use it in earnest. Antonia seemed amused by his efforts, and stated that he must teach her English. Will was not too sure this was quite the thing, but let it pass. She had a surprisingly unaffected manner about her. She asked innumerable questions about the ship, and where they were headed. Her mother slept through the noisy conversation from next door. Will suspected that it might have been laudanum, which Henri had added to the brandy.

After dinner, Will leant Antonia his cloak to wrap around her shoulders so she could visit the quarterdeck and watch how the ship was handled. Lieutenant Tucker pointed out everything, attempting to translate it into Spanish, followed by the English word. When she returned to the day cabin, she had flushed checks. Will hoped they were only the result of the wind.

He showed her the Captain's Heads situated at each

quarter; which she promptly took advantage of. She excused herself and went back to her cabin.

It dawned on Will that taking the Ladies back to England was not the problem. It was what to do with them once they got there.

As evening closed in, so did the weather. The wind began to blow harder, and the waves respond. *Hound* was on a long reach, but as the wind backed to the northwest, she was increasingly on a fetch. Millward slipped silently out of his pantry and knocked on the Ladies door. He went in, and on coming out, Will raised a questioning eyebrow. Millward crossed to Will and whispered. "Both asleep, Sir."

Will nodded and putting on his foul-weather gear went out on to the quarterdeck. He looked up. Whoever was on watch had taken the precaution of taking down the topsails. *Hound* was cutting through the water, the odd wave making her shudder as it tried to force her off her course. Will popped his head into the tiny chartroom, which was on the starboard side just ahead of what had been Craddock's cabin. He looked at the last estimated position on the chart. He ran the parallel rulers up to read off the position. They were 45°N 45'21 3°51'06W: which meant they were nearly half the way up the Bay of Biscay. It was another 120 nautical miles before they would be off Ushant. He backed out of the cubby and looked around. Lookouts were posted in the bows and on the poop at the stern. Lieutenant Kemp stood firmly, legs astride near the wheel. They were about 140 miles off the French coast, and Will thought it unlikely any French vessel would be searching for an enemy out here; that was if they had managed to dodge Admiral Gambier's blockade of the French Biscay ports. Satisfied he turned in.

In the morning, he was eating his breakfast, when Antonia emerged from her cabin. She stopped on seeing him.

"Good Morning!" Said Will, first in Basque and then in Spanish, followed after a moment's thought in English. She gave him a beaming smile "Good Morning." She tried; testing the strange sound.

"Very good! Like something to eat?"

"Yes, Please".

"How is your mother?" Asked Will; in Spanish.

"She is very weak. She still feels a trifle ill."

"I'll get the surgeon to take a look at her. Rest assured, it is very common. It can take days, if you are prone to suffer. You are the lucky one. It doesn't seem to affect you."

Millward appeared un-summoned with a plate and a steaming mug of coffee.

"Excuse us mariners. We don't tend to use delicate china when at sea."

Antonia sat in the chair that Millward held for her.

"You have taken to eating off a sloping table very well. These by the way are called fiddles. Don't ask me why, they just are. Do you think your mother would like something?"

"I rather doubt it. Shall I go and ask?"

"No! Millward will ask her, save you getting up." Will smiled at Millward who was nodding his head. Millward knocked and then entered the cabin. When he came out, he nodded to the pair in the stern and disappeared into his pantry. He emerged with a plate and a mug, which he took back into the cabin. When he came out, he came to the table.

"Madam said she would try some dry bread and a drink."

"How on earth do you know that?" Asked Will realising he had forgotten about the language question when he had suggested that Millward ask Madam. Millward looked embarrassed.

"I couldn't help but overhear the Surgeon

instructing Thomas Sir. I repeated everything to myself. A kind of game, but I just picked up the lingo. I hope I haven't done anything wrong?"

"Far from it, old friend, I admire your attitude."

Antonia put her head on one side. "Are we very close to the French coast?" She asked.

"No; about a hundred and twenty miles away. Let me see that would be about 46 Leagues."

"Will there be any fighting?"

"I doubt it. The British Navy controls the sea. The French fleet are bottled up in their ports. Occasionally a brig or even a frigate manages to escape. Sometimes there are privateers, but they are mainly based on a place called St. Malo on the north coast of France. I shouldn't worry. This crew has never been bested in a fight."

"You have fought in many battles?" She asked; eyes wide.

"A few!" Will replied; modestly. "If you are worried, let me show you a little secret."

Will pulled open a draw in his desk and extracted a key. He led her over to the side of the divide between her sleeping quarters and his. He turned the key in a lock and pulled down the front of what looked like a draw. "Have a look in there."

Antonia gasped as she realised that two cannons sat hidden away there.

"They are our sting in the tail. There are two more hidden up in the bows. The cannons you saw on the foredeck are small compared to these beauties. We shall be exercising the guns shortly. If you want to, you can watch."

"Will there be a lot of bangs?"

"No, we pretend to fire them. Every few weeks we do so for real, but of course that uses up precious ball and shot."

Half an hour later, Will took Antonia forward to witness the 18 pounders in their hidden seclusion forward going through their drill. She was wrapped up in his boat cloak again. She seemed impressed. Afterwards Will wondered whether he should have allowed a young girl to watch half-naked men sweating over a couple of cannons. He worried as to what her mother might say. Then he worried more about what Isabella might think, if she knew. He cursed his own enthusiasm.

By mid afternoon, with the wind still keeping up a steady, though not too drastic a blow, they were ten miles off Ushant. Charging towards them out of the slight haze, came a line of frigates. Very early on, the lookouts announced that they were British from their rig. Antonia was sitting on the window seat of the day cabin reading, when she first realised that there was something up. She wrapped herself in Will's boat cloak and went out on deck. She watched as the lead frigate joined them at an angle. She was aware that *Hound* seemed to have slowed; she was more affected by the waves. As the lead frigate turned she watched as the huge flag hanging from the top pole of the rear sail of the frigate was lowered and then raised. There was shouting going on above, but she could not understand, and it seemed strangely echolike. Moving to one side, she saw an officer climb into the ropes holding the mast nearest the back of the frigate. He held a tube-like thing to his mouth. Then he waved, and she felt a change in *Hound's* movement. She was no longer pitching around; she was forging ahead. When Will joined her, she asked what that had all been about.

"Just a traditional British Naval practice. They were confirming that we were British, and then they saluted our flag, and we exchanged information."

"What do you mean; saluted our flag?"

Will looked embarrassed and the girl immediately recognised it.

"They were saluting you, weren't they? But, they were bigger ships. Why don't you have a bigger ship?"

Will collapsed against the rail. "I was senior to their Captain."

"Commodore, that is higher up than a Captain?"

"Yes."

"And you are a noble? Sir is noble?"

"Well I suppose so. I am a baronet; that is about the lowest form of noble you can find... except a plain Sir. A Baronet is hereditary; a normal knight is just a knight."

"And you have a big house?"

"Fairly big, I suppose."

"Is there a Lady Calvert?"

"Very much so, Isabella is my wife. I have a daughter, and another child on the way."

"You love your wife?"

"Very much. Ours was a love match, not an arranged marriage."

"The why do you fight?"

"I am a British Naval Officer. I have to serve my country!"

Antonia gazed at him for a moment. "Is Lieutenant Tucker married?" She asked.

Will roared with laughter. "No, I haven't given him the chance. I have kept him at sea for the last few years."

"He is very handsome, I think. I think he is kind as well, don't you?"

Will laughed. "I don't know about being handsome, I had not thought about it, but kind, yes he is very good hearted."

Antonia, looked slightly confused, and Will thought perhaps his Spanish was not up to it.

"He has been with you for a long time?"

"Yes, since he was a boy."

They were interrupted by the subject himself coming aft and telling Will that they were about to change course to head up the Channel. The light was beginning to fade, but so was the wind strength.

"I am thinking of hoisting the topsails if the wind abates anymore." Said Thomas.

"Good idea. I should give it an hour or so, just to

make sure." Will replied.

Back in his day cabin, he was able to get back to bringing his journal and all the other ledgers up to date. He really did need a clerk, he realised. He would try to find a suitable applicant.

Will was woken by Midshipman Manning, who told him they had Start Point in sight. Will hauled himself out of his seaman's hammock by using the rope that was threaded through two holes in the beams above. He was fully dressed except for his coat and boots. It had dawned a fine bright day. Lieutenant Kemp was the Officer of the watch. Will recognised that the fellow had placed them exactly where they needed to be.

"Good Morning, Sir." Kemp said; coming across to join Will. "Fine morning, wind has dropped. We are by my estimates about three hours ahead of high water."

"Couldn't have timed it better, if we had tried."

"If we keep on this course, we shall be two miles off before we turn."

"Very good, Lieutenant: a word if you please." Will moved away from the group around the binnacle to the larboard side.

"How is Midshipman Manning doing?"

Kemp as always thought before replying. "His seamanship is coming along satisfactorily, of course he is fine with the navigation, having been a Master's Mate."

Will thanked Kemp and strolled forward to the forecastle, and mounted the ladderway to the top. Here he had an even better view of Prawle Point and beyond it the familiar cock's comb of Start Point. Many a mariner had fallen foul of this coast in bad weather. You had to round the point at least a mile and a half off to avoid the race, which occurred at certain states of the tide. It was one of those almost unseasonably bright late October days. Everything seemed to be pinpoint sharp. They were a good two to three miles off, but it felt as if you could reach out and touch the rocky shoreline.

Millward had prepared a steaming mug of coffee for him when he got back to his cabin.

"Any sign of movement from next door?" Asked Will; quietly.

"No Sir." Came the reply; equally quietly.

Will returned to puzzle over what to do about his two passengers. He had been unable to ask the mother if they knew anybody in England. She had been too ill. He could hardly dump them in Dartmouth and leave them to fend for themselves. Once again, he decided that he would leave it up to Isabella to advise him. She was a woman, after all!

Millward brought in his breakfast and another cup of coffee from his pantry. There was still no sign of any movement, so Will put on his undress uniform coat and went through to the quarterdeck. *Hound* was turning from a run onto a reach. The watch on duty had just finished hauling in the sheets and coiling down the tails to hang neatly from their pins. Cranfield was by the wheel, together with Lieutenant Kemp and Lieutenant Tarrant. Eight bells sounded, and the new watch came streaming up from below to take over from the current watch. Will checked to see that the ensign flew from the mizzen gaff. High up at the top of the mainmast the broad pennant was in place.

The gold sands of Slapton could now be seen running in a long shallow curve from the south, north. Beyond, hidden now would be the beautiful bay of Blackpool Sands. Beyond, the cliffs rose up to block the view to the entrance to the Dart. Gulls came swooping out to greet their arrival. Will stood against the larboard bulwarks gazing at the familiar sights, which heralded their return home.

Chapter 14

Soon the mouth of the Dart opened up, revealing the two 15th century forts, one either side that protected the entrance. *Hound* soon turned, the sheets were hauled in, and close-hauled she ran for the opening. The wind would soon become fluky as the hills either side of the estuary played their games. Tarrant was doing just the right thing; he was allowing *Hound* to keep up a good speed as she passed the forts. They would be heading almost straight into the wind as they passed One Gun Point and had to turn to larboard. Once they turned opposite Baynards Cove, they would have the wind again to take them past Dartmouth town.

Millward came out to ask if the Ladies were allowed to watch from on deck. The fact that he said 'Ladies', indicating that Madam must be feeling better. Will instructed Millward to tell them they could, so long as they kept out of the way. Then behind him, the door opened and out came Madam Ybarra, followed by her daughter.

"Good Morning. I trust that you are feeling better Madam." Said Will; in Euskera.

Madam Ybarra gave him a weak smile, and nodded.

"Mother is still feeling rather weak." Said Antonia.

"Has she eaten?" Asked Will.

"I had a piece of dry bread, thank you." Replied the Lady in question.

Will summoned Tucker over. "Thomas, be so good as to explain where we are, will you?"

"Certainly Sir!"

Will wandered across to the starboard side, to be able to stand apart and concentrate on what was happening. Lieutenant Tarrant was calmly giving the orders. He knew this river as well as Will did. On the other side, Thomas was keeping up a running commentary as they sailed majestically up river. The harbour master's boat swung round as they came abreast.

"Good Morning Sir William. A fine morning. Going up to your normal place?"

"Yes thank you!" Shouted Will, with a wave.

The tide was helping them as they cruised past Old Mill Creek. The trees still had that cropped appearance parallel to the water, as if someone had gone along with a sharp knife cutting them in an orderly line. Most of the trees had shed their leaves, but a few evergreens, still gave the steeply wooded bank character.

Allwood was now at the wheel as they approached the Anchor Stone, a rock that really stood out at low water. One had to keep to the starboard side of the river as you approached Ned's Point before the small village of Dittisham. The anchor party were ready, the bower anchor hanging with its tip in the water. Flaked out on deck the anchor warp formed a pattern on the holystoned deck. Nippers were attached at intervals, so that the headlong rush of the cable could be checked to bed the flukes of the anchor well into the mud at the bottom of the river.

The sheets had been let fly as *Hound* turned into the widening part of the river. Here the depth was at least four fathoms, but very abruptly, it would shelve steeply. Tarrant brought his arm down from the upright position where it had been a moment before. The first of the nippers was cut and the anchor cable began to snake out. Then the second nip was cut and still more followed. Then the third nip held and *Hound* slowed right down to a stop. Then as the deck-crew secured the sail-ties round the courses, then the booms and gaffs to their crutches; the jollyboat crew were already lowering their boat into the water.

Will turned to see awed expressions on the two Ladies. Thomas was smiling broadly. The whole manoeuvre had been completed without any shouting or fuss. Tarrant had a smug expression, but then it was his first time as the officer in charge, bringing his vessel to anchor.

The side party assembled as Allwood followed his oarsmen into the jollyboat. Cranfield came across to Will, who was waiting to climb down when the boat was ready.

"Excuse me Sir, what do we do about the Ladies?"

"Nothing at this moment. I shall decide later what we do."

Cranfield stood back, and the pipes shrilled as Will climbed over the bulwarks and dropped down into the jollyboat.

It is about half a mile to the landing stage below Calvert House, which overlooks this part of the river on its northern side. In perfect rhythm, the oars dug into the water to drive the boat ahead. Normally a Midshipman would have been in charge, but Will preferred to have just Allwood at the tiller.

"I suggest that the crew come up to the house and have a noggin, so that I can send a message back to the boat."

"Aye, aye, Sir." Acknowledged Allwood; without looking down. It was quite normal for the crew to be invited up to the house after a stiff row. It was one of the reasons that there was such great a rivalry to get a place in the boat.

Once they touched the landing stage, Will was out and striding up the hill to his house. As usual he entered by the servant's entrance. The staff must have been alerted to *Hound's* arrival, as they just said 'Good morning' as he passed the kitchen. He found Isabella sitting up in bed with a tray on her lap. Mary Elizabeth who had been sitting on the end of the bed leapt up and grabbed him round the legs as he crossed to kiss his wife. He hoisted her up onto his hip and then bent to embrace his wife. It was an emotional homecoming. Will had worried about his wife's health the whole time he had been away, but now she seemed to be blooming. He admired the bump, which was now self-evident.

"So how are you feeling?" He asked.

"Fine, absolutely fine. Whatever it was that Henri gave me, seemed to do the trick. And you, how are you?"

"Oh, fine!" And he proceeded to give a full rundown on what had happened since he left her last time. He finished by explaining how he had ended up with two Ladies aboard.

"So what are these Ladies of yours like?" Asked Isabella; with a raised eyebrow. He knew she was teasing him, but never the less it felt awkward.

"The mother was sick for the whole trip, except for when we were coming up the river. The daughter though did not seem to be effected. She must be about sixteen or seventeen, I should think. Pretty thing - much taken with our Thomas. I think she is a bit of a tomboy, because she seemed to take a real interest in the boat and all that went on. Of course neither speak English, just Euskera and Spanish."

"So what are you going to do with them?"

"That my love is the question. Frankly, I have no idea. There was no time to discuss that with their husband, and the wife has been abed. I rather wanted your thoughts on the matter."

"Mine! I haven't any idea what you do with émigrés. Surely Henri must know, after all he was one once."

"Ah, but he was a qualified Doctor. These are two women, and I have no idea if they have any friends in this country or any money, for that matter. They had to leave their homes in a hurry. I don't think there was much time to organise anything. Signor Ybarra de Hondarribia was frantic for them to leave the country because the French soldiers were raping the women."

"What a tongue twister of a name! Were the French really raping the women?"

"The Signor had no reason to make it up. They were all very distressed by their parting. He thought that they would be going to America."

"I suppose we better have them to stay, but we cannot keep them here indefinitely. We shall have to move them on. I shall be giving birth soon, and I don't want to have to worry about guests then."

The subject changed now to the birth and family; the Ladies on the boat were forgotten for a moment or two. The nursemaid came and claimed Mary Elizabeth and the couple were able to spend time alone together for an hour or so.

When Will finally came down in civilian dress, he called for Allwood and instructed him to fetch the two women and to bring Millward, Henri, plus a Midshipman back with them, as he, Allwood would need to stay ashore. They were going to have to go to London the next day or day after.

When the two Ladies did arrive, they were shown straight up to two of the smaller guest bedrooms by the servants. Isabella came down to join Will in his study as he went through papers relevant to the estate.

"I suppose we better have them down for a drink before eating." Suggested Isabella.

"Suppose so, though it is going be difficult to hold a conversation if they do not speak our language. Hopefully Henri will be here."

"He will have to interpret!" Laughed Isabella. "Going to be very hard going!"

Will pulled the bell rope, and almost immediately, Clarkson the butler opened the door.

"Would you get one of the maids to invite the ...."He stopped and laughed at his own mistake." Pardon me, Clarkson; I had quite forgot that of course the Ladies don't understand English. I suppose I better go up."

"I think, Sir William; that I might be able to sign sufficiently for them to understand."

"Good for you Clarkson. Give it a try."

Clarkson backed out; shutting the doors behind him.

"I suggest we go through to the sitting room." Said Isabella. "I haven't been in there since you left. It will be strange."

"Will there be a fire?"

"I am sure Clarkson will have organised one, especially if we have guests. It would offend him greatly if we received in the Yellow room."

Will gave her his arm and they moved to the doors to the Sitting room. Isabella had been correct; a lovely roaring fire spread its warmth across the room. Isabella seated herself on one of the settees as Will poured her out a glass of wine.

The doors opened and Clarkson; a smug look on his face, announced. "Madam Ybarra de Hondarribia and Mademoiselle Antonia Ybarra de Hondarribia."

Madam Ybarra swept into the room, but slowed as she looked around. She was obviously taking in the gracious surroundings. She looked surprised. Antonia's expression was one of awe.

"Madam, let me introduce my wife; Lady Isabella Calvert." Said Will; in Spanish.

Madam dropped a curtsy, which was immediately copied by her daughter. Isabella smiled graciously and indicated with her fan that Madam should sit on the settee opposite her. Antonia went and sat beside her mother.

Will wondered what had happened to Henri, but he could not just sit there, so he had to use his not too perfect Spanish.

"I trust that you found your rooms to your satisfaction?" He asked.

Madam who had been affecting a rather rigid smile

turned towards him.

"Gracias Signor. It is very fine. Your whole house is very impressive."

Will translated for Isabella's benefit. Isabella smiled and nodded. Just then, Henri came through from the hall, unannounced.

He swept a leg to Isabella and went forward to bow over her hand.

"This is going to interesting!" He whispered. "Sorry, I am late, my humble apologises." He said aloud. Then he turned to the two Spanish Ladies.

"You are comfortably settled?" He asked first in English, and then immediately in Spanish. Both nodded their approval.

"Do you know anybody in England?" Asked Will in Spanish as Clarkson presented a tray with wine glasses on it to the two Ladies.

"No, nobody." Replied Madam; shaking her head sadly.

"Nobody in London?" Asked Henri; taking upon himself the task of interrogator.

Madam shook her head. There were tears in her eyes, and it was obvious she was fighting her emotions. Will observed Isabella's expression soften. She had noticed as well.

"We must teach the Ladies essential phrases in English as soon as possible." She said; looking to Henri to translate.

Henri explained in Spanish. Both Ladies nodded together. Henri started to point at various things and say the English word. The Ladies caught on and repeated each word. This was still going on when Clarkson announced that Dinner was served. Will presented his arm for Madam who obviously was not used to English etiquette. Henri followed with Isabella. Isabella directed Madam to the seat on her right. Antonia followed and sat opposite her mother. They were in the Breakfast Room, which had an oval table. Henri explained that they were in the small dining room, as it was cosier. He also explained that the Calvert's did not dine in the usual manner. They preferred each course to be presented separately, rather than the soup and fish course to be placed together on the table. They liked the food to be hot.

This seemed to break the ice a bit with Madam Ybarra. The meal was a strain for all, but the Ybarra's were beginning to learn a few words of the language. It was after the sweet course that Will brought the conversation round to more pressing matters.

"Did your husband provide you with any money to live on in America, or as you now know England?" He asked.

"I was able only to bring my jewels; that is all. I do not think he had considered how we should manage."

"Henri, when you arrived in this country, was there any help offered?"

"No, nothing! I was lucky, although I was considered an aristocrat by birth, being the third son, I went into medicine and then the Navy. So I had what you might call a 'trade' to fall back upon."

The Ladies looked bewildered, and Henri repeated what he had said in Spanish.

"What are we to do?" Cried Madam Ybarra; bursting into tears. Isabella was at her side immediately.

"Well the jewels might help for a short time, but they must be valued in London, for the best price." Said Will.

"Do you sew?" Asked Henri. Antonia nodded, but her mother just sobbed.

"Don't worry, we shall look after you. You won't starve." Said Isabella; rocking with the distraught woman. Henri translated, and Madam Ybarra held onto Isabella and crooned. "Gracias, Oh Gracias! Senora."

Isabella's eyes met Will's and he knew that they would now be responsible for these two émigrés. He would have to have a long talk with his wife, to decide what was best.

That evening they sat up in bed and discussed their problem.

"You will have to ask around when you are in London. The Government surely must have funds to help such people." Stated Isabella.

"The trouble is that they do not come from a city, they come from a small town about the size of Totnes. Which gives me an idea! What if we check if there are any properties in Totnes that would be suitable. They would then be near enough to ask for our help, without being on top of us."

"It would certainly be an answer, but not until they can speak more English." Replied Isabella.

The next morning Will summoned his Steward to ride around his estate with him. During their ride, he asked him to seek out any properties that might be suitable for a couple of single Ladies on their own in Totnes.

He then spent the rest of the day with Isabella and his daughter. The Spanish Ladies joined them at meal times, but otherwise kept to themselves.

The following morning Will left with Allwood for London and the Admiralty. He left behind Millward, just in case Henri had to return to the ship, which would leave nobody who spoke Spanish in the house. As usual, he found the trip tiring and boring. He was all alone inside the coach, since Allwood rode beside Jeffries the coachman, with two footmen behind. As always, he travelled light.

In London he stayed at a hostelry, rather than travelling all the way to Highgate and his London home. He reported to the Admiralty, leaving word that he could be found next door in the Aliens Office. Here Mr. Granger debriefed him, following closely everything Will described, and then asking questions. Will left him with a very detailed report.

Lord Castlereagh was in his Palace Office, and greeted Will with his usual bonhomie.

"God it is good to see you Will. Had a good trip I hope."

"Interesting; I have just left the Aliens Office where I left a detailed report. I must say it is the first time I have seen the enemy on the ground so to speak. I wasn't too impressed by Junot's forces; more a rabble to my eyes, than an army. They are not doing themselves any favours. They are surviving off the land, which in turn means pillaging and raping as they progress. I suppose all armies are prone to do just that! I left Caspar and Patxi there, who have joined up with a local Spanish, or rather Basque nobleman. He virtually dumped his wife and daughter on me; he was so frightened that they would be raped."

"That bad? I always thought Napoleon kept strict discipline."

"Not this time it seems."

The friends then travelled together to Castlereagh's London House, where Emily clasped Will to her bosom and asked tenderly after Isabella. Whilst there, Will took the opportunity of seeking their advice about the Ybarra jewels. His Lordship told Will to leave the jewels with them. They would get their jeweller to value them.

Will's visit the next day to the Admiralty did not go too well. Wellesley Pole seemed rather distracted, and Will had the feeling that he was an irritant.

"Not sure that we can spare you for much more of this travelling backwards and forwards to Spain. We need experienced Captains. Frankly, the First Lord feels that your First Lieutenant could easily command your yacht, which would leave you free to take command of a ship-of-the-line. I know he means to have a word with the people next door and Lord Castlereagh. Anyway, what is it like down there at this time of the year?"

"We were lucky, but with winter upon us, it is going to be a very difficult coast to service. *Hound* is ideal, but with the French now in northern Spain, it won't be too long before there are no ports or shelter. I managed to contact influential Basques, who are prepared to fight the invaders. We left Captain Caspar, together with Signor Patxi, to help them. I actually witnessed the French Army marching south. General Junot is in command, but his troops are apparently untested. What the Spanish are going to say about their ally marching an army across their country is difficult to imagine."

"So from a naval stand-point, how do you assess the situation?"

"In my opinion it is essential that we are seen to be aiding any resistance. They call themselves *Partisans*. We left behind all the French and Spanish muskets we had taken aboard, together with shot and powder. They will need more, as more people join their bands. I instructed Caspar to concentrate on capturing their couriers. The intelligence could be vital. They are also to attempt to hinder their supply chain, though it appears that from their pillaging and raping, they are intending to live off the land, which is what Napoleon's armies always do; I am led to believe."

"Would you be prepared to let *Hound* continue to be in His Majesties service, even if you were no longer in command?"

"We are at war. Of course she must continue as she is the most suitable vessel available in my opinion."

"Thank you. That makes my life much easier. What are you intending to do next?"

"Lord Castlereagh is keen to get more muskets to the partisans. I think that we might just be able to do that before the weather gets too bad. We have established a bay, where if the weather is not too awful, we can off load onto a beach which their mules can reach."

"I see. In the light of what you have said, I suggest that you leave as soon as possible, and report here the moment you get back. Good luck."

Chapter 15

Back at Calvert House overlooking the Dart, Will found that all seemed peaceful. The Spanish pair was desperately trying to learn English. Antonia, probably as she was younger was beginning to put sentences together. Isabella seemed to have accepted them, but tried to remain remote, except for meal times, so that she did not get too tired. Will allowed himself a whole day with his wife, before returning to *Hound*.

Plymouth Gun Wharf had been alerted to their arrival, and again a large quantity of captured muskets had been brought together for the Basque Partisans. By the time, *Hound* was loaded she was a floating powder keg; she was so full of barrels of the stuff. Will was extremely worried about any sparks reaching the powder, so had a completely new bulkhead constructed across the ship to divide the cooking area from the rest of the ship. All flints were removed from the marine's rifles, and all pistols.

It was lucky that *Hound* was a fore-and-aft rigged vessel, because the winds shifted significantly to the south-south-west, so were right on the bow. With her centre-plate down, and all sails sheeted tightly, she managed down the Hamoaze before turning to larboard and freeing the sails for the passage through the Narrows and on to Drake's Channel. Because the wind was veering to the south, they were forced to sail close-hauled on a course far more southerly than they would have chosen. Will wanted to gain time so they sailed to within sight of the cliffs of Brittany, before they tacked.

Just as they were about to put over the helm, a lookout cried out that a brig was being closed by a bigger ship. When questioned the lookout thought she was a small frigate, but judged her to be French, and the Brig to be British. Because of the fading light, it was difficult to make out exactly what was happening. Will decide to take a look. Instead of tacking, they continued on their previous course.

As they closed the two ships, it was clear to see that the lookout had been correct. The bigger of the two ships was a French privateer and the smaller a British Brig-sloop. The Brig-sloop was obviously trying to get away from the privateer. Neither seemed to take any notice of the three masted schooner, which was bearing down on them. *Hound's* long barrelled 18 pounders were charged and ready. Her stern chasers manhandled to their positions pocking out through where Will's widows would normally have featured. The sea had a moderate swell, but due to her shape, *Hound* was cutting through the waves, rather than breasting them or climbing over. The privateer fired and the brig-sloop's top mizzenmast collapsed. Will stood close to Allwood who was at the helm.

"We can't wait to get around to her stern. We shall have to attack her beam." Said Will to Allwood, who nodded.

"Number one, We shall have to attack her at extreme range and then turn to try and get behind her." Said Will; to Cranfield who had just returned from checking the bow chasers.

"What calibre do you think she might mount?" Asked Cranfield; his eye to a scope.

"I should imagine 12s. Hope so anyway."

Everybody was poised ready. They just had to be patient. It seemed like hours, before the gun captain up in the bows put down his quadrant. Then the starboard gun roared. All the officers on the quarterdeck held their telescopes watching to see the fall of the shot.

"Bugger!"Said Tarrant; reacting to a splash short of their target. Then they all gave a sigh of relief. The ball had hit the water short, but it had bounced like a five stone to crash into the side of the enemy ship. Instantly the second 18 pounder barked, this time the shot hit the enemy smack below the quarterdeck. Because they were sailing close to the wind, the acrid smoke came rolling back down the deck making everybody cough and the eyes smart. The enemy broadside sounded impressive, but all the telltale splashes were well short. The long powerful guns had given *Hound* the advantage on her first taste of action.

Immediately after the second gun had fired, Allwood had spun the wheel and *Hound* came through the wind and onto the opposite tack. The British Brig was fighting for her life, but the intervention had obviously unsettled the Frenchman. He could not turn across the stern of the brig, as he was too far forward, abeam of his target. If he turned away, he would present his vulnerable stern. The fact that the Frenchman now needed to man the guns on both sides of his ship, probably helped the British brig. Also the French privateer had sustained damage to his hull. The first of *Hound's* shots having struck amidships just above the waterline. The second had struck the gundeck.

It did not take long before Will judged that they could turn back and go for the French stern. The bow chasers were already reloaded as he gave the order. *Hound* gybed round and on a broad reach sped towards the target. There was ample time to make sure that each shot scored a damaging hit. Will had both hands up indicating to the gun captains to wait. Then much closer in, he dropped his hands and nodded. Both cannons fired almost simultaneously on the beginning of the upswing. The ornate carving over the stern windows of the privateer disappeared. There were no windows left. Still *Hound* charged forward and the 12 pounders on the forecastle spoke. They had been loaded with grape. If anybody was still willing to fight aboard the Frenchman, they must have survived by a miracle. To make sure Will gave the order; Allwood spun the wheel and the cannonades opened up, their heavy balls crashing into the privateer's quarter. The Brig had held her ground bravely and now the foremast of the privateer collapsed, bringing after it the maintopmast. *Hound* did not wait to see the obvious outcome; she turned onto the course she would have taken if they had not come across this challenge.

"We wait to see if the Brig captain is honest!" Remarked Will; checking to make sure that the ensign and his pennant were still flying.

It had been their first skirmish, and Will went forward to thank his crew for their efforts and to promise them that their part would appear in the official records. If the Brig managed to tow the French ship back to a British port, there would be a slice of the prize money for the crew.

"Wonder where that fellow managed to escape from?" Murmured Cranfield.

"Probably gave the Channel Island squadron the slip." Replied Kemp; still looking back at the now stationary ships standing yards apart.

Will checked to see how the midshipman had handled their first taste of action. Mr. Manning was trying to look nonchalant, whereas Mr. Surprise looked stunned by the whole affair. Neither had flinched from their station.

Night was now closing in on them. Will ducked into the tiny chartroom. The midshipman of the watch had clearly marked the position of the encounter. On this reach, they were making a good average of between 12 and 14 knots.

"We shall turn south in four hours from now." He stated for the benefit of the officer of the watch, who happened to be Lieutenant Tucker.

"Very good Sir." Said Thomas; with a wide grin. He was used to the challenge of the fray.

The Bay of Biscay must have remembered that it was winter, for soon after their turn at around midnight, the wind backed and began to increase. This meant that *Hound* was being pressed forward with a quarter sea running. It was not a very comfortable point of sailing as the waves built. There was nothing they could do about it, but to put in reefs and slow their headlong dash. Two mornings later, still with a typical Biscay sea, *Hound* closed the North Spanish coast. The only port that might be open to them was Santona, but that faced north, so was still dangerous in this wind and sea state. They would just have sail up and down in a near gale to wait for the wind and sea to relent. To counter the conditions, Will ordered that they should head into the waves before meal times, so that the stove could be employed to provide some hot food. It was a week before things calmed down enough to consider approaching the shoreline.

The Bay of Biscay is deep and there is no ledge to that part of the Spanish coast. With no sights and no sight of land, everything was guesswork. Will hoped that they were about 44° 30 N. Their estimate by log, course, and wind, was that they were somewhere north of Santona. When they did see land, there were sheer cliffs that feature all along the coast. They had to sail in to nearer the coast, to try to pick out a reference point. As they worked their way east, it was the teeth like rocks jutting out of the sea, which gave them their first clue. They had to be a couple of miles to the west to the promontory that protected Santander. Soon the mouth of the river opened up and they could see into the wide safe harbour. Their problem was that it was the most likely port for the French to try to capture. Will did not feel like risking everything. Another hour and a half and they were off Santona, where the masts of a couple of brigs suggested the French had already arrived. Keeping between two and three miles off the coast, they continued following the coast in an easterly direction. By mid afternoon, they were off Ogella Bay. Here they dropped their anchor on an extended hawser, as the sea was not too rough.

Telescopes were trained on the bay and the headlands on either side to see if there was any sign of life. When nothing transpired by dusk they hauled up the anchor and worked their way out to sea again to try again the next day.

When they sailed into the bay in the morning, they could see activity on the beach, but no flags where they should have been. Cautiously they crept in, guns ready to give anybody who challenged them the shock of their lives. As far as they could see, mules were being brought down to the beach, but still no recognition signal. Was this a trap? Had Caspar and co been caught and forced to reveal the landing spot?

As *Hound* turned to sail out of the bay, a lookout cried out. "Flags." The flags had appeared where they should have been in the first place. Will gave the order and they came around in a tight turn and dropped their anchor. The cutters were manned; but as a precaution, Will sent in the marines. They were in civilian dress, with their Baker rifles ready to counter any ambush. It was Lieutenant Kemp, who was in charge of the cutters. Will felt that he was the most stoic of his officers: most likely to react calmly to any situation.

When the first cutter returned, it brought Captain Caspar of the Marines. He was dressed in peasant costume and looked filthy. He did not smell any better.

"God, what a mess!" Were his first words. Will waited to let him expound.

"The French are animals! I really did not expect them to be quite so brutal. They strip everything, or kill what they cannot eat. No woman, however ugly is safe."

"How far south do you think that they have reached?" Asked Will.

"Have no idea! Ybarra and his men will not move out of their own area, which rather makes sense. They know the ground. We have to rely on word of mouth from the next partisan group to the south, and so on. You are never sure if they are exaggerating or not."

"So what have you been up to?"

Caspar grinned. "We have managed to ambush quite a number of couriers. They now have to have guards riding with them, which must tie up resources. We have built up an intelligence network. In virtually every village, we have partisans who pass on information. We know when a baggage train is coming; we even know the numbers of troops and its size. The partisans ride over the mountain tracks; hand over to the next partisan who carries the information along the network. The beauty is that the first partisan is back trying to till what he has left. The French cannot work out how we know where to be at a given time, and the resources we need to deal with them. The result is that the French have to guard their supplies. They have taken to sending troops back along the route to escort the next lot of supplies."

"How are Ybarra and Patxi?" Asked Will.

"Ybarra is in his element. Patxi was nearly caught the other day. I think it has un-nerved him. I would be happier if you took him off for a time. I don't think that he is cut-out for this type of warfare."

"But Ybarra is?"

"Oh yes. He is respected by the partisans from his area. They trust him. He also has that ability to understand when he should ask advice. A quality that makes it much easier to plan. He reacts fast, and can organise well; but he also considers the risks."

"You have obviously been living rough!" Commented Will.

"Is it that bad? Yes, we have to keep moving to surprise the enemy. I have not slept in a bed, nor had a bath for weeks. I apologise if I am a trifle ripe!"

"You better come through and show me on the map exactly what you have been up to."

Over the map of the area, Caspar inked in numbers; then wrote on a separate piece of paper with the number at the top, what action had taken place. It seemed to Will that they had been remarkably busy. The numbers grew down the line of the main route from where it turned south near Deba onwards as far as Vitoria. Then they began to be added to more remote passes. At first, it was mostly the ambushing of the couriers, then more and more ambushes of supplies, and even ammunition. It would appear that the partisans now had more than enough muskets and powder, even without *Hound's* new supplies. At Arrasate, they had even managed to 'lift' a complete gun carriage and limber from under the noses of the French troops. It was now hidden in a remote farm; the horses being ridden by partisans. It was the interruption of supplies, which Caspar was keenest to invoke. He had taught the partisans how to blow out the sides of mountains to block them.

"The trouble is that the French are now trying to bring supplies further along the coast. Ybarra does not have so much influence that far west. We have had meetings with groups who are beginning to operate south of Bilbao. The French use fishing boats so they can unload at Getxo. Sometimes they have brigs to guard the supply boats. Lately though the weather has stopped this chain of supplies. Your new Muskets will help, because we can offer them to these new partisan groups."

Caspar was delighted to be offered a wash with fresh soap and a towel. He had to change back into his peasant clothes though for the return to the land. Just as Caspar was finishing his ablutions, Ybarra arrived in one of the returning cutters with Patxi. Ybarra clasped Will to his chest, tears in his eyes.

"It is so good to see you and your lovely ship. How is my wife and how is my daughter?"

"Good to see you alive and well. Your family is

doing well. They are staying at my place whilst they learn English. Then we will consider what is best for them. The problem is of course their maintenance. Do you know anybody who can assist them in England?"

A worried Ybarra shook his head. "We know nobody! Graciosa took her jewellery with her. Other than that, I am at a loss as what to do. Our house was looted, there is nothing left."

"Attack a French pay wagon! That is the answer!" Cried Caspar; slapping his thigh. Ybarra looked bemused.

"How do we know what the wagons are carrying?" He sighed.

"Can't you see? The French will guard their gold with many more troops. We attack anything that is closely guarded."

"At the moment, Signor, I suggest you do not worry about your wife and daughter. They are well clothed and fed. They ask for nothing, I assure you."

Tears came to the big man's eyes and he looked as if he might hug Will again, so Will moved to the other side of the table pointing at the map.

"You have been very busy. I shall take this back to London. Unfortunately, now that winter has set in, bringing you supplies will be very difficult. You did well to get here so quickly."

"That is what I meant by our network. You were seen off the coast to the west of Santander. We had the news the next day."

"But no flags!" Will pointed out. Caspar looked confused.

"I am sorry, I was not here. No flags you say. That needs to be looked into. Glad you stayed!"

"Si! Thank you!" Added Ybarra.

"Patxi, I need you to come back to England with me. They will want to have a firsthand account of what has been going on here." Will said; and Patxi could not hide his relief. Will noticed Ybarra give Caspar a great wink.

Chapter 16

Unbeknown to the crew of *Hound,* back at the Admiralty, a report had come in from one of their Brig-sloops operating as a courier for the Channel Fleet. It now lay on the desk in front of William Wellesley Pole, the Secretary to the Admiralty. He sent for his deputy and asked.

"How many three masted schooners do we have in our navy?"

"We don't!" Came back the immediate reply. Then after a short pause, the man added. "We are leasing one from Sir William Calvert. It is operating independently for the Aliens Office."

Wellesley Pole smiled. "I thought so; thank you for confirming my suspicions. It appears that *Hound* went to the aid of HMS *Gretna* off the coast of France. *Gretna* was attacked by a French privateer, but *Hound* came to the rescue. As a result, *Gretna* was able to capture the Frenchie and bring it to port as a prize. I shall take this to the First Lord; we could do with some good news. But since *Hound* is operating secretly, we shall not be able to publish the letter in the Gazette."

"True, but we can leave out the mention of *Hound*; after all *Gretna* never named the helper, did she?" The Aide responded.

Wellesley Pole thanked his number two and went down the passage to the First Lord's room.

He placed the signal on Lord Mulgrave's desk, so he could read it.

"What's this? So which ship could that be...... Good

God, not Calvert?"

"Could only be the same!"

"Why didn't he stay and reveal himself to *Gretna*?"

"Anxious to get on his way? Who knows? But it was a timely intervention." Pondered Wellesley Pole

"I quite see why St Vincent thought so highly of him! Now I have Lord Gardner asking to have him in his command. Did you raise the matter of him rejoining the fleet?"

"I did say you were anxious to have him back in command of something rather larger than a schooner." Replied Wellesley Pole.

Hound's trip back to England was once again uncomfortable. The Bay decided that it was not going to allow this little ship to have it all its own way. A Southwester blew up soon after they had left the Spanish shore. The wind increased as it backed to become a full gale. Under storm sails, *Hound*, on a broad reach spent most of the time with the water sloshing about in the scuppers. Everything had to be battened down and secured, which meant that life below decks became very uncomfortable. Lifelines were fitted, but anybody venturing on deck was liable to find himself upended in the scuppers. The helmsmen were lashed to the binnacle, the officer of the watch held firmly by a rope to the mizzenmast. Salt water blinded you as it scoured your face. Will ordered that nobody be allowed to stay on deck for more than a half-hour at a time. Once below, there was no way of getting dry, or having a hot drink. Rum for the crew, brandy for the officers, was the only relief. Because of the heaving seas and strong winds, it took twice as long as normal to reach the western approaches.

Because the wind was coming from the west, they were clawing their way westward to make sure they were not driven right into the Bay and a lee shore. They had no way of knowing their position. It was all guesswork. The log was unreliable because of the wave height. All they had to go on was the compass bearing they had been on for a period and a rough calculation of the effect the wind and waves were having on the ship to plot a water track. The Traverse Board was kept up-to-date, but it was sheer guesswork.

There was one consolation; tidal streams out here in the middle of the bay could be ignored.

When they turned to run up the Channel, it was slightly more comfortable, as *Hound* running was on a more even keel. The stove was lit and for the first time hot food could be served. There was a crowd around the stove, trying to dry out. So bad was it that the cook had to ask the boatswain to order the crew away. It was now more uncomfortable for the officers as they were in the dark down below, because the shutters were up over the stern windows. Will was equally in the dark. The best place to be was in one's bunk or cot. In the Channel, rain added to their difficulties, cutting visibility down to less than a mile. At least now, the lookouts that were sent to the forecastle did not have to endure a soaking every few seconds.

Eighteen hours after turning to run up the channel a lookout spotted land. Since it was getting dark, they had to continue, assuming from dead reckoning that it was Prawle Point or Start Point. Now tides had to be considered, but Will was sufficiently confident to turn north, but with an extra number of lookouts as the light faded away. He reasoned from the sea state, that they were now in the shelter of Start Point and the Hams. They reduced sail and lay to a sheet anchor until soon after first light, the dim outline of the Devon coast could be seen. By Midday, they were safely anchored in the Dart above Dittisham.

Will took Surgeon de Cornes with him when he was rowed ashore. They climbed the hill to Calvert House together. The rain was still coming down, but the trees gave them some shelter. Will discovered

Isabella in the Yellow Parlour, with Mary Elizabeth playing at her feet. Picking up his daughter on the way to his wife, he asked Isabella how she felt.

"Ready to give birth at any moment; I have the midwife on call in the servants' quarters. Oh! Hello Henri! So good to see you." She added as she spied the doctor over her husband's shoulder. "Do you have to go to London immediately?" She asked, turning back to Will, desperation showing through.

"No, my love, I shall send Signor Patxi. I shall make a clean copy of my report; it was too rough to write a clear one on the trip back. I shall add a note to say that I am at my wife's bedside."

The look of relief was evident to both Will and Henri. Henri excused himself, to go and change; he wanted a word with the midwife; that meant that Will and Isabella had a moment to themselves and their daughter. Over supper, Will and Henri told Isabella and the two Spanish Ladies of their adventures. Will made sure that the engagement with the privateer sounded as if they had just lobbed a ball at the fellow and he had given in. He was anxious not to cause Isabella any alarm at this time.

It was still a miserable day when Signor Patxi was brought over to Calvert House. The Ybarras were delighted to have a fellow Basque to talk to, but Will had other ideas. He invited Cranfield to dinner and asked him which of his officers could accompany the Basque to London. Cranfield suggested Thomas, as he spoke Euskera and Spanish, after a fashion. As Will's servant, he had also been to all the places they needed to know about in London. Will therefore dispatched Thomas and Signor Patxi to London in one of the Calvert coaches. Thomas had strict instructions as to whom he was to try to see and in which order.

Three days later Isabella gave birth to a baby boy. This time she had more difficulty, and was grateful to have Henri on hand to make sure everything was handled properly. It was a long labour, and Will was banned from the room. He had never felt so inadequate in his life. Henri called him in as soon as the boy had been checked, and he was sure that Isabella was tidy.

"Strapping young fellow; no wonder Isabella here had a bad time." Henri said, as Will went straight to Isabella's side.

"Aren't you going to take a look at your son? After all, that is what I have been going through all this agony for!" Rebuked Isabella, but it was said with a tired smile. Will pulled aside a part of the soft blanket that the child was wrapped in and was able to see a grizzled looking little head, with a tightly clenched mouth.

"Please don't say he looks like me!" Laughed Will. "He looks really pugnacious."

The midwife handed the child to Isabella, who cradled him. "You're right! He does look as if he is about to take on the whole world!" Laughed Isabella, all the trauma forgotten.

Chapter 17

It was ten days before Thomas reappeared with Signor Patxi in tow. As Will had suspected, doors were slow to open for a mere Lieutenant. Only Viscount Castlereagh had immediately responded. He had spent a whole morning with Thomas and Patxi, asking very pertinent questions. Thomas had spent three days waiting to see the Secretary to the Admiralty. It turned out that the Admiralty employees had taken it upon themselves to delay the meeting. Castlereagh had however sent Thomas and Patxi to the Alien's Office, where Patxi had been interviewed at length.

Thomas brought mail from both Lord Castlereagh and the Admiralty. Will settled down in his study to read Lord Castlereagh's letter first.

London

1st December 1807

My Dear Will,

I hope all is going well with the birth. Emily and I are thinking of you both at this time. Let us know as soon as possible the outcome.

I have read your report with great interest. You have as usual exceeded in all that we asked of you. As you of all people are aware, Politics is not an easy option. The Opposition are constantly trying to score political points rather than concentrating on what is best for the Country. I have passed a copy of your report to the Prime Minister. We are due to hold a Cabinet meeting in three days time; but so near Christmas, it may very well be ill attended. Directly I have some news I shall be in touch.

Hope all goes well, and that you have a very good family Christmas. Emily and I send all our love, and look forward to seeing you all in Town in the New Year.

Yours truly

Robert

Will put the letter aside and slit open the next sealed epistle. It was from the Aliens Office. Short and sweet; it just acknowledged the arrival of the report and said they would be examining it with interest. There was a third missive that he was loaf to open from the Admiralty. He feared he would be ordered to sea immediately. Instead, he was grateful to discover that it was virtually the same in intention, though not in words as the one from the Aliens Office. Thomas had also brought back a heavy carpetbag with wide leather handles for Isabella. It came together with a letter from Emily Castlereagh. Isabella read it out to Will when he went up to visit her in her bedroom.

"A letter from dearest Emily; Absolutely typical. I can almost hear her rushing through it!"

My dearest Isabella,

I do hope that you are in the best of health ready for your lying-in -what a stupid expression!

At least you now have a proper doctor on hand. Do let us know how you are – we miss you dreadfully. Of all my friends you are the one I truly adore being with. I love your down to earth approach to life as well as your incisive wit! I miss all the laughter!

Dear Robert has been wonderful, despite having to work so hard. He had a brilliant idea about the jewels for those poor Basque Ladies of yours. He suggested that we would get a much better outcome if we auctioned the jewels. I sent for our Jeweller and got him to give a valuation, as it is called, because Robert said we should not sell for less. I invited a whole crowd of Ladies with money to spare! I had asked Robert to be the auctioneer, but he said he was too busy. I think he was frightened of facing all those Ladies! Anyway, I plied the assembled with plenty of alcoholic beverages; I even allowed them to try on the jewels with looking glasses to preen in front of. I had never been an Auctioneer before – such fun! I gave a rousing speech about how hard it was for displaced Ladies to survive in a strange land. I vow some of the audience were in tears. Perhaps I should have been an Actress! The result was that we managed to obtain twice the amount for the gems than the Jeweller's valuation! Dear Robert now calls me his Auctioneer to tease me.

I am intrusting the results of our efforts to your delightful Lieutenant Tucker; such a handsome young man!

Do you have a birthing bed? I am told that they are de rigour. I have no idea what such a couch would look like! I am sure that your Henri de Cornes will insist on a bright sunny room for the birth. Here in town it is now the done thing to have a Doctor in attendance. None of those beastly vile smelling midwives!

Must rush, your Lieutenant is leaving and I have to give him the bag.

All my love

Emily.

The carpetbag, when opened revealed a sealed bag inside. Once the seal had been broken they found that it contained golden guineas wrapped in cloth to stop them rattling. This would mean that some of the responsibility for the Ybarra Ladies would now be lifted from Will's shoulders.

There were just two weeks to Christmas, so Will took Hound on a short trip to sea, to keep the crew on their toes. Patxi was now installed in Calvert House teaching the Spanish Ladies English. The Estate Steward had located a House just on the North side of Totnes, which would be suitable for the Ladies. Will had arranged to purchase the house in Totnes, as he reasoned he would be able to sell it again without loss, whereas if he had rented it, he would have had to charge the Ladies. Isabella had not yet seen the House so it remained a secret from the Ybarra's. On the 19th December, Isabella felt well enough to take the short carriage ride to view the House. It was not large, but it boasted all the amenities that were needed for the two Ladies. This then would be their Christmas present. The house was furnished, so the only problem was staff. The Ybarras had to be able to speak enough English to run the establishment.

Isabella's mother Laura Kenton, had been staying at the Calvert House for the birth, but left once everything had settled down. As usual, the Kentons would be present on Christmas day, but this time they were even more involved, because the staff would be given the day off, so Laura would be responsible for making sure there was food on the table. This would be a cold collation prepared from the meal the day before. Presents were exchanged on Christmas Eve. This year a puppy for Mary Elizabeth was the highlight. When it came to the Ybarras, they were overcome to find that their hosts had done so much for them. On Christmas morning, Will had himself rowed across to Hound where he delivered a case of fine wine for his officers, and a couple of barrels of specially brewed beer for the crew. An extra Rum allowance also went down well. Before there was any indulgence though, Will held a short service on deck. On Boxing Day, two carriages carried the Calverts and Ybarra Ladies to the Totnes house, where Isabella and Will, accompanied by Mary Elizabeth and the puppy, showed the Ybarras around the property. They were ecstatic.

Antonia had become Mary Elizabeth's special friend. The young woman did not seem to mind, entering into the games with enthusiasm. Mary Elizabeth had proved an early learner. Will suspected that it was because she spent a lot of time with her mother, rather than being hidden away in the nursery. She was even picking up Spanish and Euskerian words. The amusing part of it all was that Antonia was using childlike words in her speech. At first, Isabella had been worried, but Antonia, thought it was very funny, and soon corrected herself. Senora Ybarra, being older was finding learning a new language difficult, so Antonia was taking it upon herself to act as interpreter half the time.

On the 30th December, a fast rider arrived from the Admiralty. He carried dispatches for Will. Obviously, Lord Castlereagh had been in conference with Lord Mulgrave. Will was required to take Hound to Portugal, to make a survey of the Portuguese coast for possible landing sites for an army. Hound was taken down to Dartmouth for extra victuals to be taken aboard. Will remained at Calvert House; he wanted to spend as much time as he could with his wife and his family. He had been approached by his father-in-law on behalf of their vicar., He had asked if there was any chance of Will taking the vicar's second son as a Midshipman. He had also been lobbied by the Mayor of Dartmouth. If they were to do a thorough survey, they would need more junior officers to handle the chart work and copying. Grooms were dispatched to the two families, informing them that their sons could join, but that there would be no need for uniforms until Hound returned. On January 1st, Hound hoisted her anchor and made her way out past the castles at the mouth of the Dart.

When they rounded Start Point, they were facing a gale blowing up the Channel. The Courses were replaced by staysails, but it took twenty-four hours of hard tacking to clear Ushant sufficiently to be able to turn south. The Bay of Biscay was no better. Because they were on a long reach down the bay, Hound was broadside on to the waves, which made life below extremely difficult. The two new midshipmen spent a miserable time in hammocks, to try to lessen the effect of the motion. There was no hot food, as it was too dangerous to light the stove. Luckily, because they had just taken on victuals, and Cranfield had predicted that they would face heavy weather, they had taken on a large number of cooked ham joints and freshly baked bread. Wedges were the order of the day, washed down with weak tots of rum. It took two days of this miserable existence to reach Cape Finisterre. Here the wind tended to veer to the south and fell back. For the first time the staysails were replaced by the courses and the stove could be lit. It was not until the start of the forenoon watch (8am) that they were off Cape Roca. Here they were met by a sloop from Admiral Cotton's command off Lisbon City. By now, the sea was moderately calm, and the sloop had no trouble rushing to intercept the strange three masted schooner. Once the sloop had identified Hound as being British, it rounded up to sail close by on the leeward side. Will had anticipated being challenged so the largest red ensign was flying from the mizzen gaff and the broad pennant from the mainmast peak.

The sloop saluted Will's flag and a Lieutenant sprang into the shrouds with a speaking trumpet.

"Good Morning! Are you bringing dispatches, supplies or joining us?"

Cranfield climbed up onto Hound's small poop deck. "No! We are on special assignment from the Admiralty. We do have dispatches for Admiral Cotton."

"Understood! Pity you aren't carrying supplies; we desperately need fresh water. The Admiral is aboard Minotaur. You will find her anchored off the estuary."

The sloop wheeled away, off on another errand, no doubt. Hound continued on round Cape Roca towards a small group of naval ships. Some were anchored, but most were under sail. Minotaur was easy to spot; she was the only ship-of-the-line amongst the group. Hound came smartly up into the wind, and even as the anchor splashed into the water, the jollyboat was lowered and hauled round. Allwood had his crew over the side and ready for Will, as the call went out that the anchor was holding. Will, in full Commodore's uniform dropped easily into the boat and it was shoved off and the oars thrown in the air and then lowered in perfect unison to pull smartly towards the flagship. Will was received with the customary honours. Admiral Sir Charles Cotton's expression when he realised how young Will appeared, amused Will, but he kept a grave face.

"Sir William Calvert." Will announced himself.

"Delighted to meet you. You bring dispatches from the Admiralty?"

"I do Sir."

"Come through." Sir Charles led the way to his quarters, which were surprisingly small. Will realised his own were positively luxurious in comparison.

Will handed over the waxed canvas bag with its big red seal.

"Are you to join us?" Asked Admiral Cotton.

"I am afraid not, Sir Charles. We are on a special assignment for the Admiralty, hence the Commodore bit and the pennant. The Admiralty don't want us to be sidelined by other commands, demanding we do their bidding."

"I am not quite sure I understand their reasoning. You are if I may say so Sir, extremely young to hold such a rank!"

"Temporary, I assure you." Laughed Will; which seemed to ease the tension.

"So where are you off to next?" The Admiral asked. Will hung his head.

"I am afraid, Sir that it has to remain secret."

The Admiral looked perplexed, but offered Will refreshment. Will thought it wise to humour this senior officer so accepted. He was able to reveal to the Admiral that he had recently had meetings with the Secretary of War himself, as well as the First Lord. This seemed both to impress and placate the Admiral. Will apologised for the fact that he would be unable to carry any dispatches back to England. Will hoped, when he left, that he had done as much as was possible to sooth any antagonistic feelings that his youth might have had on the Admiral. In less than an hour, Hound was under sail again.

They continued south, following the coastline, making notes, and drawing outlines of the coast. Although there were sandy beaches, these were wide open to the power of the Atlantic. Also, Will judged it inexpedient to land an army on the peninsular to the south of the Tagus Estuary, as it would be forced to fight its way right round, so exposing its rear when trying to capture the city. So, Hound came round and started to retrace her path, but this time much closer inshore. Will had opted for sailing at a distance of between a mile and a mile and a half off the coast, except where there were forts to be seen. The charts they had aboard were very rudimentary. Before leaving Dartmouth, they had purchased every box compass with a pelorus that they could find. This meant that at least four could be employed at any one time. As they slowly made their way up the coast, constant bearings were taken on anything remotely identifiable. At first, there were high cliffs north of Cape Roca for about a mile and a half, then came the first small beach with an arch in the cliff. Here there was a narrow defile down to the beach, but the cliffs behind meant it was totally unsuitable. It was also far too near Lisbon in Will's opinion, as troops from the city could be called up to repulse a landing in a very short time. There followed more beaches, but they had high banks behind them which would make unloading artillery and horses difficult. This was followed by more cliffs, with the sea breaking against them.

They were comparatively lucky for January as the sea was moderately calm and the wind was from the south. The Atlantic swell still drove long breaking waves against the coast. Any landing on this coast at any time of year, was going to be hazardous. Right the way up the coast to Peniche, the cliff faces made a landing impossible. Peniche itself was a promontory with a large fort guarding the southern side. A French flag flying from the fort showed that the French were in residence. It was an impressive fort, which would be difficult to assault even from the northern side. It was also so near Lisbon that re-enforcement would be speedy. Even though Hound was out of range of the fortress guns, there was still activity as they sailed by, showing that the gun crews were in place. North of Peniche there were more beaches, but they were backed by low cliffs. Here the rolling surf broke onto the sand below the cliffs showing that even with a calm sea, the waves were likely to cause loss of life. There was an estuary with a sand bank across it marked on the chart as Arelho, but it was only four miles from a small town inland. There followed cliffs until a small inlet came into view. It was well protected on either side from the weather except from a westerly wind. The entrance was only a couple of hundred yards wide, with only about a quarter of a mile's radius of water for ships to anchor in.

Next, a long sandy beach led to a small south facing cove with a fishing village. This was followed by more beaches with high sand dunes behind. Again, it would be difficult to land artillery and horses along this length of beach. The surf was rolling in from the Atlantic. Will doubted the wisdom of attempting a landing here, because of the heavy surf.

The mouth of the Mondego River appeared to be the most feasible landing spot so far. There was a small fort on the northern side; a sand bar that looked as if it might shift, but there was a wide beach. The fort once occupied, would be difficult to retake, as the river would have to be crossed at least ten miles inland.

Whilst the midshipmen took the bearings, the lead was being constantly dropped from either side. At intervals of five minutes off more suitable sites, the lead was greased to check on the type of bottom. After Figueira da Foz, the village at the mouth of the Mondego, there were no possible landing sites until Porto. Porto, or Oporto as the British seemed to call it, was a harbour that was well known to British Merchant fleets. The town was still under Portuguese control, but was over a hundred and seventy miles, as the crow flies, from Lisbon.

They continued to chart the whole coast right up to the Spanish border. From then on, it was trickier, because there were Spanish Naval ships at most of the possible harbours. Will did not want to come into conflict with anyone. He considered that the Chart work they had carried out must be important. They did come across a Spanish sloop that was off Cape Finisterre. The sloop changed course to intercept Hound, but after a couple of shots from the sloop fell short, one long range shot from one of Hound's long barrelled 18 pounders, which took away the sloop's mizzen boom, persuaded the Spaniard to retreat.

Since the weather was holding, Will decided to try to find out what was going on in the north. They sailed into Santona, which still flew Spanish flags from the fort. Once again, they were sporting the American Ensign. Patxi was landed as before on the beach opposite the town as it became dark.

In the middle of the next morning, after a visit from Spanish officials, who were plied with supposedly American hooch, had passed off amicably, Patxi was spotted signalling in the distance. The cutters, which were already in the water, were manned, and Will with Henri, were rowed over to the sands on the east side of the estuary. Here the oarsmen of the two cutters pulled up their craft and proceeded to exercise, running races, and playing games, whilst Will and Henri crept away under the cover of the scrub.

Patxi had three horses, so they mounted and rode off in the direction of the hamlet of Guriezo. Here they were met by Signor Ybarra. After much embracing and kissing by the Spaniard, relieved to find that his wife and daughter were prospering, they were taken to meet a Spanish Army Brigadier under mysterious circumstances. From what the brigadier said, Will gathered he was second in command of the Spanish troops in Galicia. What he was doing two hundred miles away to the west amongst the partisans soon became apparent. The man spoke fluent English. He admitted that his mother was Irish, which intrigued Will. He apparently was well known to Signor Ybarras, and his priest friend. He had fought against the French the last time Spain had been at war with France, and was remarkably anti-the French.

He suggested that the people of Galicia, Asturias, Cantabria, as well as the Basques, deeply resented the French sending troops into Spain. There was talk of the Galicians forming a Junta to control their area in defiance of Madrid. He seemed particularly resentful of some fellow called Godoy, who he inferred advised the King. The reason for his being so far from his base only came out when Ybarra mentioned muskets and powder. It appeared that this military gentleman, had been instrumental in smuggling Army weapons and powder to the partisans, now forming in the Cantabrian mountains. Their whole discussion was about the possible supply of arms to a Spanish army in the north, if such a body could be formed. Will liked the man, although neither was permitted to know the name of the other. It was only on the way back to the ship, that Patxi admitted that the Brigadier was a well-respected General by the name of Joaquín Blake y Joyes. He had in the past, trained elite troops of the Spanish Army.

Chapter 18

As *Hound* made her way back to Britain, in increasingly bad weather, Will tried to write up a report. He was very conscious of how Admiral Cotton had reacted on their meeting. He realised that ever since he had been made Post, he had only once come up against an Admiral, and that had been Lord Nelson, who himself had been made a Commodore at an early age. He remembered that questions had been asked in the House about the appointment of a Captain so low down the Navy List. Luckily, there had been no names mentioned. Lord St. Vincent had come down heavily on the Officer who had instigated the question. The looks of other Admirals and Captains at the funeral of Lord Nelson had been an indicator as to the jealousy such early promotion could bring. It was going to be difficult to go back to being a mere Captain, and be so low down on the list. He contemplated resigning his commission and seeking a seat in the House of Commons. He was wealthy enough to pay for such a privilege. Perhaps he should buy into a Merchant Fleet and take on the role of a ship owner as his father had been before him. The difference being that Will would not command any of his own ships.

A battered *Hound* slipped up the Dart as the light

was fading almost exactly a month after she had left. Isabella and the two children seemed to be in good health, which was a blessing. Awaiting Will was a letter from Lord Castlereagh asking him to come up to London as soon as he got back. He would be needed in London for a series of meetings that could last a fortnight or more. Isabella was adamant that she would accompany her husband despite the fact that it was one of the worst times of the year to travel. She was breast-feeding, which added to the complications. There was no way she was staying put. As a result, the Calvert convoy set out two days later to make the laborious trip on muddy lanes, and across flooded rivers. They took their time, so it was not until three days later that they finally rolled up at Calvert House in Highgate. A groom had been sent on ahead, so the beds were aired, and there was food on the table. It was the second trip that Mary Elizabeth had been on; she was so excited by all the unfamiliar sights and sounds.

The following day, with the rain tumbling down, the Calvert coach rolled up at the door of Castlereagh's St James Square, London home. When they were announced, there were shrieks from above, and Emily nearly fell down the stairs, she was in such a hurry to greet her friend. Emily showed them into the Drawing Room which she had laid out herself.

Her two Bull Dogs hefted themselves to their feet to pad over to have their ears tickled. Since Isabella was breast-feeding, they had brought both children. Mary Elizabeth was very quiet; she was not used to meeting strangers. Emily though was delighted, and took both Mary Elizabeth's arms and ran round in a circle, which brought giggles and then laughter from the child. The baby was much admired. The Castlereaghs had been the butt of many snide remarks and innuendoes, because they had not had any children. Will thought that Emily had put on weight since he had last seen her. She was still a very vital and charmingly unaffected person, even though she was now so well known in Society. They did not stay long as Lord Castlereagh was working, but Emily invited them to dinner the next night, and Will left his report for Robert on his return. Will had that morning left a copy of the same report at the Admiralty. He had not bothered to ask to see the Secretary to the Admiralty.

The next night they arrived from Highgate just after the appointed hour of seven o'clock in the evening. They were shown into the Drawing Room on the left of the Hall, where other guests were already standing in groups chatting. Immediately they were announced both Castlereagh and his wife broke away from the guests they had been talking to, to greet them. It was sometime since Lord Castlereagh had last seen them. Emily took Isabella off to meet some guests, whilst Robert whispered to Will.

"Read your report. I want to arrange a meeting, will let you know when." Then he led Will over to introduce him to other members of the party. At eight o'clock, Dinner was announced and they all trooped upstairs to the first floor dining room, where the table was set with silver candlesticks and table centres, that reflected the candle light to make the whole room full of reflected silver light. As usual, Castlereagh took the seat at the head of the table, but Emily, always her own person, sat halfway down the table with Will beside her. She was very discreet about his movements, and Will knew that she shared Castlereagh's desk, so knew all that was going on in government and elsewhere. As usual, he tended at such functions to listen and to speak only when asked a direct question. He felt that because he spent so much time at sea, or in Devon, he had little to add to the conversation. As an observer, though he stored away details about the people he met. He was an avid reader of the Gazette as well as all the novels he could get hold of, to read at sea. Ever since first meeting Lord Castlereagh, he had taken the trouble to research the Irish question and the characters involved. It had surprised Robert Stewart, Lord Castlereagh, when he had been able to comment on the works of some of the Irish writers and Politician's of the time. They had even debated William Godwin's *Caleb Williams* novel, and its real intentions.

Just after the main course had been cleared, a gentleman sitting next to Isabella cried out and shot up knocking over his chair. Will turning to see what was the cause of the fracas, realised that Isabella was blushing. Castlereagh leaned forward to her and said something, which made her shake her head. The gentleman had stormed out of the room. Castlereagh remained his urban self and smilingly waved a hand as if to dismiss the whole episode. The conversation resumed. Emily turned to Will.

"I wonder what all that was about? Izzy looks upset, do you think I should go to her?"

Will said he thought it was best to let whatever it was pass, as Robert seemed to be in control of things.

On the way home, the whole story came out. The middle-aged gentleman sitting beside Isabella had been making suggestive remarks which Isabella had ignored. He had then placed his hand on her leg, which she had asked him to remove. He had continued to suggest that they might meet and again put his hand on her leg and started to run it up towards her groin. She had tried to remove his hand, but he was too strong. She had remonstrated with him asking him to desist, but he had continued to molest her. Finally, she had taken a fork and plunged into the back of his hand, which had caused him to shriek and knock over his chair. She had explained her actions to Lord Castlereagh, who thought she had acted courageously.

"For God's sake I'm still breast feeding. Why would I want to get into bed with a reprobate like him? I have a husband who satisfies all my needs!"

"Is that what you told him?"

"Exactly, but he would not stop. What was I to do? I acted on instinct!"

"Well the fellow has taste! I'll give him that my love." Replied Will. For indeed Isabella looked radiant, and with fuller breasts was even more curvaceous than usual. He skin glowed with health. Will thought how lucky he was to have such a wife.

The call came two days later. After having had his boat cloak and hat taken from him, he was shown into Castlereagh's study, where a roaring fire gave a warm contrast to the miserable January weather outside. It was so dark even with the curtains open that candles burned at strategic points about the room. Will knew most of the Gentlemen present.

There was Edward Cooke and Alexander Knox, both colleagues and old friend's of his lordship. In an armchair near the fire, sat Sir Arthur Wellesley, recently back from Denmark, where he had defeated a Danish Army. Will had thought that he was in Ireland with the nucleus of an Army about to be sent to South America to support Portuguese aspirations on that continent. Wellesley Pole, his younger brother and Secretary to the Admiralty, and therefore Will's boss rose from another chair.

"Ah Will, glad you could join us! Read your report; as usual - straight to the point. You know everybody here don't you?" Said Sir Robert; waving his hand to indicate the people present.

Will nodded his assent. He knew that Sir Arthur was an old Irish friend of Castlereagh's; he had met him socially a few times.

"The Corsican is definitely about to launch yet another army into Spain. The Cabinet have decided that we must confront the French ambitions. Perhaps you would expand on your report, which some of us present have not had the chance to read yet." Castlereagh said.

Will hauled his leather chart tube out from beside his chair and walked over to the desk. Castlereagh immediately started to clear it of books and an inkstand, so that the charts could be spread out. The others crowded round.

"I was sent to bring the charts of the Portuguese coast up-to-date and to consider a possible landing place for the relief, as I understand it, of Lisbon. As you know Gentlemen, the City is on the north side of the estuary of the Tagus. It is my opinion that any attack on the city would have to come from the north to succeed. One might be tempted to land at Setubal, here to the south, but you would have to fight your way rather a long way inland before you could cross the river Tagus and attack the city. You would therefore have a very long supply train, and your flank vulnerable to attack. I therefore carried out the survey from Cape Roca north. We are talking about probably the worst coast for landing an army on of any in Europe. The coast of Portugal faces the full brunt of the waves that have travelled all the way across the Atlantic. This means there is nearly always a swell, which causes the rolling surf that one would have to face. Any landing in my opinion would have to take place during the summer months to be successful. Even then, there can be considerable difficulties in bringing a small boat onto the beach. The first place one could possibly land a force would be here, there is no name, but it is a very small beach and only seven miles from Lisbon. Far too near in my opinion, because it would be repulsed before any sizeable force could be landed. This is Peniche; a small harbour that has some protection from the surf. But; and I accentuate the but; there is a very strong fortress overlooking the harbour, which would be very difficult to assault, even from the North. It is only some forty miles from Lisbon, so the French could force-march to upset things whilst one was still trying to take the fortress.

All along this coast running north, we have cliffs behind the beaches, so making it impossible to get horses and artillery ashore with any ease. Therefore, we have to move fifty miles north before we come to any possible landing site. This is Figuera da Foz at the mouth of the Mondego River. There is a small fort here, but I think that it would be easy to take. One has to travel at least ten miles upstream, before you can cross the river, so any relieving squadron, would have to come from that side of the river. There is a bar across the mouth that moves, which makes it difficult to get anything of any size into the estuary. The land here is flat, so it gives plenty of scope to drive inland to protect any landing. It is some a hundred and twenty miles by road from Lisbon. I would suggest this is the only practical landing point."

Will stood back, so the others could inspect the chart more closely.

"Would a fleet be able to anchor off to land an

Army? Asked Sir Arthur; without looking up.

"The holding is good in all but anything approaching a gale. But it is a still a lee-shore, after all!"

"Did you test the bottom?" Asked Wellesley Pole. Will was amazed that such a question should be asked, but just replied "Of course!"

"What about anything further North?" Asked

Castlereagh.

"The coast is made up of cliffs until one gets to Porto. We sailed into Oporto or Porto, under the American flag. We purchased a few barrels of their wine, which gave us the opportunity to check out the situation at first hand. The French could have taken the city by the time we are able to land an army. It is heavily fortified. There is nowhere to land anywhere near to put an army ashore to assault the city. It would have to be a sustained barrage, much like Copenhagen, but without an army to lay siege. Where we thought there was a possible site, we made sure we went in as close as possible. In some instances, we were less than half a mile off. That might sound a long way, but we do have telescopes. To get that close in to a lee shore in winter can only be achieved by a fore and aft rigged vessel, such as Hound."

Sir Arthur straightened up and ran his fingers down his aquiline nose. "How close were you able to get to the shoreline elsewhere?"

Will pulled out the sketches that he and others had made of the Mondego entrance."I hope these give you a better idea of what is to be expected, if one was to land at that point."

"You are very certain this is the best possible place?" Alexander Knox asked, as Sir Arthur poured over the sketches.

"These are extremely detailed! Who drew them, might I ask?" Sir Arthur asked; without looking up.

"I did those ones, and Lieutenant Tucker those three." Replied Will; pointing to the relevant pictures. Sir Arthur just gave a 'humph', and continued to gaze at the sketches.

"What about the meeting with the General?" Asked Castlereagh.

"General Blake. Yes surprising!" Commented Will.

"How exactly did you come to meet him?" Asked Knox.

"We put into Santona under the American flag. Our cover was that we were purchasing Spanish wines to take back to America to see how they travelled. Signor Patxi went ashore to see if he could join up with the partisans again. They were hiding in the Cantabrian Mountains, so he was able to get a message to Signor Ybarra, whom we had met before. He has raised a quite substantial band of cut-throats. It was Ybarra, who asked me to meet with this General Blake. A General of Brigade is I believe equivalent in rank to our Brigadier. I was wary at first, as I thought it likely that he was a spy for the Spanish Government. The more we talked, the more I came to like the fellow, and be convinced that he was genuine. He had been the commander of some of the most elite troops in the Spanish Army. He had resigned, as he did not like what was going on at Court. Later, he had been returned to duty to command the forces at Ferrol, He had just been to Madrid, but on his way back, he had stopped off to meet up with Ybarra, to find out for himself exactly what was going on up North. He was very worried about the threat to Spain from the French Army there. He has contacts, who had advised him in their correspondence that Napoleon was bringing an Army south to cross into Spain.

That is another army, not Junot's one. If Napoleon was to annex Spain, Blake would definitely try and raise an army to resist French rule."

Everybody was absorbed by what Will was saying.

"So you think this fellow Blake would be able to achieve such a feat?" Asked Cooke.

"I have no way of knowing. All I can say is the fellow is very charismatic. I should imagine he would be an inspiring leader."

"Did he ask what you were doing there?" Asked Sir Arthur.

"I am not sure what Ybarra had told him. He did ask if Britain was likely to intercede. I told him I had no idea. I was not a Politician, just a humble ship's captain following orders."

Castlereagh laughed. "And did he know you had armed the partisans?" He asked.

"It was not mentioned. He did ask if the British would be prepared to help with arms and powder, if France does send an army into Spain. I just said I could but ask."

"These Partisans. Exactly what are they doing?"

Asked Sir Arthur.

"We advised them not to confront the French; just to pick away at their supply chain, and to concentrate on trying to interfere with the chain of command. I brought back a whole bundle of orders and signals that the partisans had relieved from couriers. The main aim is to get the French to divert troops to protect their supply chain and courier service. This has been quite successful I understand. The French have to provide much larger escorts for their wagons. The couriers now have to have outriders, which slows them down. Where possible, the partisans cause landfalls to block routes south. There are a number of places on the route from France, where the roads or tracks are quite narrow with high banks and rivers on their sides. These are ideal places to interrupt things. It can take days to clear these landslides. The French try to use local labour, but these have to be guarded. We also supplied Ybarra's partisans with some of Hound's Baker rifles. These are issued to the best shot. They aim to shoot the lead ox or horse of the leading wagon. This slows the whole convoy. We trained them to cover the marksman, so he can get away. Being local, they know their ground. When the French come after them, they ambush them. It is very effective."

"You say 'We'. Who exactly thought this type of operation out?" Asked Sir Arthur.

Will felt embarrassed. "Well Sir, I suppose I did; now you come to mention it."

"And where did you learn these techniques?"

"Nowhere Sir. I just thought of the best ways in my opinion to make life difficult for the French and to try and keep the reprisals and loss of life as low as possible."

For the first time Wellesley Pole spoke up. "Is it not so, Sir William, that you were the instigator of the use of the long barrelled cannons in the bows of your ships?"

Will nodded. He realised that Wellesley Pole probably had sight of the Top Secret reports of his taking of the Spanish treasure ships four years before. Since it was Top Secret, he obviously was unable to reveal this to his brother. It was Castlereagh, who changed the subject.

"This correspondence that Blake was talking about, it confirms rumours we have been getting about Napoleon. Where do you think Blake got his information from?" Castlereagh asked.

"I have no idea."

Chapter 19

Will was told to stay in London. Not being sure of his rank, when called to the Admiralty, he chose to arrive in civilian clothes. He was surprised to be referred to as Commodore Calvert. He was set the task of devising a new codebook using Admiral Popham's flags, to be used by a future fleet of troop carrying vessels, which had been requisitioned by Lord Castlereagh. The problem was that to hoist a signal required so many flags that it was difficult to read them without making mistakes. In bad weather, this was compounded. Will set about working out every conceivable move such a fleet of ships might be required to make. He got Allwood to get hold of a set of flags, which they took to nearby Hampstead Heath and hoisted one at a time to be observed at a distance through a telescope. He was then able to distinguish which were the most easily recognised flags.

He brought back into service a couple of Lord Howe's origin flags, to make the ordering of course changes easier. The three sided pennant style flag of blue and yellow squares was to be the signal to change course. If the command ship hoisted this flag with a numeral flag beneath, this indicated that the fleet was to change onto one of thirty-two principle compass points. For example, the pennant with the flag for zero beneath meant change course to North, since north was zero on the compass. The pennant with numeral eight beneath meant change to due west. The rest of the fleet were supposed to hoist the affirmative flag (a white cross against a red background) to indicate they understood the signal. When the commander lowered the hoist, all the ships were supposed to alter course. Having disposed of the simple course change procedure he had to come up with every other combination, using as few flags as possible. By placing the Substitute flag or the Affirmative flag at the bottom of a hoist meant it increased the number of combinations, without resorting to the making of more signal flags.

To make sure he had covered every possible manoeuvre, he sought out retired Captains and Admirals to enlist their help. He was aware that there were many unforeseen problems, that he probably had not thought of; but by seeking this help, he was sure he had covered most of the ground, before presenting it to the Board of Admiralty.

This had taken up the whole of February. During this period, he and Isabella invited a broad spectrum of polite Society to dine at their Highgate home. Will was very careful not to be seen to back either the Whigs or the Tories, so both sat at the same table. As a result, there were many invitations to others' tables.

At the beginning of March, Will was called to the Admiralty to be given the command of a captured Danish 80 gun ship-of-the-line. The ship had been taken to Chatham to undergo repairs. Will insisted that she had her bottom covered in copper as was normal for all British ships. He was extremely grateful to discover that the Admiralty had for once thought to crew her by dint of taking crews from ships that were going in for refits. It meant he did not have to try to find a crew himself. He asked that Surgeon de Cornes join him. This meant that besides Allwood his coxswain and Millward his servant, he also had a friendly face. The ship had been called *Byen Copenhagen* meaning the City of Copenhagen. Because the British Navy was superstitious, even captured ships tended to keep their original names where possible. This, the second largest captured, was now known as *HMS Copenhagen*.

She had a crew of 738 including Officers. She boasted the usual 7 Lieutenants, 24 Midshipmen, a Master, and second Master, with four master's mates. Although over three quarters of the crew were seasoned seamen, there were also a number of

'Landmen' to be trained.

Will had reverted to the rank of Captain. He was sorry to have to leave his schooner behind, but at least he had the knowledge that she was now under the command of a newly promoted Commander Cranfield. In the middle of March, *Copenhagen* was finally warped out of Chatham Docks and Will took her into the Thames Estuary to work her up. Despite the stormy weather, he made them sail on every point of the compass in all winds, evaluating her sailing properties. The Master was very surprised to find that his Captain knew quite so much about handling such a big ship. There was no let up; they practised firing their guns at least twice a day, with prizes as to which crew were the fastest. After four days of relentless pounding backwards and forwards within the confines of the estuary, he took *Copenhagen* back to anchor in the comparative shelter of the Medway. Here he had the Purser and the two Masters reposition the stores down below. Once this had been completed, the ship set sail again, this time being far more manageable. It was a lesson to all; the chat below decks was all about their new skipper and his apparent seamanship. Allwood was quizzed about Will's past, which he was happy to expound upon, though being careful not to mention anything about their time in the Caribbean. The fact that Will was amongst the leading prize money winning Captains delighted the crew.

When he had read himself in, he had stressed that he believed in discipline, but fair discipline. He had the vests issued for the landmen, so that the quartermaster's mates could easily identify them. He stressed that the starter was only to be used in extreme circumstances. The lashing of the tongue should be enough to 'encourage' the laggard.

Finally, at the end of March *Copenhagen* sailed for Plymouth. Isabella had stayed in London, so that she had company. When Will was finally ready to depart for Plymouth, she left for Devon.

At Plymouth, a whole convoy of troop ships were to gather, and would sail for Cork in Southern Ireland. *Copenhagen* would be the command ship, with a couple of frigates and a group of brig-sloops to guard the convoy.

It was whilst they were sailing to Plymouth from Chatham and were two days out at night and closing the coast of Devon that fire broke out down below.

"Fire! We're on fire!" Shrieked mess men from up foreward near to the galley. There was panic amongst the junior ratings.

"Man the pumps!" Shouted the boatswains' mates.

"Get buckets on lanyards!" Shouted Mr. Cropper, the Boatswain.

The officers were streaming up from the wardroom in various states of dress.

Will, wearing just a shirt, pantaloons and boots strode forward. "Clear the lower decks; Number one! Hoist out the boats, Furl the courses! All hammocks to be brought up and taken aft."

Smoke was beginning to come up through the forward ladderway. Fire was one of the greatest dangers a ship could suffer. If the fire reached the forward magazine, the whole ship would blow up.

"Lieutenant Articus!". He was the second lieutenant aboard. "Get water soaked clothes down to those fighting the fire, to put round their faces and bodies." Ordered Will. He grabbed a soaking cloth from a passing seaman and dropped down the forward ladderway to see for himself what was happening. Flames were beginning to catch everything around the galley stove. The smoke was curling under the beams like strange octopus tentacles. The flames were feeding on long forgotten grease, which spat as it caught fire. The men playing the hoses were desperately trying to pour water on the flames.

Will shoved his way forward. "Wet the deck around

the flames and the deck head NOW!" He ordered. "You there, don't just stand there, get anything you think might burn easily out of here. Lieutenant Crumble, find the sailmaker and get him to bring up to the top deck any spare canvas. Get him to soak it with water and bring it down here. Mr. Saintly, find the Carpenter."

Lieutenant Crumble was the sixth in line, and Mr. Saintly was one of twenty-four midshipmen.

The heat from the fire was intense. Could they get enough hoses from the fire pumps to tackle the blaze? The smoke was rolling as a cloud around their faces, constrained by the height of the deck-head.

Simms the first lieutenant made himself known to Will.

"Get as many hammocks on ropes dropped over the side and get them as wet as possible, then get then down here. We must build a firewall around the fire." Ordered Will.

The fire fighters were shouting and coughing. "Keep playing the hoses on the deck-head and the deck!" Ordered Will as tears streamed down his cheeks. There was a tap on his shoulder; he turned to find the Carpenter beside him.

"Mr. Bottom, when the wet canvas comes down tack it to the cross beams and the deck-head in between. Then hold the bottom down with the wet hammocks. I want a wet screen all round the fire."

Will went up on deck and made his way to the quarterdeck. Mr. Howard, the Master was beside the two quartermasters at the wheel.

"How far are we from land?" Asked Will.

"Eight miles, Sir!" Came the instant reply.

"Get us as near a beach as possible. If we have to abandon ship, I want to be within a stone's throw from land. I am not sure how long we have got, but pile everything you have got on!"

"That will be Slapton Sands, Sir. About one hour."

"Very good!" Came Will's automatic reply; it was delivered calmly.

The Boatswain had furled the main course and was getting the main yard ready to hoist out the cutters. With over seven hundred men aboard, there was no way they could all get off safely. Will had to get the fire under control. Luckily, fire drill was one of the exercises that he had insisted upon being carried out, before they left Chatham. Now it was time to see if the crew remembered all they had been taught.

Will walked calmly forward and dropped down the ladderway again. Steam as well as smoke was pouring up in the opposite direction. It being night did not help, although the flames lit the area, it was difficult to see past the flames.

"Anybody forward of the galley?" Will asked. At that moment, flames reached towards one of the forward cannons.

"Turn the hose on that larboard forward cannon." Will instructed. If the charge box next to it were to catch, there would be an explosion, which could blow out the side of the ship. If the cannon ignited, it would blow out the gun-port.

"Number One; appoint an officer to take control of each side of the fire." Will ordered; as Simms reappeared.

At long last, a bucket chain had been established. The buckets were being brought down the forward ladderway and back out, after use, by the aft one.

The fire fighters were struggling to breathe, and their efforts seemed to achieving nothing. It was as if the fire had a hold on the dry timbers and was not going to give it up.

"Keep rotating the men on the hoses, Number One. Let them get air before they try again. Get extra men to beat the flames on the deck with anything to hand."

The Carpenter and his mate, followed by some seamen from the forecastle came down the ladderway hauling wet canvas after them. Will indicated where the carpenter and his mates were to nail the canvas to the beams. They put up the screen about a yard away from the flames using the screen to protect themselves. The hoses were used over the top and underneath, until the wet hammocks were brought down and used to hold down the bottom of the screen. Finally, the gaps at the top were nailed up and anything damp used to fill the gaps. The hoses were left to pump water into the area, now completely encircled by the canvas.

"Cover the stove pipe!" Will ordered; realising that it was funnelling air down to the fire.

The screen stopped the air getting to the flames, and they gradually seemed to sink down and snuff out.

"Keep the pumps going to cool everything down. The fire could re-ignite at any time." Commanded Will. He was peering through a grommet hole in one of the canvas screens. He could see the flames flicker and die.

"Keep a guard on it until morning. If it starts up again get the pumps going immediately. We only need a couple at the moment." Will could hear the discordant sound of the bilge pumps, pumping out the water that was flowing into the bilges, because of the hoses above.

"Who is the officer of the watch?" Will asked; as he strode back to the quarterdeck.

"I am Sir." Lieutenant Fanshaw, the third lieutenant stepped forward.

"Get her back on course for Plymouth."

"Aye, Aye, Sir."

"Number One, I need a report as to the cause of the fire first thing this morning."

Will was having breakfast in his cabin when the First Lieutenant was announced.

"Have some toast, Number One?" Asked Will; indicating that Simms might take a seat at the table. Millward had already produced another cup and saucer by the time the First Lieutenant took his seat.

"I have written a report on the fire, Sir."

"Good, now tell me what happened." Replied Will.

"Apparently one of the new boys; a powder monkey

felt cold. He thought he would warm himself up by going to the stove. Of course, it had been dampened down for the night, so he piled wood on the officers' spit. It took off; he had piled it too high. A flaming log fell out. It was too hot for the boy to put back. He panicked and the fire spread to the deck."

"How old is this villain?" Asked Will.

"Twelve years Sir. Least that's what he says he is, but I think he probably is only eleven, or so."

"How come a boy could sneak up to the stove and nobody noticed when he piled on the wood?"

"I questioned those whose hammocks are nearest, but they all claimed they were asleep. Of course they were above him and tucked in." Replied Simms.

"So we shall have to punish this fellow. All pomp and circumstance; Number One. Question is; what sort of punishment do you hand out to a mere child? If I had my way, there wouldn't be such young children aboard. Trouble is we need them when it comes to battle. Anyway, he is probably safer and much better fed aboard one of His Majesty's ships, than in a Poor House. Have him up before me at six bells of the forenoon watch. You will see him officially first as usual."

When the boy came before him shaking with fright, Will handed down his judgement. He docked him a month's pay and he had to climb up and down the shrouds of each mast twice a day. The gravity of what the boy had done was explained graphically, pointing out that by his actions; he had put the entire crew at risk to their lives.

Once *Copenhagen* was moored to a buoy in the Hamoaze, Will had to report the incident to the Port Admiral. The ship would have to have the stove lifted and new planking put down where the original had been burnt. The Master Shipwright declared that the beams and deck-head might be scorched, but need not be replaced. This meant that the ship had to wait its turn for the work to be completed. The bonus was that Will was able to travel to the Dart and spend a few days with his family, who had returned to Devon a week before. It was not until late May that the ship was ready for sea.

Cork Harbour on the southwestern coast of Ireland is about two miles wide and five miles long. *Copenhagen* anchored near the mouth, so that she provided a gun platform protecting the anchored transports in the bay, from any marauding Frenchman.

Here they waited for orders. Will hated this time.

He was a man of action, he hated sitting around waiting for orders that never seemed to come. He insisted that his crew was kept busy and had the guns exercised each day. In the middle of June, he decided that the escorts should put to sea to keep up their training. Whilst the weather was fair, he led his small command out to sail up and down off the south coast of Ireland, much in the manner of the blockade of Toulon.

Then whilst anchored in the bay, on the 8th July, Will had a visitor. It was Sir Arthur Wellesley, the General commanding the troops. They dined in Will's cabin in style. Sir Arthur brought news that there might be a change of plan. Originally, the convoy was being held ready to sail for South America to support the exiled Portuguese government. Now it seemed more likely that they would be sent to support the Portuguese on their own territory.

Lisbon was in the hands of the French. Lord Castlereagh and the Government were keen to try to wrestle the city and the whole of Portugal from the French stranglehold. Sir Arthur was enthusiastic about the idea. He had been promised more troops if he was sent south. They discussed over dinner the merits of the few ports on the western coast of Portugal, but Will still favoured Mondego as the most suitable landing site. Will was firm in his contention that it was the only suitable place to put a whole army ashore, other than Oporto. He was very definite about the difficulties they could face if the weather was inclement. Sir Arthur was particularly interested in the partisans and their ability to interfere with the French logistics.

The next day more ships joined them including the 74 gun *Donegal* under the command of Captain Malcolm. Since Malcolm was senior on the Navy List to Will, he would now be in command. Then a week later, a boat brought over dispatches. Will was surprised to find that he had been relieved of his command of *Copenhagen*. Another Captain would soon be coming across to take command. Will was to act as an adviser to Sir Arthur, the Commanding General. Once the new Captain had arrived aboard, Will was rowed across to *Donegal* taking with him Allwood and Millward. Will had suggested that the new captain of *Copenhagen* should utilise his furniture for the time being, as Will had no need of it aboard the other ship, as a supplementary officer. Sir Arthur was not aboard when Will climbed in through the entry port of the *Donegal*. Captain Malcolm being the senior officer on the Navy List, did not greet him; that was left to the First Lieutenant. Will was taken straight to Malcolm's day cabin.

"Sir William; welcome aboard. You must be rather

perplexed by the turn of events. Sir Arthur told me he had asked for you, but was not sure if the Board of Admiralty would allow such a senior and distinguished officer to act in such a capacity."

"Thank you. It was rather a surprise to me too!"

"I understand that you have knowledge of the Spanish partisans and speak the language. Is that so?"

"Yes, I have spent time arming and advising the partisans even before the Spanish nation woke up to what had happened to them."

"Well obviously a good choice. I am afraid we shall be a bit cramped aboard. We have run out of senior officers' cabins. I am afraid I shall have to ask you to use one our lieutenant's cabins off the wardroom."

"Don't mind about me. I actually prefer a hammock to a cot; much cosier."

Malcolm looked closely at Will and then laughed. "Sir Arthur described you as a down to earth individual. I gather he doesn't suffer fools lightly. He is ashore making sure that the troops are fresh and able to exercise, rather than being cooped up in the transports for too long. Now tell me: Sir Arthur says you recently up-dated the charts for the west coast of Portugal. You must know the coast well."

"We surveyed the coast north from Cape Roca. I hear rumours that a landing south of Lisbon has been proposed. I would strongly oppose such an idea. The Tagus is too wide and too long. The enemy would have plenty of time to oppose us. Mondego Bay would be my choice; but then it is not up to me!"

"Interesting! Sir Arthur was of that opinion himself." Malcolm added.

Will then tactfully asked Malcolm to describe the action off San Domingo where he had captured two enemy ships. This he did with great relish. Malcolm had spent much of the last year off Finisterre, so was knowledgeable about the coast of that part of Spain.

They were still talking when Sir Arthur was announced. "Have you joined us, Sir William?" Were the first words he spoke as he caught sight of Will.

"Aye Sir. Arrived but an hour ago. I understand I am to be with you."

"Yes! Sorry not to have broached the subject the other night, but Castlereagh was doubtful as to the Admiralty releasing you so soon." Then he turned to Captain Malcolm. "Would it inconvenience you if we were to stop off at Corunna on the way south? I would like to get a firsthand account of what is happening up there."

"Not at all, Sir Arthur. I suggest that you transfer to a smaller and faster vessel and then rejoin the fleet off Finisterre. How would that suit?"

"Very fine, very fine!"

Chapter 20

Donegal and the fleet started to prepare to leave on the 10th July. However, the weather decided otherwise. They finally left Cork on the 12th. Even then, the sea was in a foul mood.

The next day, with some difficulty, the general's party transferred to the smaller HMS *Crocodile*, a 24 gun frigate. Once again they were cramped so Will found himself sharing a cabin off the wardroom.

Will was surprised that Sir Arthur Wellesley always referred to him in company aboard as Commodore Calvert. Will supposed this was because he knew no better, but it could be so that the Captain of

Crocodile who was about the same age as Will, so might be higher up the Navy List, treated him with more respect. Because Will had no idea exactly what rank he was supposed to hold, he dressed in civilian clothes, which the General seemed to approve of, commenting on Will's modesty.

The weather was still bad and it took six days for them to reach Corunna. Will reflected at how fast the *Hound* had been in comparison in such seas.

It was a hectic couple of days in Corunna. They met up with a Mr. Charles Stuart, who was a special envoy, just out from London. Together they met with members of the Galician Junta who were able to pass on what information they could about the situation in the rest of Spain, though Will doubted its accuracy. Apparently, most of Spain was in the grips of an uprising against the French. They stated that Navarra and the Biscay province appeared to be under French control. Will later pointed out to Sir Arthur that the reason for this was that the Partisans would be attacking in Cantabria, where it was easier to ambush the French, and further away from the French border.

In many places, the Spanish had overcome the local French units. However, sadly the Castilian and Galician Army under General Blake together with a Partisan called Cuesta, had been routed by the

French around Burgos. Of the supposed 50,00 Spaniards, 7,000 were said to have been lost. Exactly what 'lost' meant was not explained. At first they had been winning the battle, but the French had brought up cavalry on what was a divided mixture of Spanish troops and partisans under no single command. The remnants of Blake's troops had fallen back to Manzanal, to the west of the battle, yet the French had failed to follow up.

They were advised by the Junta that the British should keep a fleet off the North West coast of Spain, because the Junta thought that Napoleon would try to break out his ships to aid Asturias. The Junta said they had intelligence that General Junot had 12,000 troops in Lisbon, with a further 3,000 in Almeida, near the Spanish border further north. And so, the flow of information came; not all to be regarded as safe in Will's opinion.

During these briefings, Will stayed in the background, able to hear and take notes, but not speaking. He was heartened to hear the members of the Junta strongly advise against trying to land troops near Lisbon. They recommended Vigo or Oporto, so that the Portuguese troops who held sway in most of the north of the country could be allied with any British landing. On being offered troops, the members of the Junta opposed such an idea, asking instead for arms and ammunition,

A Secret Assignment

together with money. A 'species' of the Asturian Junta demanded that the British should drive the French out of Santander. When this was raised later with the Galician Junta, they stated that relief was in hand. What would be best for them was the occupation of Portugal, so driving out the French and allowing Northern and Southern Spain combine their forces.

On the afternoon of the second day, Will slipped away and using his knowledge of the Spanish language was able to find out much, that the members of the Junta had failed to communicate. He learnt, in much more detail, exactly what had occurred at Rio Seco. It appeared that General Blake had been ordered by the Galician Junta, not to take orders from Cuesta. The later, being a proud man, refused to take orders from Blake. As a result Cuesta had not risked his partisans, so leaving a critical area in the centre uncovered, forcing Blake to retire.

It was not until they were back on *Crocodile* sailing to rejoin the fleet off Finisterre that Will had a chance to confer with Sir Arthur. He waited until the General asked his opinion. Then he passed on what he had learnt and suggested that intelligence over such long hostile distances, should be treated carefully. Sir Arthur just nodded.

On the 22nd July, they managed to join up with the invasion fleet. Back aboard *Donegal,* there were signals from Admiral Cotton, whose fleet was blockading Lisbon. After conferring with Captain Malcolm, it was back to the *Crocodile* and to Oporto, where they met the Bishop of that City who seemed to be in charge. He was of the opinion that the Spanish troops under Blake were unlikely to cross the border to aid the Portuguese, as had been rumoured. When asked, Will gave his opinion on the Bishop as being power hungry. This got a sharp look from Sir Arthur. Back aboard *Crocodile,* Sir Arthur received further dispatches from Admiral Cotton. These advised that they should sail straight to the Tagus to meet up with the Admiral.

Crocodile sailed down the Portuguese coast to meet up with Admiral Cotton on the 26th July. Much to Will's embarrassment, Sir Arthur insisted that he be at the meeting with the Admiral. The Admiral was not introduced to all the party, so Will kept in the background and listened. They were given a briefing on the disposition of the Spanish forces in Lisbon and the surrounding area. As they poured over the charts, it became obvious that to try to land troops so near the enemy in such a heavily defended area was out of the question. The issue of the heavy surf and its effect on the small creeks around the Tagus was also mentioned. General Spencer had landed troops further down the coast in Spain, but they had not joined up with the Spanish Armies. Sir Arthur was strongly of the opinion that it would be ludicrous to land his troops to join Spencer's, and then try to join up with the Spanish. The French held such strong ground, with a plentiful supply line. Wellesley ordered that a signal should be sent to Spencer to re-board his troops and bring them to join the rest of the fleet off Mondego.

In the main cabin of the frigate, Sir Arthur sat reading the dispatches. He looked up and said. "Sir William, hear this. 'I recommend that any landing should take place at Porto (Oporto) or at Mondego'. Admiral Cotton recommends Mondego. You are vindicated! I think that your choice is the best. It means we have less ground to cover and we can be supported from the sea; which was your point all along. We shall also be far nearer the Portuguese troops. Humph! He has put 100 marines ashore to capture the fortress at Figueira. That settles it. Mondego it shall be! Or if the fortress is taken, perhaps Peniche."

Later that evening in the Captain's cabin, Wellesley came over to Will. "Ever put troops ashore, Sir William?"

"I have put Marines ashore, but only in small numbers. Getting an Army ashore is going to be a nightmare, I am afraid. Even at is time of year the surf is going to make things very difficult. The mouth of the Mondego River has a bar. I doubt if any ships with a draft of over a fathom will be able to get beyond that bar. The transports have flat bottomed boats, but those are very unstable."

Sir Arthur rubbed his nose, nodded and walked away, deep in thought.

On the 30th July, they joined up with the fleet off Mondego. Will was extremely surprised to see amongst the numerous ships, a three masted schooner on the northern fringes of the fleet.

General Wellesley's group rejoined *Donegal*. The orders went out to prepare to land. Will kept out of the way; it was up to Sir Arthur's staff to arrange the order of landing. Late on 1stAugust, *Hound's* jolly boat came alongside and Allwood brought Will mail from England. There were twelve letters from Isabella, but there was also an official dispatch from the Admiralty. He was ordered to continue to be available to Lieutenant-General Sir Arthur Wellesley, to give any service within his powers. It was addressed to Captain Sir William Calvert Bt, so Will knew his place in the pecking order. There was also a dispatch from Cranfield, saying that Hound had been in action on the north coast of Spain, but had not been damaged nor had there been any injuries.

The landings had started, and Will observed them with a certain degree of annoyance. He was privately critical of the methods employed. There was no doubt about the bravery of the seamen who ferried the troops, horses, and supplies ashore. It was the lack of forward planning. Will had formulated a plan of his own, but being too junior could not put his ideas against aged and much senior officers. He would have sent in pioneers with stacks to be driven into the beach amongst the waves and then tied flat-bottomed barges between them, providing a pier for unloading beyond the surf.

Will was ordered ashore on the second day. His cutter was grabbed as it ran in, by seamen up to their armpits in the surf, steadying the craft. He was able to get ashore with just wet feet. Millward followed him, hefting a couple of heavy bags, containing their clothes and a couple of blankets. Will was led to the Command tents, pitched a little inland. He discovered that he was to share with two of the General's staff officers. It was not an auspicious time to have arrived. According to Lord Fitzroy Somerset, the General's nineteen-year-old aide-de-camp, Sir Arthur had received news that the Government was sending more troops, and that a more senior General was to arrive with them.

Yet here they were with the French in chaos. According to intelligence, Junot was still in Lisbon, where the local populace were getting extremely restive. Junot would be hard pressed to collect enough troops to face the British, if Wellesley was able to march south and attack.

Sir Arthur had ridden to Montemor Velho to meet with the General Don Bernardin Freire de Andrada, the Portuguese Commander-in-Chief. Freire was all for combining and attacking Beira. Will sat on the fringes, concentrating on the Portuguese General's manner and facial expressions.

On the way back, Lord Fitzroy Somerset, who had been riding close to the General, peeled off and came to ride beside Will.

"The General would like a word, Sir William." Will was very surprised, but spurred his mount forward to join the General.

"Ride to hounds, Sir William?" Asked the General; who had not slackened his pace.

"Unfortunately I have little opportunity, but I do when I can."

"Thought so! Never seen a sailor who could ride well before!"

Sir Arthur was not someone who handed out compliments that often, Will was very surprised.

"What you make of Freire?"

"Frankly I would not trust him further than I could see him."

"Thank you. You have confirmed my own opinion. I should like you to make your way north and find General Blake. You know him; you speak his language. See if you can persuade him to move south. It could draw off Bessières and his troops. We don't want him trying to join up with Junot."

"If that is not be possible after Blake's defeat, perhaps I could try to get the partisans to spread the word that his is about to do so, even if he is unable or unwilling."

Sir Arthur turned in his saddle to stare at Will. "I am beginning to realise why Lord Castlereagh advised me to have you on my staff. Any other ideas?"

"Well it did occur to me, that if we were to send about twenty of the empty troop transports, with covering frigates close inshore south of Peniche, it would lead to speculation that we were about to land troops near there, and therefore might just get Junot to split his forces to cover such an eventuality."

"You Sir, are a devious fellow! You really do think differently! Castlereagh was right."

As General Spencer's troops were being landed, Will managed to get a boat returning to Captain Malcolm's ship to take him and Millward. When he was taken to see the Captain, Malcolm was extremely surprised to see him.

"I thought you were with Sir Arthur!"

"I am. He wants me to visit General Blake at Corunna; or wherever he happens to be. I came to ask if you could supply transport, so to speak."

"My dear fellow, of course. As it happens, the Admiralty have sent me an extra schooner with explicit orders that it is to be made available for use if you require to visit other parts of the Spanish coast. I am sure you will be pleased to hear that the schooner is none other than *Hound*!"

"Good God!" Will exclaimed. "That is marvellous!"

Malcolm sent for his signals Midshipman, and ordered him to make a hoist for *Hound* to send a boat.

"How are things ashore?" Malcolm asked; turning back to Will.

"As you are well aware the landing of the troops was extremely difficult. However, the army seems to be in good order. Sir Arthur is extraordinary. He is on top of the minutia of everything. His planning is a revelation. I must say I find it difficult to understand why they are sending out new Generals to take charge."

"The Army is very like the Navy now in its way of promoting. The Duke of York laid down that the Generals' line of promotion runs from the date they are made a Lieutenant-Colonel. Same as naval promotion; is from your first Post-Captain appointment. Sir Arthur is relatively low down the list. Problem is similar to the Navy, just because you have served time, doesn't mean that you have battle experience. As I understand it, Sir Arthur had a lot of experience in India, but for some reason Indian battles don't seem to rate highly at Horse Guards."

"I fear you are right. From what I learned, I have a feeling that Sir Arthur will be tested before the new fellows arrive. Intelligence has it that the French are beginning to move elements of their forces north to meet our army."

"Really? So am I allowed to know why you are

travelling north to meet General Blake?"

"We don't want the French to bring their armies in the north of Spain to join up with their southern forces. If we can get General Blake to make the signs of moving onto the field; that might keep a large proportion of the French strength up north."

"And why a sailor, might I ask?"

"I have already met General Blake. I helped to organise the resistance to the original French invasion."

"I am beginning to understand why Sir Arthur has you on his staff! Lord St. Vincent once told me that you were the next young blood to be watched. He likened you to the late Lord Nelson."

"I am flattered, but I assure you, Lord Nelson had far more experience than I have had during my career in this man's Navy."

Hound's boat was announced, and Allwood stood open mouthed as first Millward dropped down with his heavy bags, and then Will came over the side to sit in the stern.

"You back in command Sir?" Asked Allwood, directly they had cast off.

"No, old friend, I shall be a passenger."

The same question was asked by Cranfield as he greeted Will.

"No Oscar, I am still attached to Sir Arthur Wellesley's headquarters staff. I need you to take me to Corunna as fast as possible."

Chapter 21

"So what's this about Hound being in action? Asked Will when they had the privacy of the day cabin.

"The Admiralty sent us down to patrol the north coast of Spain. They wanted to deter the French from sending troops and supplies by sea, now that it is summer. We spent some time cruising, but we only came across a few small craft trying to sneak in. I decided to take a look at the nearest French ports to see if anything was brewing. There was quite a collection of masts sheltering behind the sand spit at Hendaye. I decided that a pre-emptive strike might be in order. I remembered you had used Congreve rockets in the past, so we hauled our cache up from below and fired them at the masts we could see. We must have hit a transport loaded with gunpowder, because there was a God Almighty explosion, and we could see flames leaping in the air. Trouble is, we could not see over the sand dunes, so we have no idea exactly how much damage we did. It was though, very satisfying!"

"Good thinking! What did you do about the boats you did see along the coast?"

"We challenged them, to make sure they were not Spanish. When we knew for certain they were French, we ordered the crew to take to the boats, then we used our carronades to sink them."

"So how come you joined the fleet?"

"We went back to Corunna, for victuals. Whilst we were there, a Brig-sloop arrived and we were ordered south."

They could have been on a pleasure cruise, the weather held fair and the sea was relatively calm. They had a spectacular sunset as they pressed north under full sail in a southwesterly breeze.

Will had his first good sleep for days; waking much refreshed. On land at night, it was cold and damp lying on the hard earth, even when one was under canvas. Not being an Army member of staff, nobody had thought to provide the Naval Officer with any camping equipment. Will had even ordered Millward to come and sleep in his tent, because the poor fellow was discovered sleeping with the soldiery in the open. The ground at night became extremely damp from the dew. Horses had been another problem, only solved when Fitzroy Somerset had learnt of Will's lack of a mount and ordered the commissariat to find a suitable mount for a Staff Officer. Will had paid over the odds, but managed as a result to get two good beasts, one for himself, and one for Millward, who accompanied him wherever he went.

It was mid afternoon, when *Hound* dropped her anchor off Corunna. Once ashore, Will made his way to the headquarters of the Junta. He discovered that General Blake was there in Corunna, for meetings with the Junta. That evening Will was able to sit down with the General and explain what the British hoped he would be able to achieve.

General Blake explained in detail what had happened at Rio Seco. How the partisan troops of Cuesta had failed to move up, so that the French had been able to divide the Spanish. He was apologetic, but was of the opinion, that the Galician Junta would not allow him to move his army too far east. Will then put forward his own proposals. These he had not discussed with Sir Arthur in detail, because he feared that they might not fit into a regular army officer's idea of warfare. Blake listened with amusement as Will explained exactly what he wanted.

"So you want me to send out skirmishers, to at least appear that an army is on the move? What happens when the French discover that there was no army in the first place?"

"If there are enough reports of troops moving, how are they going to be able to divide fact from fiction? They will have to send out their own spies, which not being native to the area will be spotted immediately. If you can get word to Ybarra and co; they will notify their people that they must capture these spies. Plant rumours that you are moving your army in small divisions through the countryside, so that the French will be unable to gauge your strength."

"You want more *Guerrilleros*! You know, that is the word we use for small wars. Wars like your friend Ybarra has waged against the French. I see much merit in what you suggest. You want the French to believe that there are more of us, and that we shall attack if they try to assist their troops in the south. That I think we can manage, my friend. You know that Joseph Bonaparte is being sheltered by Bessières and his troops up in the north nearer the border with France. If Bessières decides to move south, he will be opening his flank to us! That is the message that we must get across to him. I already have troops from our old army, held ready to move south to attack if he so much as moves towards Salamanca"

"Thank you! I know London had hoped that you would march south to aid the British army, but that would leave both our flanks exposed!"

"Exactly! But you have given me an idea. We have a spy in our midst at my headquarters. I am certain that he has been passing information to the French. I shall make sure that he is at a meeting, where I shall outline plans for a move southeast as part of a pincher movement on the French at Valladolid. He will be ordered to go and prepare for them. I shall of course counter the order directly he has left."

It being summer, *Hound* was able to leave Corunna that night. Will spent part of the night writing up a succinct report for Sir Arthur, before turning in. Late the next evening *Hound* came up with the British ships supporting the British Army. They had moved further down the coast keeping pace with the army's march south. Will was rowed across to *Donegal* Malcolm's ship, to inform him of his next move. He left his report for the General to be delivered ashore with the mail the next morning. He also asked and got permission to 'borrow' a frigate.

Will boarded the frigate and explained his plan to the young Captain in command. Will did not mention to either Malcolm or the young Captain that this was solely his own idea, and had not been discussed with Sir Arthur. In Will's opinion these were naval tactics, so had nothing to do with the army, although if successful would help the British army considerably.

The next morning *Hound* sailed westwards followed by the frigate. Twenty miles off Peniche, *Hound* turned to start her run in. The frigate waited for a short period and then began to follow her. At ten miles off the coast, the frigate fired one of her cannons, although it was not loaded with shot. As they raced towards the land, the frigate began to fire more often. *Hound* was forced to spill the wind slightly so that the frigate appeared to be keeping in touch. As they passed the island of Berlenga, the frigate began using shot, but she made sure that they landed to the seaward side of the schooner. To make it seem that *Hound* was in danger, the crew of *Hound* dropped charges over the side, so the splashes would appear to be very close.

Two miles off the fort of Peniche, the frigate turned away. *Hound* , flying the American flag, luffed up between the mainland and the fort at the entrance to

Peniche harbour.

Immediately, as Will had hoped, a boat was seen to put out from beneath the fort. When it was within hailing distance, Will using the speaking trumpet called to the officer in the boat.

"That was close! There is a fleet of about twenty to thirty British ships sitting just out of sight over the horizon. They did not take kindly to our taking a look."

"What sort of ships?" Asked the French officer

"Looked like transports. They look as if they are preparing to land troops. Is it alright if we wait for darkness before we leave?"

The French officer waved and the boat immediately returned to the fort. A few minutes later, it came rowing across again to the hovering *Hound*. This time an older, more senior officer asked to come aboard.

"What are you doing here?" He asked.

"We are on our way to the Mediterranean. We are American."

The Officer seemed to accept this without questioning further.

"Can you describe the ships you saw?"

"Certainly. They were big transports. They seemed to have a large number of flat-bottomed craft on their decks. The British ignored the fact we are neutral and started to fire on us."

"Thank you. You think they are heading towards the shore?"

"Well that is what we thought. Why wait out there if they are intending to go to Lisbon or Cadiz? So is it permissible to anchor here until sunset?"

Permission was given, and *Hound* lowered her anchor in the gently rolling sea. Even in the middle of summer under a bright cloudless blue sky, the Atlantic still heaved up and down, even though the surf on the shore was quite mild.

Discreet telescopes, trained on the fort, soon picked out a number of riders leaving the fort and turning inland.

That evening *Hound* set sail heading south. Directly the light had gone, she turned and headed in a circle to return to the north and await the dawn. Only twenty odd miles up the coast off a small village called Nazareth, they found Malcolm's ships still unloading supplies for the advancing British army.

The British were already on the move early in the morning, and the entire fleet moved to anchor off the small inlet of Caldas. Here; Will left *Hound* and was put ashore with the faithful Millward. They discovered that their horses had been brought down with the other staff baggage. This time they were better prepared. Millward had brought more blankets, together with Will's and his own wet weather gear. They managed to persuade the stores to let them have a couple of camp beds, generally reserved for staff officers. Will had to accompany Millward to explain that he was on the staff. Luckily, a staff officer was nearby and confirmed that Will was indeed attached to Sir Arthur's headquarters staff.

At the Headquarters near Caldas, Will heard that four companies of rifles had been sent to drive back the French outposts, which were reported to be a few miles to the south. Apparently, they had been over enthusiastic and had very nearly been cut off, but that General Spencer had come to their aid, and the forward French pickets around Obidos had been driven out. Intelligence was coming in that the French had advanced as far as the village of Roliça on the road from Lisbon. Roliça sat where the flat sandy coastal plain meets the hilly region to the east. Here the road climbs up a steep escapement to the plain above. Will listened as Sir Arthur gave his orders for the next day.

Colonel Trant was to take three battalions of Portuguese troops and some fifty horse on a wide arc, crossing the road to Peniche and then to gain the heights to the west. General Ferguson and General Bowes were to take their second and fourth brigades up a valley to the east, where they would be hidden from the French, and then to cut round so as to gain height to the east. The rest of the British army would face the French in the centre. The French were commanded by a General Delaborde; but how the British Commander came by this intelligence, Will had no knowledge.

Will wondered what he was doing here once again. He could see no reason for his attachment. He decided that he had best keep out of the way of the main staff group, as he would only get in the way. Studying the map after Sir Arthur had finished his briefing, Will informed Fitzroy Somerset that he would position himself on a wooded outcrop directly to the north of Roliça, where he could observe and write up a minute-by-minute report of what he was able to see. This the young Aide thought was a good idea, and appreciated that Will did not want to distract the General, by asking what was required of him.

Very early on the 17th August, after the British had

moved forward, Will with Millward in tow, cantered over to the rear of his chosen position. They tethered their horses amongst the trees and made their way to a forward position where they could see the area laid out before them. They were less than a mile away from the French positions. Of Trant's Portuguese soldiers, there was no sign. There was no sign either of the two brigades that were circling to the east. Below them, the British army was advancing in two rows. General Hill could be seen with his staff on the west side. General Fane's small brigade, with the rifles, was to the east, with General Nightingale's foot in the centre. The heat was appalling. The soldiers' boots kicked up a cloud of dust as they advanced. Myriads of flies took a delight in descending on the poor afflicted horses. Already one's mouth was parched. Millward had thought to bring ashore a firkin of beer and had filled canteens with the light ale. Two other canteens of water hung either side of his saddle for the horses.

Early on, Fane's rifles seemed to be having an effect on the French; the French troops withdrew from the hillock on the northwest of the village in an orderly manner to the ridge of the escarpment beyond the village. This would mean that the British troops would have to fight whilst trying to climb the escarpment. Will noted that General

Delaborde's troops had acted in a disciplined manner.

Below, Will could see Sir Arthur on his horse, closely followed by Fitzroy and his other aides move from side to side. The British moved forward and repositioned themselves. Fane advanced to just south of the village. Hill mean time had advanced his troops to the small hamlet of Columbeira, which was right at the bottom of the escarpment, facing the French left. Nightingale's Brigade moved forward in the centre.

It was like watching a game of chess. Will decided that their position was now too far back. They retrieved their horses and moved forward to the road, crossed the bridge to the north of the village and into the village of Roliça. The small village was a surprise. The houses were well kept and had gardens full of flowers and vegetables. Here they turned up to the hillock to the northwest of the village, previously occupied by the French, where they had a superb view. Laid out before them were olive groves and fields of vines, with variously sized Holm oaks. Millward took the horses back to the shade of a tree and gave them some water from a canteen. Will found shade from a bush and sat with his portable writing desk, his back to a convenient rock. He started to sketch the scene. Just as they settled, things started to happen which were completely unexpected. A battalion of foot from General Nightingale's 29th regiment started to advance. They appeared to be Colonel Lake's foot soldiers and they moved forward without, as far as Will could see, any support. Will had expected Fane's rifles to move in before this charge up a gully. The gully was full of tall dried grass, with brown bracken and evergreen bushes. To Will's horror the regiment was now attacked from both sides. Yet they kept pressing on, reaching the top, where they were met by more French fire. As it unfolded before him, the British regiment was then assailed from three sides. At the top, but without support, they were trapped. They had to fight to retreat down the gully. Of Colonel Lake, there was no sign.

Then there was action to the east and the west. British regiments were trying to force their way up at either extremity in the available gullies. Will could only see clearly the centre and eastern gullies through his telescope. Each time British troops appeared to achieve the top of a gully, they were charged by the French. Both attacks appeared to fail; Will could see the English soldiers retreat and regroup. The smaller French force was using the terrain to deadly effect. There was another push by Hill's brigade to the west, Nightingale's in the centre and Fane's to the west. Each attempted to fight their way up one of the three gullies leading to the summit. but they were beaten back. Will was in despair. Whatever the British did seemed to have no effect on the French positions. Where were the two flanking moves?

Below him, Sir Arthur seemed to be everywhere. The British regrouped and yet another assault was started. This time the sound of gunfire could be heard to the east. General Ferguson must have managed to fight his way up the eastern side and was now targeting the French eastern flank.

The French began to retreat, but to Will's eyes it was a brilliantly executed manoeuvre. Each of the French battalions retreated, then turned to cover the retreat of their friends. It was a rolling retreat.

The battle as far as Will was concerned was over. He closed his book, put away his writing desk, and rode up the central gully, which the 29th had contested so expensively a couple of hours before. There were dead and wounded on every side. From seemingly nowhere the Portuguese peasants were arriving to revenge themselves on the French. The British had forced the French to retire, but the French had cavalry, which on the flatter ground could be used against the British.

Will waited on the high ground to see the outcome,

but finally gave up as the dust and smoke made it impossible to see what was happening.

Back at Headquarters there was quiet satisfaction that the French had been forced to retreat the field. A British army had overcome the invincible French on land at last. Sadly, when the British were chasing the French from the field, the Portuguese cavalry had failed to support Taylor's small cavalry force of the 20th Dragoons, not wanting to face the French mounted *Chasseurs*.

The Army started a slow move south following the seaward route and on the evening of the 19th August, General Anstruther's 7th brigade, consisting of a battalion of foot, two light battalions and a Highland battalion landed. The Navy managed to get most of them ashore through the surf by a supreme effort. Many of the sailors working up to their arm pits in the water trying to make sure the boats did not turn over in the surf. Will watched from his horse on the shore and was proud of his own service. He considered that the troops landing appeared to be extremely vulnerable, but later learnt that General Spencer had positioned troops to deter the French cavalry.

The next day there was another arrival: General Acland with two battalions of foot and two companies of rifles. Fitzroy Somerset in passing told Will that General Burrard had arrived aboard one of the ships. The young aid seemed upset. Apparently, this General was to take over command. Sir Arthur braved the surf to be taken out to meet this new General.

Will once again was watching the troops being landed. He was trying to see if *Hound* was anywhere out at sea. There were so many masts and such a hustle of boats bringing the troops ashore, that he could see no way that she would be anywhere within signalling distance. When he rode back to the new headquarters position, he was at a loss as to what to do. He wandered over to the command tent. Here a line of smart horses was lined up, their bridles held by grooms. There was a constant coming and going of aids bringing and taking messages to the various brigades and their commanders. As one arrived and threw his bridle to a groom, another would come rushing out grab his horse's reins and leap on its back to gallop off. Inside he found Sir Arthur pouring over a map that was spread out on the large folding table. Around him were his generals, including the new arrivals, Anstruther and Acland. Will kept in the background, but was conscious of a nagging feeling. He was not sure what was odd, until it suddenly struck him. There was no sign of General Burrard. Sir Arthur was giving orders as if still in complete command. Fitzroy, in passing, whispered in his ear.

"General Burrard is not coming ashore!"

As he listened, he realised that the French were on the move. Sir Arthur expected them to attack the next day. Intelligence had been brought in that the enemy force was increasing in size as various units joined the main force.

"We are in strong position where we are. We shall use this ridge here above the village of Vimeiro to face any attack. I suspect that if it is General Junot in command he will attack our seaward side to try to cut us off from naval support. The main attack will probably be aimed at breaking through in the centre here behind the village of Vimeiro, to drive up the valley and spread out behind us. If I were the French I should move up tonight so as to try and catch us on the hop." Stated Sir Arthur; looking from one general to the next. Heads were nodding.

Sir Arthur cleared his throat, then continued.

"General Burrard disdained from coming ashore today. He wanted to spend another night aboard. He wants us to wait for General Moore's troops to join us. Unfortunately, he changed their landing site. He ordered them to come south and land here. (He pointed at the map). I very much doubt if the French will be prepared to wait! They probably have intelligence about Moore's division. I feel certain they will attack first thing tomorrow morning. So we must be well prepared! General Hill, we need your brigade, the 5th, 9th and 38th Foot to be on our right hand flank. General Acland, if your brigade will cover this area to the west of General Hill, here. You will be in reserve behind General Nightingale, who will be further forward here, with General Crawford between Hill and yourself. General Anstruther, I should be obliged if you would take your Brigade and take up a position on Vimeiro Hill, here. General Fane, I should be obliged if you would place your brigade across the road from the south, beside Anstruther's brigade. You shall have artillery to supplement your strength. General Acland, General Bowes, and General Ferguson, I should be obliged if you would cover the western side of the river on the hill here. You should be able to see any threat to our western flank from there. Keep your battalions in two lines and behind the ridge so the enemy has no idea of your strength. General Crawford, your 5th Brigade will cover the eastern flank higher up the ridge here. Again, don't let the enemy have the advantage of being able to assess your strength until they are right up to you. The troops must all be in position before first light, ready for any action. Colonel Trant, I require that your cavalry and Portuguese troops be kept here at

Maceira as reinforcements and the cavalry to be ready to oppose any break in our line. I trust that the Portuguese can be persuaded to fight this time!"

There were general murmurings amongst the distinguished Gentlemen around the table. Colonel Trant looked embarrassed. As the Generals moved away in bunches talking together, leaving Sir Arthur at the table with only his staff around him, he looked up and caught sight of Will standing in the background.

"Sir William, I understand that you made a minute by minute report on our battle at Roliça the other day."

"Sir! I did just that."

"Tell me from your observations; can you think of any good reason why Lake should have charged the ravine when he did?"

"No Sir Arthur, I was very surprised when they started forward unsupported. I had thought that your plan was to make a concerted attack up all three ravines, or gullies at the same time. I saw no messengers, nor what I would have taken to be your messengers, joining him before the charge. I had a very good view through my telescope of that part of the action. I was less than a mile away, and on raised ground."

"Ah yes! You were on Roliça Hill, were you not? An ideal observation point! Well, it seems that we shall never know why Lake acted as he did, poor fellow." Here he seemed to ponder for a moment, then he looked up again.

"I should be grateful if I might read your reports when this action is over. Please do the same again. I suggest you position yourself on the higher road out of the Vimeiro to Ventosa."

"I shall do just that General."

Chapter 22

Millward shook Will awake at three in the morning.

"They are on the move Sir." He said, handing Will a scalding cup of hot chocolate.

Even as Will scrambled out of his tent, soldiers were pulling out the guy ropes to the tents.

Will finished his drink, put on his coat, and left Millward. Finding his mount, he saddled it himself, as the grooms seemed very preoccupied. He then trotted out to join the stream of soldiers moving south in the semi-darkness. He followed the road to

Vimeiro turning left to cross the bridge, before the village, then he turned left again to take the track over the smaller stream, named as Toledo Brook on the map, and up onto the ridge. He left the track, as groves of olive trees interrupted his view of the village of Vimeiro and the plain beyond. He found a suitable spot and tied his horse with a long rope to graze what little weeds and grass had survived the heat.

Laid out in front of him was a view across the village of Vimeiro to the ground beyond. The village sat on a junction of roads, on the south side of the Toledo Brook tributary to the river Maceira, where it joined at the village. To his right, was the steep valley cut through the hills with the river at the bottom through which he had arrived in Vimeiro. On the far side of the village, there was a hill with a wood just visible on the south side. He knew from Wellesley's briefing, that Generals Anstruther and Fane's brigades were positioned on that hill. Slightly below his position was part of Acland's 8th brigade. Straddling the road behind him on the army's left flank, was General Crawford, and beyond him Ferguson and Nightingale's 2nd and 3rd brigades. They were there to prevent the French from circling around towards the hamlet of Ventosa and attacking the rear of the English positions. He knew that General Hill's 1st brigade were on the

Western Ridge, out of sight, to prevent the French from an attack on the coastal side of the English.

As it grew lighter, Will could see Anstruther and Fane's troops taking up their positions on the hill to the south of the village. They were joined by horse artillery that positioned themselves at either extremity of the line. Raising his telescope, he realised that he could see clouds of dust on the horizon. Much perplexed, he lowered it to witness the same on the plain before him. Almost immediately, columns of British foot came marching up the slope in front of him. He recognised the flags of some of the battalions. Ferguson's 7th and 40th of foot came in an orderly column up to turn behind him to go off to the east. Crossing in front came Nightingale's brigade of foot. Then came General Bowes troops.

By eight-thirty, Will could see clearly the French advancing down the road towards Vimeiro from the south. The leading group then turned to their left and fanned out into lines facing Vimeiro hill. By nine o'clock, the British artillery was in action pouring their shot into the French ranks, which started to advance. Despite the devastating fire, the French continued to move forward. Will saw two groups who must have been British riflemen, because they would drop, fire, then scamper to another cover. After a while, the sheer relentlessness of the French foot, made the skirmishers fall back. Their retreat was covered by Anstruther's highlanders and another battalion of foot. Eventually they too had to pull back. The enemy could now be seen on the edge of a copse. Suddenly the highlanders rose from their concealed position and poured relentless fire into the French. Under this pressure, the French fell back. Another of Anstruther's foot neatly turned the French left and they were forced back to the other side of the coppice.

Will was glad to see that Anstruther's men halted, because he could see French cavalry ready to support if the British were to move onto the open ground. Then another French brigade advanced down the road from the southeast, this time facing Fane's troops. Down in a sunken lane a column of French tried to advance on the village of Vimeiro. A battalion of Anstruther's troops crossed behind Fane's and together with a small group of cavalry went to face this new threat. To Will's surprise, the new troops filtered into the Village and waited, then poured a withering fire into the oncoming French. The later faltered and were chased as they retreated leaving their guns and supplies behind.

By now, the smoke from all the guns was beginning

A Secret Assignment

to obscure Will's view. He was able to see that a group of the British had become carried away and gone too far forward, where they suffered greatly.

After a short pause, the French made another attack on the village. This time they were met by fire from three sides as well as shot from guns just below Will. The French got halfway up the hill, then faltered, as rows of their soldiery fell. Again, there was a pause, and then a third attack was made. This time the French arced round to try to reach the village by out flanking Fane's brigade. The French could be seen reaching the village church, but the British troops held their ground. Foot and riflemen using the buildings as shields to fire round the corners at the enemy. It seemed almost as if it was a stalemate. Then General Acland, until now, in reserve on the hill immediately below Will, sent in his troops, pouring down the hill firing as they went. The sheer weight of numbers was too great for the French soldiers; they withdrew. Then down charged the small troop of British cavalry. A magnificent sight; unfortunately they went just a little too far, and their French counterparts, in much greater numbers opposed them. It looked as if about a quarter of the English cavalry fell.

An eerie calm settled over the proceedings. It appeared as if the French were licking their wounds. To Will's left, the sound of new gunfire erupted.

A Secret Assignment

Will packed up his writing desk, and ran to his horse. He untied its tether and rode to the top of the hill, only half a mile from where he had been. It was difficult to make out what was happening, but he saw a whole line of red coats rise as if tied together in a line and fire their muskets. Then the sound of cheering reached Will, which surprised him. Who had won? Shortly there came more gunfire and musket fire. The British troops seemed to remain impassive, only a few dropping from their line. The firing came in waves, as if the British were just waiting for yet another attack.

To Will's right, he could see General Wellesley sitting on his horse, telescope to his eye watching and issuing orders at the same time. Aids would ride off to the Generals with Sir Arthur's instructions. Then it all came to a lame ending. Suddenly Wellesley turned his horse and started to trot away. Will edged his forward, until he came across a staff member he knew.

"Bloody man! Bloody, bloody buffoon!" The staff member shouted out for anybody listening. His face was red with suppressed anger.

"What's happened?" Asked Will.

"Bloody Burrard has happened, stupid fucker!"

"So what's he done?"

"We had the enemy routed; we were all ready to drive them back to Lisbon. Then Burrard shows up and takes over command from our General. In the middle of Battle! Would you believe it? Burrard refuses to harry the French when they are in full retreat! What sort of a General is he? I say a frightened old fool."

"I shall forget that, I think. Luckily, we are alone." Will turned his horse around so he was riding alongside the staff officer. "You know, all this noise of the guns; makes you quite deaf, doesn't it?"

The staff officer shot him a sideways look and then laughed. "You're a rum one, and that's for sure. What is a naval officer doing here anyway?"

"Good question! I have absolutely no idea!" Laughed Will.

A storm blew up that night which meant that those ships that were able to do so hoisted their anchors and put out to sea to avoid being driven on a lee shore. Many of the transports were unable to do this, so lost most of their anchors. Luckily, there was little damage done. Will was anxious to get back to *Hound,* as he could see no real reason to stay. Unfortunately, it took a week of waiting before *Hound* reappeared of the coast. Finally Will was able to get a message passed to her, and was taken off with Millward in tow. He then sent a signal over to Captain Malcolm asking permission to take *Hound* back to England. He was summoned to attend the senior officer.

Malcolm welcomed him with good grace when Will went aboard *Donegal*.

"Ah! Sir William, thank you for attending. I was just curious as to exactly what your roll is on the staff."

Will was not sure what to say. "You might well ask! To be frank I have been asking myself the same question. I can only suppose that it is because I had dealings with the Spanish opposition in the north. I had met General Blake, so I was asked to meet him again to try and get him to provide what I would call a threat to the French in the north, so keeping General Bessières tied up there."

"So it as I thought, you are not just a Naval Captain, you are part diplomat."

"I should never call myself a diplomat. I have acted for the government in, shall we say, rather unusual circumstances in the past."

"I admire your reticence. I shall not push you further. You want to take *Hound* back to England.

Of course, you have my permission. After all as I understand it, you were a Commodore until very recently." Malcolm gave a knowing smile. "I hope you will join me in a drink. I should be grateful if you could take back my dispatches. I understand *Hound* is uncommonly fast, so I should imagine that Sir Arthur would like you to carry his mail as well. Is that possible, or would that place you in a difficult position?"

"I should be delighted to take back Sir Arthur's dispatches. Perhaps the new Commander-in-Chief and his immediate predecessor would prefer their dispatches to be carried in the normal manner!" Will said; accepting a glass of claret.

Malcolm laughed. "I can see we are like minded!"

Will returned ashore to say goodbye to Sir Arthur and his immediate staff. He came away with private correspondence and other papers that Sir Arthur wanted to get to England as soon as possible. Just as Will was leaving, Sir Arthur came out from a meeting especially to see him.

"Sir William, my thanks for all that you have achieved. I consider that you are worth at least two Battalions. Your liaison with Blake, and your inspired trip to Peniche, both managed to keep

French forces occupied elsewhere at a critical time." He shook Will's hand vigorously. Just as he was turning away, he turned back with a smile. "I appreciate your taking back just my papers!"

Chapter 23

The wind was kind to *Hound*. It remained a strong southwesterly for the whole four days that it took to reach Portsmouth. During the voyage, Will spent the whole time writing up his journals in clear script, from his notes. He also copied his sketches, so that the final version would be easy to read and for the reader to comprehend the lie of the land at the time of the two battles. He was not sure, when Sir Arthur would be able to return to England, so he put off making the second copy, which he proposed to present to the General so that he had an outsider's unbiased view of the battle for future reference.

Directly *Hound* reached Portsmouth Harbour, Will had himself rowed ashore and hired a chaise to take him direct to London. He arrived on Sunday 11th September. The Housekeeper at Calvert House in Highgate managed to get in a cook and some servants, so that Will was able to relax in comfort. He wrote to Isabella, saying that he was not sure how long he would have to remain in London, but that if it was to be more than a couple of days, she should be prepared to come up to town and join him.

On the Monday, he was taken to Downing Street and asked to see Lord Castlereagh. His lordship was already at his desk, so Will was shown straight up.

"Will; how wonderful to see you! You have caught the sun I see! What's that under your arm?"

"I kept a journal as an observer of the battles. This is for your eyes only. I hope it explains very clearly what happened and when."

"That will be extremely useful; thank you! Already there are mutterings over the Convention of Cintra. Were you present?"

"No. Sir Hew Dalrymple was by then the Commander-in Chief, so I was not involved in the party. I did however follow proceedings each day when the staff returned. I have to say that I personally agree with Sir Arthur. The reasoning behind signing was well thought out. He objected to the detail. No doubt, you will already know this from his correspondence."

"I think may be this package contains some of that. I shall read it with interest. I am afraid I cannot stay to talk; I have to be in the House very soon."

"One thing I should like you to know, before you go. Burrard was a complete disaster in my opinion. He did not know the positions of our army or the enemy when he took over command, and as far as I was concerned, I thought it was premature. We could have chased the French, and won a war, not just a battle! I know I am not an army man, but for God's sake our brigades in the east were still engaged! Poor Sir Hew, he found himself in an impossible position, taking over from Burrard the same day that Burrard had already made a fatal decision. At least Sir Hew took advice from the man on the spot, although it was too late. If Sir Hew had countermanded Burrard's orders and gone after the French, if could already have been too late. The French could have reformed."

Lord Castlereagh stared at Will for a long moment. "Thank you Will. You have confirmed my own suspicions. Unfortunately, Horse Guards sticks rigidly to the reforms the Duke of York put in place. I just hope that this will change their opinion of Sir Arthur as a General! Quite why it has taken Dalrymple so long after the signing to send us the Convention details, I have no idea. We have yet to received them, so are still trying to come to terms with it and the reasoning behind it." His lordship stood up. "Walk with me to the House; if you will.

We can continue our discussion."

They walked down Downing Street and turned right into Whitehall. "I'll have to report to the Admiralty." Stated Will.

"Leave that to tomorrow, will you?"

"If that is what you want. I should really have gone there first."

"Good thing you didn't! I need to have a word with the First Lord." He did not expand on the subject, so Will let it pass.

"How did you get on with Blake?" Asked Castlereagh.

"Oh fine. He was very annoyed at the way that Cuesta had behaved. However, he was very keen to be of help, where it was possible. He trained the elite Spanish military before they changed sides, you know. He was intent on bringing the Galician Army up to the highest standards."

"Good. What about Cuesta? Do you think he would be of help?"

"Ybarra thought so. If we help supply them with arms and ammunition, I can see no reason that they would not be amicable to the idea of playing our game. Although I should add that the man is maddeningly arrogant and fails to listen to any advice. I know Blake thought him totally un-trust worthy."

Castlereagh turned and gave Will an appraising look.

"Would you be prepared to go back and see?" Castlereagh asked.

"If I am asked to do so for King and Country, it would be my duty."

"That is not quite what I meant. It is dangerous and I know that you are a family man, Will."

"I doubt that it is any more dangerous than an engagement at sea." Replied Will.

"Ah yes! The Navy works in the same way as Horse Guards. It doesn't matter how brilliant an officer you are, you have to wait your turn in the queue."

"Nelson didn't!"

"He had influence. The Earl St. Vincent was responsible for his promotion. I doubt that there are quite such far seeing Admirals in the Admiralty at the moment."

"It was the Earl that promoted me." Remarked Will. There was a pause then Castlereagh said.

"So what rank do you hold now?"

"Captain."

"I thought you were a Commodore."

"It was a temporary rank. One reverts to your place on the list."

"That seems wrong. You should not have to revert."

"Well a Commodore is in charge of a devolved squadron. If one is no longer in that position, you have to revert."

"Right. Now come and see me after you have reported to the Admiralty tomorrow. I shall be in Downing Street. "

"I shall do that."

Will left Lord Castlereagh and crossed St James' Park to dine at his one of his clubs and to pick-up on the gossip. In the afternoon, he called in on the Alien's Office and was able to meet with Mr. Granger. They discussed the situation in Spain. Will filling in the gaps, to give the spy-chief a clearer understanding of what life was like in the north of Spain. The discussion went on to include the late battles in Portugal, so Will was able to give the man a full description of the two battles and Sir Arthur's handling of the troops. Will asked if he could make an observation; but that it should remain privy to just the two of them. He then roundly castigated the Horse Guards and the placing of Burrard over Sir Arthur. Granger sat back and smiled enigmatically at Will.

"I have always found you to be a shrewd observer. We don't have direct influence here, you realise. However, we do have the ear of some very influential persons in Government!"

The next day Will reported to the Admiralty. He was met at the door by the usual porter, who immediately recognised him. It had obviously been wise to tip handsomely in the past.

"Sir William, a very real pleasure to see you again. If I should make myself so bold, I am surprised to see you in a Captain's uniform!"

"Thank you, my friend. We all have to revert at some time."

Instead of being shown up to the usual waiting room, he was taken to a small office, where a clerk apologised, stating that because the Board were having a meeting that very morning, it would be better if he returned in the afternoon. The Clerk insisted he would appraise the Secretary of Sir William's arrival. Therefore, it was back to another club, before he reported to the Admiralty again, where he was shown straight up to the Secretary's Office.

Wellesley-Pole stood up as Will was announced. "Good Afternoon Sir William. I apologise about this morning: there was a meeting of the Board, which took up the whole morning. So how are you? Fresh back from the Peninsular, I gather."

"Thank you. I have a letter from your brother: he asked me to deliver it in person."

"Thank you! So tell me all!"

Will gave a short version of events as he had seen them. The Secretary was on the edge of his seat. Will must have been the first eyewitness of the two battles, able to report on the action.

"Now about you, Sir!" Wellesley-Pole said. "Your name came up this morning. The First Lord was saying that it was rather hard on somebody like you who served his nation in more than one field of operation. He pointed out that if it had been two sea battles, it would go down well on you record. As it is, the War Office has requested that you are kept available for their employment. That being the case, we cannot offer you a ship-of-the-line. So, the First Lord has ordered that you are to be made a Commodore once more, in command of a special secret unit. I gather that the War Office hasn't any plans for you at this moment, so you are free to take *Hound* back to the Dart to await orders."

On leaving the Admiralty, Will made his way to Downing Street to see Lord Castlereagh again. He had to wait as his lordship was with the Prime Minister, but soon his friend was bursting into the room. "Good, you haven't left for Devon!"

"Not without reporting to you. I understand I am seconded to the War Office."

"Quite. Will, I have just got news that Napoleon might be collecting a new army to invade Spain. It is imperative that we arrange a reception!"

"Any idea which side of the Pyrenees he will cross the border?"

"No! Not yet. We must help the Spanish partisans. What do you call them?"

"Guerrillas. It means little war in Spanish. It is their term for irregular fighters to distinguish them from regular army units."

"Oh, right. Anyway, I shall order that all captured muskets shall be delivered to Plymouth, along with specially cast ball and powder. I know it is the wrong time of year, but I want you to get those weapons to those guerrillas, that you think will achieve the best results. It will take at least a fortnight to prepare, so you can take your yacht back to the Dart and see Isabella and the children."

"Might I ask that we also provide Baker rifles for some of the Guerrillas? They are far more effective, and have far greater range. It would mean that in an ambush, the guerrillas, would be more likely to be able to get away to fight another day."

"Baker rifles for Plymouth. Got that. Will you be able to land them?"

"I doubt that very much. Probably safest if we go to Corunna. I can leave the muskets for Blake and Cuesta, whilst taking the rifles to Ybarra and his people."

"Well you know the country: I shall leave that up to you. I shall write to Charles Stuart, informing him of your imminent arrival, and asking him to aid you in any way possible. You've met him, haven't you?"

"Yes in Vigo with Sir Arthur."

"Good. I shall ask him to send a representative to wherever you decided to land your weapons."

"Corunna would be the safest at this time of year. It will take time to get them across to where they are needed, but it could take even longer waiting for the sea to be calm enough to close the North Coast of Spain."

Chapter 24

For Will it was a well-earned rest, being able to be with his wife and family. *Hound* could be seen putting out to sea every few days to keep the crew up to scratch. Finally, a rider brought news that the weapons and powder would be waiting for them in Plymouth. The flag was hoisted on the pole atop the house to summon the jolly boat. Will said a fond farewell to Isabella and his children. He was then rowed out to *Hound* and they immediately set sail down the Dart for the Channel.

On arrival late that evening off Plymouth, they had to drop anchor and wait for the morning and an incoming tide. Using both tide and the light wind, they coasted up river. A boat from the Port Admiral swung alongside, and a Lieutenant instructed them to berth at the far end of the dockyard. Here, covered wagons were brought up and their contents loaded straight aboard *Hound*. The schooner's booms being used to hoist the crates off the quay. The crates contained both the promised muskets and Baker rifles.

Once the wagons had left, further orders arrived, commanding them to anchor in the centre of the Hamoaze. Next day a dumb barge was worked down river to lie alongside. This was a powder barge, and the small barrels were hoisted aboard and stowed as low down near the bilges as the design of *Hound* allowed. By early afternoon, they had also loaded as much fresh meat and vegetables as they could muster, together with cooked hams, cold beef joints, and freshly baked bread. This would mean that the crew would be able to eat if it was too rough to light the stove. They hauled up their anchor and made their way out into Plymouth Sound to set sail for Northern Spain.

The weather was not kind to them. It was late autumn, and the Bay of Biscay seemed to take exception to their trying to cross it. Even under storm sails, *Hound* was racing at break neck speed straight through every wave that faced her. Even with duckboards at the entrances to Will's suit aft, the water found a way through. Millward had taken up the rugs, but anybody in those cabins had to put their feet up to keep them dry. Not only was it impossible for the cook to provide any hot food, it was also impossible to take any type of fix. The sky was full of low damp cloud expelling any chance to use a sextant. Cranfield was taking no chances so had erred on the side of caution and kept to a westerly route.

When the sun finally peeked out at midday, four days after leaving Plymouth, they discovered they were on the right latitude for Corunna, but at least a hundred miles too far to the west.

A cold and damp crew greeted the sight of land with relief. Still in stormy seas, they entered the Bay of Corunna and dropped anchor behind the narrow headland on which the forts sat guarding the town. Here at least they had some protection from the waves, although there was nothing to stop the wind causing any loose halyard frapping in the wind. To Will's surprise, there were very few ships at anchor, and only one British frigate that was slow to salute the Commodore's pennant flying from *Hound's* main mast. Later a jollyboat came from behind the frigate to be rowed to where *Hound* lay at anchor. An elderly Captain was piped aboard, who on seeing Will's comparative youth scowled, before adjusting his expression to salute and then proffer a hand. Will had seen the look of resentment, so set about trying to charm the man.

After two large glasses of Will's finest wine, the Captain mellowed slightly. He was intrigued to find

A Secret Assignment

that Will was on a special assignment. Will was deliberately vague, but suggested that his rank was only temporary, which seemed to mollify the Captain.

Once the visitor had been shown over the side, the jolly boat was prepared and half an hour later carried Will, in his oldest Commodore's uniform to the shore, with Lieutenant Tucker and four Marines in attendance. It took quite a time to establish the whereabouts of Charles Stuart, the English Agent. When finally shown up to that gentleman's apartment Will was greeted with great courtesy. Mr. Stuart let Will enjoy a glass of wine, whilst he read the missive Lord Castlereagh had sent.

"Off course I shall endeavour to do everything within my power to aid your venture, Sir William. Pray tell me, how I can be of the greatest assistance?"

"Thank you! Because of the uncertainty of events, or indeed the whereabouts of the parties that I need to meet, I aim to try to find somebody who can provide an adequate number of the local ponies best suited for the terrain. That is the most pressing matter at the moment."

"I am afraid I am not even aware that there is a local breed of pony. I shall of course ask about – put out the old tentacles, you know!"

"That is very kind of you. My ship is anchored off the town. She is the three masted schooner: so you cannot miss her. Do you by any chance have any idea as to the rough whereabouts of any of the Guerrilla bands? I especially want to locate a Signor Ybarra."

Stuart studied Will for a moment before replying. "Signor Ybarra is my main source of information on the French Army. He has established a regular courier service to bring us captured signals between various French forces. Do you know this Ybarra fellow?"

"His wife and daughter are under my protection back in England. He is, or was, advised by my Captain of Marines. London considers him to be one of the most effective 'Guerrillas' operating against the French."

"He certainly seems to be able to interrupt their couriers! I understand that the French now have to provide heavy guards for all their communications, but still he manages to intercept them!"

"So you would have some idea as to where he is currently operating?"

"Vaguely so, yes. He moves about a lot, you know. I suggest you dine with me tonight, I shall hope to have discovered something about his whereabouts and have enquired after those ponies you are after."

Just in case, Will left Thomas Tucker ashore to ask about ponies. That evening, Mr. Stuart was able to point out on a map of the north of Spain, the rough locations of various groups, including that of Ybarra. On the subject of ponies, he was unforthcoming. It took Thomas four days to come up with a name of somebody who just might have enough of the right type of pony for the rough terrain they would face. At a further meeting, when Will explained to Mr. Stuart that they were going to try their luck inland from the village of Cabanas further up the estuary to locate a possible source for ponies, Stuart brought him up-to-date with the latest information he had on the situation in Spain.

"Napoleon himself has taken charge of his troops in Spain. He has just taken Madrid, and now apparently is going after Sir John Moore. Moore had his army in Castile Leon to try to cut off Napoleon from reinforcements reaching him from the west. The latest information that I received was that Napoleon is about to head north to destroy the British army, so Moore is attempting to retreat into Portugal, but that could be difficult. Your friend Ybarra was last known to be operating further west than before in the mountains to the north of Leon itself. Do you have maps of the areas?"

"We have obtained maps, but frankly they are not very clear. I hope to pick up guides on the way."

"Not a time of year to be travelling the mountains! I wish you all the best in your endeavours Commodore!"

"Quite so! If I had the choice, I should rather spend Christmas with my family, than up in the mountains of a foreign land. Frankly, I would even prefer the sea!"

Late that afternoon *Hound* dropped her anchor off the sandy beach before the small fishing hamlet of Cabanas. Cabanas is at the extreme north eastern area of the Corunna Bay, at the mouth of the river Eume. Lieutenant Tucker had brought with him an interpreter who spoke English, but also spoke the local dialect. In the village, they were able to find a fellow who was willing to take them to the farm of the horse trader. Hiring local beasts, Will, together with Tucker, the interpreter and four marines set off up the thickly wooded slopes behind the hamlet. At first, they had to follow the course of the river, before the track wound, snake like up the side of the mountain. Finally, their guide branched out through a narrow path none of them would have recognised.

Suddenly they were in the open, in a wide area of pasture. There were groups of ponies nibbling what remained of the grass. Here and there were tripods with the remains of hay hanging from them, around which more ponies were grouped.

The ponies were mostly a dark dun colour with sturdy legs and intelligent eyes, which followed the party's every move. Breasting a rise amongst a group, they could see a long stone building backed by trees about a quarter of a mile ahead of them. As they rode forward, two figures emerged from the building holding muskets across their chests.

The Guide called out a greeting, and the muskets were lowered. As Will's small group advanced, it became clear that one of the figures was a woman. The other, a well built man of middle age, with a beard. Both were dressed in the drab brown cloth that every peasant in those parts seemed to wear. Drawing up in front of the couple, the Guide dropped of his mount and went forward to embrace first the man and then the woman. Will slid from his saddle, and advanced hand outstretched

"¡buenos días." Said Will, smiling in the hope that it would show the scowling man that he came in peace.

The man grunted in reply and turned to the guide to speak in the local dialect. Will had no idea what he said, but the reaction was encouraging. He turned to face Will and said in Spanish. "English! Come to fight the French! You are welcome signor!" For the first time the man smiled. Will felt a surge of relief. He even roughly understood what the man said. He decided to try out his Spanish, learnt in the middle of the Atlantic.

"I am Sir William Calvert, Commodore in his Britannic Majesty's Royal Navy. I am here to aid your fight against the French. We are in need of strong ponies to carry arms to the local guerrillas. We understand you have a ready supply of suitable beasts."

The man took off his cap with a sweep of his arm and bowed to Will.

"Signor Antonio Miramontes de Rua Tella, at your service, Signor!"

The formalities over, Signor Antonio asked what Will wanted exactly. Will explained that he needed to carry muskets, rifles, powder and shot over the mountains to various groups to the north of the plains of Castile, where the French Army was about to face a British army.

"You will need a guide as well as pack ponies, I think!" Said Signor Antonio; with a broad grin. Will conceded the point.

"Antonio Miramontes de Rua Tella, late sergeant of horse in the Royal Army of Spain, will be your guide and you shall have as many pack and riding ponies as are needed. You have saddles?"

"I am afraid we only have a few. We shall also require panniers for the pack animals."

"I do not have enough, I think. You will have to return to Corunna to buy what extra are needed, I am afraid. So how many of you will there be?"

Will had no idea. All he knew was the number of men, the number of packs of muskets, rifles, and barrels of powder and shot.

"We shall need at least 4 extra, in case any go lame." Added Antonio; who seemed to be relishing the idea. His wife spoke up in the local dialect, and Antonio was all arms explaining what was happening.

"My wife does not like the idea of my going, but I tell her it is my duty as a patriotic Spaniard. Also I need some adventure, you know!" And he winked at Will.

Will was warming to this big boned Galician.

"You need to purchase the local garments; we need to fit into the countryside." Antonio continued.

A Secret Assignment

Will had been busy working out in his mind the number of animals required.

"I estimate that we shall need about eighteen ponies, plus your extra four. That would mean that each rider would have two ponies normally in tow. Can you supply that number?"

"Give me a week and I shall have more than enough, so you can choose. However, I suggest you take my advice, because I know the country and you are a sailor; no?"

Will laughed." I agree, I shall take your advice. We need though to know how much you will charge for the ponies."

"You are expecting to come back?" He asked, with exaggerated raised eyebrows.

"Of course!"

"Then I charge you by the day. At the end, you pay for any that we have lost, yes?"

Will nodded in agreement.

Suddenly Antonio focused his attention on the weapon slung from the shoulders of the nearest marine.

"What is that?" He asked pointing.

"That is a rifle. It is three times more accurate than a musket." Explained Will.

"May I try?"

The marine looked to Will for permission before handing over his weapon. Antonio studied it with care. He then shouldered it and aimed at a tree. He squeezed the trigger. And looked startled at the recoil.

"It was loaded?" There was a comical expression on his face. He looked rather ashamed of himself, as he handed the weapon back to the marine. Then he walked forward to examine the tree he had aimed at. He then paced out just over two hundred large strides from the tree and turned with amazement writ large across his face.

"Two hundred Vara? That is incredible! Who in the English army uses such weapons?"

"There are special units called Rifles. The weapon is known as a rifle. It takes longer to load than a musket, but is far more accurate, especially at a distance."

"You give me one?"

"Of course!" Replied Will, with a smile.

"But it is bad to carry such a weapon over your

back, when on horse-back. It take too long to free, you need both arms, so you lose control of the horse – or pony. You need a funda. A long funda." Antonio walked up to Will and pointed at the holsters that hung over the neck of Will's horse.

"A very fair point my friend." Will said.

"Now you come join with me in a toast to our little expedition."

Antonio's home was a long substantial stone building with a straw roof, held down by ropes and heavy stones. It had a stone floor, with a large fireplace at one end, where huge logs smouldered. In the centre of the space was a rough table with benches down either side. Piled against one wall were various saddles, with tack hanging from pegs driven in between the stones of the wall. To the side of the fireplace, a rough cloth hung like a curtain, showing that there was more beyond.

Antonio's wife had left them and was now found stirring a giant pot that hung from a chain over the embers. Standing ready on the table were a group of horn mugs and a 'relags bota' leather-drinking bottle.

"Local brandy – very strong! You only drink a sip

at a time if you want to stay on your horse!" Laughed Antonio.

Antonio's wife produced wooden bowls, which she slid onto the table, for Antonio to separate. Then she took one at a time and ladled out a portion in each.

"Lacón con Grelos." She said, indicating the rich stew in the bowls. Antonio produced wooden spoons, and they all sat down to eat. The wife then adding to the table flat bread, The stew was surprisingly tasty, and Antonio explained that it was made from the front legs of a pig with turnip leaves.

It was agreed that Antonio would be paid in gold, part being paid when the ponies were loaded, and the final part when the ponies were returned to the farm. Meanwhile there being too few packsaddles, it was agreed that Will should try and purchase the missing number from a supplier in Corunna. Will took away one of the saddles to see if his sail maker and carpenter could between them come up with a solution, if all else failed. Antonio suggested it would be best to meet on the southern side of the river Eume, which fed into the bay where *Hound* was currently anchored. They agreed to meet in five days time, although Will was impatient to get going as winter was already settling in.

Chapter 25

In the end, the required saddles were partly constructed aboard, and the rest bought in Corunna. Cranfield took *Hound* in as far as possible to the mouth of the river Eume, without charts. The cutters were loaded with the weapons, powder and shot; and accompanied by the jolly boat with Will aboard, were rowed to where a stone slip appeared. Just as they were turning to head for the slip, they saw a column of ponies coming from behind a wood, towards them. Soon a smiling Antonio appeared at the top of the slip.

"You make good time!" Antonio cried as the first of the boats ran its prow up the slip. When Will made it to dry ground, he was surprised to find that Antonio and his wife between them had managed to bring thirty-five sturdy ponies with them. The wife was busy tethering the ponies to trees.

"I show you the best ponies for riding." Said Antonio; giving Will a gentle slap on the back. "You know how to ride, I trust?" He laughed.

"I do, but we had to check on the Marines!" Responded Will.

Meanwhile Antonio had changed his attention to the ever-increasing pile of arms and barrels that were being unloaded. "Good, you have kept the powder to small barrels. I was afraid, you being a sailor, that they would be too big for the ponies. Now I think this one, and this one....." Antonio untied each selected pony and handed the lead rein to one of *Hound's* crew to take to where the barrels were stacked. Then he hurried back to supervise the loading of each barrel.

Meanwhile Antonio's wife measured each member of the party and allocated them a pony. Henri de Cornes spoke with an exaggeratedly English accent as he showed a Marine how to strap the rifle holsters over the withers of his pony, then his saddlebags and roll. The roll contained a thick woollen blanket, which was wrapped in an oilskin. Nobody wore uniform; they were all dressed in the local drab brown cloth. Millward, having been allocated a pony to ride then managed to convey to Antonio's wife that he needed an animal for the canteen. She chose a particularly strong looking fellow. Millward then set about carefully mounting his wares so that they were well balanced. The Marines meanwhile, tried out their mounts. It had been difficult to find four marines that had any knowledge of horses. It being essential they would be able to sustain days of riding in difficult terrain.

It took all morning to sort out the party. Antonio was very much in charge, deciding which pony should carry which rider or load. It ended up with the four marines leading two ponies each, and the rest four. Cranfield had come over to wish them well as they set off. They went via Antonio's farm, where they left the wife with the surplus ponies.

Antonio had discussed their route with Will, but it was really up to him as he was their guide. Each member of the party had pistols in holsters at their side; with the Baker rifles hung either side of the front of the saddle in canvas holsters. In addition to the roll at the back of the saddle, each had a double strapped bag on their backs containing the extra clothes that Antonio had pointed out would be necessary at that time of year in the mountains. Because they had no up-to-date information as to the progress of the war, they kept to the mountains that run across the northern coast of Spain. At first, they were forced to keep to the south of the river Eume. Then they swung north to head for the higher mountain area, as this would take them well clear of any possible French encroachment. Below them at one point, they were able to see in the distance the town of Vilalba, before they really started to climb. Once they had breasted the mountains, their route tended to work its way east. Nothing was straightforward. They would descend one narrow track and then seem to turn back on themselves to negotiate another track climbing back up.

It was surprising how much the seemingly remote farms seemed to know about what was going on to the south. Various guerrilla groups operated out of the different regions. On their way, they made detours to drop off muskets, as well as powder and shot to small bands. It was tricky to locate the groups, so progress was of a necessity slower than Will would have wished. Will left it to Antonio to ask the questions, which might lead them to where a guerrilla band was hiding. In return for the muskets and powder, they were provided with meals and provisions as well as information. Small farms seemed to cling to the side of the mountains, providing barely a living, for the very independent minded residents. They crossed rivers, swollen by the rains. They sought barns or stables to sleep in at night. Wherever possible, Antonio directed them along valley bottoms, to ease the riding. The four marines suffered most, as they had hardly ridden before in their lives, and therefore got cramp and sore bottoms. At night, the ponies were tethered to a long line, generally tied between two trees, so that they had an arc of poor grass to munch. Wherever possible, hay was bought at extortionate rates, to give them better nutrition.

They spent Christmas Day 1808 camped in a barn, just outside the village of La Robla, situated in an open valley on the road from Leon to the sea.

Antonio and Tucker were able to purchase extra provisions for the party, as well as some locally produced brandy to enliven the proceedings. The barn being empty, the farmer was happy to let them have firewood and to start a fire inside the barn, so they were able to warm themselves and to cook.

It was in the village of La Robla, that they first got any concrete news of Ybarra and his band. There were rumours of a large group of guerrillas who moved about the mountains. It was according to their source, a recent arrival. The band had moved west covering the French army's progress. The Mayor was able to pass on the information that the British army was in retreat. They seemed to be retreating towards Astorga and the valley that would ultimately lead them towards Corunna. They spent the night, courtesy of the Mayor, in a hostelry, which made a great change from sleeping in barns or the open.

The next morning, as they set out, they were aware that they were being watched from above by a couple of figures on horseback who moved in parallel to them. Through his telescope, Will was able to make out that they were dressed in the same drab brown dress as their own. Will dispatched Thomas Tucker and one of the better marine riders to find out who they were. As the two ascended the hillside, the two riders climbed further up. Then they disappeared from view. Tucker could be seen waving from the crest of the hill; then he stretched out his hands as if to indicate that he had lost his quarry.

When he rejoined the party, Thomas said. "Followed the blighters to the top, but blow me if there was nothing to be seen the other side. Where the hell they disappeared to, defeats me!"

"Probably hidden in a barn or somewhere well known to them." Commented Antonio.

"Who do you think they might be?" Asked Will.

"I should be surprised if they were French pickets. They might be guerrillas, but they must know the terrain well to be able to disappear so quickly." Commented Antonio; borrowing Will's scope to check, in case there were others.

Now that Tucker and the marine had rejoined them, they continued on the narrow track, which started to climb into a precipitous valley. They had repeatedly asked locals if there were any guerrillas about, and mostly the countrymen had been willing to point in the direction where they thought there might be a band. Toiay the locals had been extremely reticent.

Suddenly as they rounded a cliff side corner on the steep path, they were faced by two men with muskets poised blocking the way. Antonio, in the lead, held up his arm to bring the others to a halt. Whatever language the two guardians of the route spoke in, it was totally incomprehensible to Will and the others. Only Antonio responded, and there was quite a lengthy question and answer session, before the two men put down their muskets and turned to walk away in the same direction as Will's party had been heading. After about five minutes of plodding up the track, it suddenly widened and there sitting around on the ground, with their ponies behind them, was a group of men, who rose up as Will's party came into view. Their muskets were held loosely at their sides, but covered Will's mounted group.

One of the men; all of whom were dressed in the familiar drab brown cloth, came forward. "You are seeking Signor Ybarra?" He asked in passable Spanish, with a strong Basque accent.

"We are!" Replied Antonio.

"And who are you?" The man asked.

Will edged his pony forward. "I am Commodore Sir William Calvert."

The man pointed at Will and broke into a wide grin. "I did not recognise you, Sir William. You have a beard! I was Signor Ybarra's manservant. Now I command this group of brigands!" He chuckled. "We did not expect you at this time of year and with the French chasing the British. Why do you come?"

"I bring arms from the British government."

"Then you are doubly welcome; but you are heading in the wrong direction! We have moved west to a new base, so we shall be closer to the French as they advance."

There were about a dozen men, all with similar sturdy ponies to those Will and the rest of his party rode.

Instead of going back by the way they had come, the leader of Ybarra's group headed straight up the side of the mountain to a higher plateau, where they turned to head west.

The rain started coming in from the west, driving into their faces and those of the ponies. Neither man nor beast was too happy as they made their way across a high ridge before descending into the comparative shelter of a valley. When the rain ceased and the clouds parted, they could see that they were riding along the ridges of a series of high hills and mountains. The valleys were thickly forested with fast flowing streams that bubbled and splashed around rocky outcrops. Here and there, there were waterfalls, which left a low cloud at the bottom of their valley. The party did not stop, even as the light began to fade.

It was almost dark when they came to a crossroads. Here the tracks divided into five different routes. The leader did not pause; he took the second left path, which had to be ridden slowly as the ground was of rock or screed.

Finally, just as it was getting too dark to really see where they were going, there was the call of an owl. One of the riders near the front could just be seen to let go of both reins and cup his hands in front of his mouth. He made an answering call, which was responded to immediately. Then from either side figures surrounded them in animated conversation. Bridles were grabbed and the ponies led off sideways from the path through the trees whose branches threatened to swipe the unwary across the face. Suddenly they were in an open space facing a stone built building of some size. Two thick walls came out from either side, like crab's claws to virtually encircle the group, as they reached the front of the imposing building.

"Sir William?" The loud booming voice of Ybarra cut through the darkness.

"Signor Ybarra?" Called Will.

A big figure emerged from the darkness and gave Will a huge hug the moment he had dismounted.

"How are you, my friend?" Demanded Ybarra; stepping back, still holding Will by the arms.

"Fine ... and yourself?"

"I am well, thank you. How are my wife and daughter? You have seen them recently?"

"They are fine. They stayed with my wife until they knew a few words of English. Now they are living in a town house on the edge of Totnes, within easy reach of my home."

"I am eternally indebted to you Sir! Come, come inside and get warm." With that, he led the way up the wide steps and through the great door of the building.

"This was a monastery. We have taken it over. If the French come, we are monks, no?" He winked at Will. He then turned to greet Henri, Thomas and the rest of the party. Antonio was introduced and greeted like an old friend. Hot food and cups of wine were produced; they were invited to sit at the great table in the middle of the hall.

"What about the ponies?" Asked Antonio.

"Have no fear my friend, they will be well cared for. We have a large cave nearby, where we keep our animals out of sight of prying eyes!"

After they had eaten, they were introduced to other members of Ybarra's guerrilla group. Sitting in front of the roaring fire, Ybarra explained the group's methods. They would spy out the ground, and attack only supply wagons or couriers. They had set up a chain of riders who took the captured orders to the British. They never struck at the same place, or used the same methods. They would go in fast and out as quickly as they had struck, always leaving a false track for the French to follow. They had suffered losses, but they had inflicted more on the French. At first, they had operated over in the Basque region, but then when they had enough recruits, they had divided themselves into small bands to cover a wider area.

"We watch out for the French skirmishers. We let them pass, then strike behind them. We teach our members the skills of the poacher."

"Excuse me, Signor? We brought rifles, powder and shot for you. Where are they?" Asked Henri; in his most English voice.

"Ha! We don't keep them here. They have been taken to the caves. They will be safer there. If the French come, they can search, but fine nobody but a

A Secret Assignment

few monks.!" Ybarra cried. "Come I show you!"

He lit a candle and proceeded to show Will and his party the rest of the monastery. The central part was the hall where they had eaten. Off it were the kitchens and then at the side the Abbott's quarters. On the floor above there were dormitory's with contemplative cells off on either side. Back in the hall, Ybarra went to a panel in the wall, which was about two feet off the ground. This he tapped and then carefully slid aside. Standing to one side, he showed them a flight of steps cut in the rock winding away down into the darkness.

"They lead to a terrace in the cliff. You see the monastery is built on the side of the mountain, with only a cliff behind it. The cliff path leads round to the back of the cave where the ponies are kept."

Sliding the panel shut, he crossed the room to the front corner, where he slid aside another panel, but this time all that lay behind it was bare stone. He pushed hard at the left hand side of the stone and it swung away to reveal a passage leading off.

"You probably did not notice the walls on either side of the front yard, but these walls have a passage down the centre. We could if we wished cut down anybody in the yard, through the slits. Now come and see our chapel." He walked to the far end of the hall away from the fire and pushed open a heavy studded door. There in a blaze of candle light was a chapel of exquisite beauty.

"What happened to the monks?" Asked Thomas.

"Oh some are still here! The rest are out acting as spies for us. The French are heathens; they abolished their clergy. Our priests don't want the same thing to happen to them."

"How long have you been based here?" Asked Will.

Ybarra paused to reflect. "Not that long. A month or so. We tend to search for suitable places to operate out of, and this has been by far the best. It was the Abbott who suggested it."

"So what is the situation regarding the British Army?"

Ybarra raised his eyebrows. "Not good I am afraid. Bonaparte himself took command of the French forces in Spain. Ever since he took charge, the French have managed to defeat one after another of the Spanish armies." Will noted he did not say 'our armies'. Ybarra continued. "Early this month he took Madrid. Now the French Army is moving north. Bonaparte is trying to cut the British army off from the sea. Sir John Moore is retreating. The French are near Valladolid we heard today. The British are near Benavente. I shall show you on a map. Directly we heard that the French were moving north to face the British, we realised that this place was going to be very important. From here, we can descend on the French supply wagons when they head through the valley to Galicia. We don't operate in open country; the French would be able to cut us to pieces. We prefer to strike where they least expect us."

They moved to the great table in the centre of the hall, and somebody produced a map. Chandeliers were provided so they could read the map clearly.

"Benavente is the most likely place that the British could defend. There is a river here with a bridge that could be held. Unfortunately, there is also a ford, which we hope no Spaniard will inform the French about. Benavente is at the beginning of the route into the mountains. If the French fail to defeat the British, they will have to send their army through this valley towards Ponferrade, as the English retreat. If they manage to do so, we shall attempt to cause them problems, by attacking from the mountains. Our ponies are ideal for this terrain. Cavalry horses are not good at the steep hills and stony tracks."

Just then, the hidden door to the back slid open and in came a group of Ybarra's men. One of the guerrillas came to Ybarra and asked a question.

"He wants to know what kind of muskets you have brought. They have not seen such weapons before. He could not understand what your marine was saying."

"Ah! They are rifles. That is to say that the barrels have grooves in them, which means that the ball is thrown far further than a musket and with far greater accuracy. We shall show you tomorrow." Replied Will; trying not to yawn. Ybarra must have noticed because they were shown up to the dormitory area where sheep fleeces were produced for them to wrap themselves up in against the cold.

Early next morning, they were shown where they could do their ablutions; after which a breakfast was served in the hall. Will and his group where taken out through the secret rear exit and found themselves being guided down a tunnel with rough stone steps carved out of the rock. The steps ended on a narrow shelf, with virtually a shear drop to the valley bottom below. A narrow ledge with the rock face above sloping out into space, wound its way to a small cave entrance. Once inside the cave, it grew bigger as you got further in, and there were the ponies tied to lines contentedly munching hay.

Ybarra nominated some of his followers who saddled up their own ponies. Will and his team saddled up the ponies they had ridden before. Then Ybarra led them through a natural fissure in the rock and they emerged into the grey morning light behind a thick growth of evergreen pines. For half-an-hour, they followed in single file a narrow track through trees and shrubs, until they came out onto a small plateau surrounded by high rocks. Some of Ybarra's men swiftly dismounted and climbed up the rocky sides to become lookouts. Then Ybarra instructed a couple of others to erect a cairn of stones.

"You show us how these rifles work, please?" Asked Ybarra. Will turned to the marines and gave the order to show exactly what was required. The sergeant of marines stepped forward, and pulled one of his two rifles out of its holster in front of his saddle.

"See here, if you look down yon barrel you will see that it has grooves down it." He said, and waited for Will to translate. He then held the rifle so each guerrilla in turn could peer down it.

"Now you hold the rifle as if about to present, then turn half to your right." He made the movements, then waited for the translation.

"As you turn you naturally bring the rifle to the horizontal position, your left hand supporting the rifle, your right hand goes to the hammer, knuckles up; elbow pressing the butt." Again he waited.

"With the lock pointing a bit towards the body, you push open the pan with your right hand, so." Ybarra's men jostled to see better.

"You slide your right hand down into your pouch, which must be in the right place. Important that! With your thumb and first two fingers, you pull out a cartridge." He followed his own instructions, retrieving a cartridge from his pouch.

"Bring yon cartridge smartly to your mouth, twist and bight off the end, so." He looked up as he finished the move, waiting for the translation to be completed.

"You bring the cartridge to the pan and shake a little into the pan, making sure it goes in correctly."

Again a pause. "Now using your third and little figure of your right hand, you shut the pan." He shut the pan.

"Now holding the narrow part of the stock, here, with your right hand, and not dropping the cartridge, you turn to your left; sliding the barrel through your left hand as you let go with your right. Gripping the base of the butt with your heels, you bends the knees and grip the rifle between them, so!" He waited.

"The cartridge is at the same time swiftly placed into the barrel. Equally smartly, you then grab the ramrod in your right hand with your thumb and forefinger. Out it comes and it is grabbed in the left hand about the breadth of your hand from bottom. Then you insert it about an inch or so before you force it down with both hands." There was a murmur from the onlookers.

"As you stand up, the left hand grabs the rifle about six inches from the end and the right hand withdraws the ramrod. Obviously you then slide the ramrod back from whence it came!"

Once the translation had been completed, the Sergeant continued.

"Now's you are ready to fire. The right hand brings the rifle to the shoulder, the left grabbing it above the hammer spring, until the right hand is in position around the small of the stock, so. You are now ready to fire. If we were in a Company, there is a drill to follow. Me thinks though that you will be on your own, so unless the Signor wants me to go through the drill, I shall end there."

"Perhaps you could fire it for us. We should like to see if it is as accurate as you fellows tell us!" Commented Ybarra; with a wry smile. Will translated.

A Secret Assignment

The Sergeant looked slightly embarrassed. "I am not the best shot. However, this is the way we fire in the open. Normally we look for a defensive position, behind a wall, or over a fallen tree. We like to rest the rifle on something; it gives us more accuracy. Anyhow, in the open we would partly kneel, right knee on the ground, left knee up, so. Then you cock the rifle with your right thumb and bring the butt up to your shoulder resting your left elbow on your left knee to give you support, the left hand supporting the rifle. Squeeze the trigger."

As he had gone through the routine, he enacted the positions. He aimed the rifle at the target and fired. A piece of shale, about the size of a man's head at the top of the cairn shook, as a chip was taken off the top right corner, which narrowly missed a spectator.

The sergeant returned to the standing position. "If you are more used to the musket, you can leave out the part about filling the pan at the start. If you have a powder horn and most of you seem to have such an item, then just bight off the end of the cartridge and push it open end down the barrel before ramming. Then when you bring the rifle up flick open the pan, use your horn to fill it. Close the pan and you are ready to fire."

Will translated. He then ordered the canvas bags

that hung from the side of two ponies to be unloaded and opened. Rifles were then distributed. At the same time, Lieutenant Tucker was supervising the unloading and breaching of one of the powder barrels. This revealed prepared paper cartridges ready for use.

"We did not bring cartridge bags. I hope your fellows can make up them up themselves." Commented Will. Ybarra nodded, distractedly. He was watching closely as his men examined the rifles.

The rest of the morning was spent with the marines supervising with sign language or demonstrating the use of the rifle.

Chapter 26

Ybarra, Will, Henri and Tucker left the marines to their instructing and returned to the monastery. Here a messenger had just arrived. He had news that General Moore, the English Commander was retreating towards the bridge over the river Esla. The French appeared to be trying to catch them before they could make it. Ybarra hauled out his map again and spread it out on the refectory table." Here is the bridge near Benavente. If the English can cross the bridge before the French catch them, they might be able to blow up the bridge. Trouble is there is a ford here, so the French, if they can find it, could still launch an attack on the English rearguard. There is nothing we can do until the French have passed Benavente and are into this valley here. Then we can really be effective. There are a lots of trees on both sides of the valley. Ideal for us to attack their supply trains. You say that the rifle has a range of, what?"

"My fellows can hit a man-sized target at approximately 200 yards. I have known them to achieve even greater distances, but the shot would not be fatal."

Ybarra did a quick calculation of his own, obviously converting yards into his own understanding of distance. He raised his eyebrows in surprise.

"A musket can only achieve a third of that – that will give us a great advantage. We can snipe through the trees at a range the French cannot match!"

Ybarra stepped back and scratched his nose in thought. "I know!" He said at last. "We shall try them out to the east, where the French send reinforcements and supplies to the corps that is positioned to attack our Spanish General La Romana's rear. The last we heard was that he was based here at Leon, but his army was last heard off covering Moore's left wing at Mansilla."

"Napoleon has come north to try and outflank Moore, is that correct?" Said Will.

"That is my understanding. Now if we can attack the French here in the mountains on the route from Gijon to Leon; that will give La Romana a small respite."

"How long would it take you to reach that area?"

"A couple of days."

Another messenger arrived. Will realised that Ybarra had set up a most proficient spy organisation.

Ybarra read the missive and then said. "New captured information from the French signals. The French are, it seems trying to press forward to outflank the English retreat. They are sending more supplies in from France to meet up with this advance. A change of plan is called for! This should give us a reasonable target, which should help our English allies greatly. We must leave today to reach the area through which they will be passing." With that, he spun round and issued a string of orders.

"I suggest you practice loading the rifles before using them!" Commented Will.

A Secret Assignment

Ybarra grinned at him. "Plenty of time when we stop to rest. Come, see what we can do!"

Back at the cave, the ponies were being loaded and saddled. It transpired that Ybarra would not be joining them. The raid would be led by his first lieutenant, a tall rangy fellow with a very aristocratic demeanour. His name was Xabier, which was the Galician form of Xavier. He was a former Spanish cavalry officer, who had decided that he would be more use working with Ybarra's guerrillas, than with La Romana's army. He gave his orders quietly, without any sign of the haste that surrounded him. He suggested that Will and his party join them as observers.

Once mounted. Xabier's legs were so long. it looked as if they would touch the ground on either side of his stocky pony. Each member of the unit that was detailed to leave was issued with two of the Baker rifles, together with cartridges. They all carried powder horns and soft cloth bags for the cartridges. As they filed out of their hiding place, the structure of the unit became obvious. Outriders or skirmishers fanned out ahead. Then the unit was divided into three separate sections with about half a mile between them. Will and his party were the last to leave with Xabier riding beside Will to explain what was happening.

They rode at a steady trot; which the ponies seemed to be happy to keep to, whatever the terrain, unless it was particularly steep. They kept to narrow tracks through the wooded areas, which because it was winter gave them sparse cover. Will did realise though how effective the muted brown garments the men wore were in blending with the background. When they stopped to rest the ponies and men, they all set about practicing loading their rifles, although nobody fired one. They travelled all the rest of that day, until the light began to fade, then they sought out barns and farm buildings to shelter for the night. Will was surprised to see that the local farmers were paid for the use of their buildings.

They must have been within a few miles of the route that they were going to survey, because scouts returned even as they were having their early morning fare. Xabier left them with one of his lieutenants as he set off to gauge the situation. When finally they were lead out, they rode for a few miles over rough terrain, before they were told to dismount. Their ponies were taken off to graze on a small patch of scrub grass. Their guide led them through meagre trees and bushes to a position high up above the road. They had to crawl to the edge of what was a sheer drop of granite, which fell away to a narrow valley with fields and willow trees by a river. The road below crisscrossed as if trying to find a flat area on which to rest.

Immediately below them, the valley widened out, so there were pastures either side of the river and road, which ran side-by-side. As an ambush site, it looked distinctly unpromising. There appeared to be better areas further away on either side. Will pulled out his scope and examined the area that their guide pointed out. He could only see two individuals who appeared to be coppicing trees by the river.

They waited for two hours, witnessing a group of French cavalry come trotting through, followed by a squad of marching soldiers. The French had skirmishers out riding the route before any modest group of the military came down from the north.

Just before midday a line of ox drawn wagons appeared. There were armed outriders in front and behind, but nobody either side as the bridges were too narrow to accommodate anybody riding alongside the wagons. Just when Will was beginning to think that these wagons would pass unhindered, shots rang out. The two oxen pulling the lead wagon dropped to the ground. The horsemen in front wheeled about, searching in every direction. Just as they got to the lead wagon another series of shots came, and the riders fell from their mounts. Panic had set in amongst the rest of the wagons and their guards. Still there was no sign of any guerrillas, even from above where Will and his party were watching. Then firing could be heard from the north. As the men around the wagons grouped around their charges, there were further shots and the French could be seen raising their hands above their heads. Then, as if rising out of the very ground, guerrillas seemed to swarm all over the wagons and their guards. The French soldiers were marched off to the far side of a paddock as one after another the wagons' ox teams were cut free and driven off. Will could see through his scope that the French soldiers were disarmed and their trousers were round their ankles.

Then the wagons started to explode. More firing could be heard coming from the north, in between the explosions. From a coppice on the far side of the valley, a group of ponies came galloping down to the action. Most had no rider and were on leading reins. Guerrillas, grabbed the saddles of rider less ponies and swung themselves up. The guerrillas guarding the French soldiers, then trotted down the gentle slope of the pasture as another wave of ponies came into view. Again, the Spanish guerrillas caught hold of the reins of the ponies from the escorting riders and the whole group galloped up a narrow defile between the rocks and disappeared. The whole operation had taken only minutes. Judging from the size of the explosions, the wagons must have been loaded to the brim with gunpowder.

Will's guide urged them to get moving and they scrambled up the rocky side of the mountain, to be met by their ponies being held ready for them. Once mounted, they rode off at a canter.

Some hours later, having ascended and descended copious narrow mountain tracks, they met up with Xabier and his party.

"That was spectacular!" Commented Henri; forgetting for a moment to annunciate his Spanish with an English accent. Nobody seemed to notice, much to Will's relief.

"Thank you. We take great care to plan. We have plotted many routes, where we can ambush the French. We try for the unexpected. Places where they least expect to be caught."

"Well that was in my opinion a really bizarre place to ambush anybody. I thought we had been taken to the wrong place!"

Xabier laughed with pleasure. "That my friend is the art your marine Captain Caspar taught us at the beginning. What is happening now though is that the French couriers are being guarded. They have soldiers riding with them. What the French don't realise is that it makes it more obvious who is a courier. The larger the guard; the more important the message!"

"I now understand why your fellows wear those cloaks. Even from above I didn't realise the rocks were your men, they blended in with their surroundings so well. However, I have one question. How did you know that was an ammunition convoy?"

"Ha! We didn't, that was just luck. You see the more we strike, the more men they have to release from their front to guard the convoys."

"Might I ask about the gun fire we heard coming from further West?" Asked Thomas.

Xabier held a finger to his nose. "A distraction! We didn't want the formation you saw pass by earlier to return. We kept them busy!"

"It is a pity there aren't more of you!" Commented Henri.

"Then it would be difficult to control. We try to keep our losses to an absolute minimum, otherwise we should have to give up very quickly, and that would be self-defeating. Captain Caspar commands another group of us to the South. We work together. We call it our pincher approach."

Chapter 27

Two days later, when they were back at the monastery and Will's party were preparing to leave, a message was passed back that the French were coming. Immediately an organised panic set in. Men and women were rushing about hiding things and cleaning up. Ybarra took Will's party under his wing. They were shown through the hidden panel and mock wall to the left wing wall that virtually encircled the front yard. They were ordered to keep absolutely quiet when the French arrived. Will was one of the last to pass through the secret doorway, but not before he had seen most of the guerrillas disappear through the secret door to the caves in the cliff. Once in the dark narrow passage that formed the centre of the wall, one was able to peer out through tiny holes between the stonework.

They had some time to wait before the small contingent of French cavalry slowly entered the front yard. They were followed shortly afterwards by a company of foot soldiers with muskets at the port. An officer dismounted from his horse, whilst an aide held the reins. Virtually encircled by foot soldiers the officer advanced to the door and banged on it with the pommel of his sword. The door swung open and there stood a monk, complete with tonsure. The officer stepped back in surprise and as if by force of nature removed his helmet.

The monk stood to one side and allowed the officer, followed by about a dozen foot soldiers to enter. Will, bending down to view proceedings through a peephole, nearly let out a gasp as one of the French soldiers dropped the front of his yellowy trousers, hauled out his penis and peed on the wall just below where Will's eye was placed. Will shot back, but managed to stifle his surprise.

It was obvious that the soldiers were tired and bored. They rested against the walls and chatted in groups, whilst trying to turn their backs on the bursts of rain that came in waves.

It did not take long before the officer and his men reappeared. The officer addressed his men.

"Les guerilleros arrêté ici il ya quelques heures. Ils sont partis quand il n'y avait pas de nourriture. Allez-y immédiatement."

The sergeants rallied their truculent men, who sloped off in a very unmilitary manner.

"Now we have then at our mercy!" Whispered Ybarra; as he turned to open the secret wall, and then the panel. He did not wait to tell Will what was about to happen, he disappeared through the secret panel to the cliff and cave beyond.

Back in the hall, Henri and Tucker were exchanging their version of events. When Will told them what had happened to him, they fell about laughing.

"What do you think Ybarra is going to do?" Asked Tucker.

"I have no idea. I only hope that he doesn't act too precipitously, it could bring down retribution here. I think we should leave as soon as possible. Where is Antonio?" Asked Will.

"He went with the others to the cave." Replied Henri.

They all followed Will, out through the back panel, down the slope and along the cliff path, buffeted by strong gusts of wind. It was a relief to make the cave. Here it was dry. They went through to the main cave, where all was calm; much to Will's relief. Xabier was organising the guerrillas into groups of about a dozen each. All had their new Baker rifles. Ybarra stood to one side listening. He might be the leader, but Xabier was the more experienced soldier.

When Ybarra finally noticed Will's little party, he came over to speak to them.

"We have our skirmishers, or what you would call our trackers following the French. They are a small enough number for us to be able to take them on. Because they have foot soldiers, we can easily overtake them."

"What do you intend to do with them?" Asked Will.

"You mean, are we going to kill them? That is up to them. They are the enemy. If they surrender, we take their weapons and their food, and then tell them to make their own way to their own country. We tell them –n

ext time we capture them, we kill them. Most don't want to fight anyway, once they have faced us!"

There was nothing that Will could say. It was not his war; nor was it his country. It was evident that their departure would have to be delayed until, whatever was about to happen, had been completed.

In an orderly fashion, the guerrillas mounted their ponies and rode out of the cave.

"How come the French were not able to track your men to this cave?" Asked Henri.

Ybarra smiled. "We make sure there is plenty of stone on the ground. The hoof prints continue, so there is no reason to think that anybody turned off over the stony ground, to what looks as if it is a sheer rock face. If it snows, we have a problem."

Will shook his head, surprised at the ingenuity of these self-trained fighters. The cave felt empty now that so many of the guerrillas had left. Ybarra was in an expansive mood though.

"We shall track the French until they reach somewhere where we know that we can surround them. With your new rifles it will be a more one sided affair than it has been in the past. We have tended to avoid confrontations where we might have a lot of casualties. It is hard to hide injured men. You see we have the advantage because there will nearly always be some of us from the area where we are operating. They have an intimate knowledge of the terrain. We use that to our advantage. What is most worrying is how far the French have come in so short a time. We shall interrogate before we let any go. It is vital we know all about our enemy."

"How do you think infantrymen managed to get here so soon?" Asked Henri.

"There is a track to the north of us that is passable for wagons. Well it was passable until a few weeks ago, when we blew out most of it, so it is now only suitable for horses or men on foot. I can think of only one logical explanation. They must have been told that they could send men through that pass to try to outflank an English withdrawal. That is precisely why we blew up part of the track. We did not want artillery to be able to use it."

"So how soon do you expect your people to attack?" Asked Will.

"Today, sometime!" Replied Ybarra; with a knowing grin.

Forced to wait, the marines took the opportunity to clean their rifles; to sort out their packs, and to sharpen their sabres, which they carried instead of bayonets.

Will, Henri and Thomas poured over Ybarra's maps. Antonio stayed with his animals, checking each pony very carefully.

It was dark when the first of the guerrillas returned through the secret door to the rear of the monastery hall. It was obvious that they had been successful from their demeanour. It transpired that they had caught the French unit resting in a valley. The officer had been wounded with the first shot. The guerrillas had remained hidden, so the French foot soldiers had no idea from whence the shot had come. Panic had set in when they realised that there was no cover. They were exposed to an enemy who could pick and choose targets. The French had fired blindly in all directions. They had managed to wing one guerrilla in the arm. This had been a ricochet off a rock. As planned Xabier's men had fired single shots from beyond the normal range of a musket. They had aimed low, to incapacitate the French, rather than to kill them. The French had tried to charge an area where they thought the guerrillas were hidden, but had walked right into a trap, where hidden barrels of powder and rock had been ignited, causing mayhem amongst the French troops. When the mounted cavalry had tried a sortie in another direction, they had been cut down by withering fire. As a result, the French had soon thrown down their weapons, when they realised that they had no hope of escape. Their weapons and powder had been taken off them. The wounded had their wounds bound up. They had been ordered to return from whence they had come. At no time had they been allowed to see the exact number of guerrillas present. Rather than keep the muskets the French had thrown down, the weapons were broken in front of them.

Will's party left the following day. Antonio had been advised on the first part of the route, to avoid running into the disarmed French party. This meant that they would have to travel further north than they would normally have done. Just as they were leaving, news arrived that some of General La

Romana's forces had been defeated. According to the report, the General had retired to Leon and left one of his Divisions to hold the bridge across the river Esla. The inexperienced commander left in charge had placed his troops on the wrong side of the river and they had been cut down by Napoleon's cavalry.

The second night was spent under cover courtesy of the monks of the Monastery of Saint Andres, just outside the village of Vega, before they crossed the river over the old bridge reputedly constructed by the Romans. The Monks were full of the news that the English army was retreating just a few miles to the south. To all the party's horror, they were regaled with stories of drunkenness and desertion by English troops.

The weather was getting worse, snow now lay on the mountains, and flurries were reaching them in the valleys. It was a roller-coaster ride. The narrow tracks they followed led them up sides of steep valleys, only to curve round and descend into another valley. The nature of the terrain was forcing them ever closer to the main route to Lugo, which was an obvious place for the English army to confront the French. Will did not want to be caught up in any action; his group would only get in the way. Antonio though only knew the route that led towards the town.

On their way down the steep side of a valley that ran north-south, they spied a group of French horsemen riding in a northerly direction, which made little sense, unless they were trying to find a way to outflank the English. There were about two dozen horse, and because they were slightly ahead and below Will's party they had not yet realised that they were being followed. If they continued on this track, they would in a mile or so, join the track that the French were riding on, but about half a mile behind them. The snow was now coming down heavily, which made keeping sight of the French difficult, but also meant that the sound of their pony's hooves was deadened.

After a quick consultation, they decided it would be possible to trot, which would mean that they would catch up with the French more quickly, but it was unlikely that they would be heard. Ten minutes later, they joined the track behind the French, but already the hoof prints had disappeared. Where the track widened slightly, Antonio pulled to one side and the Marines were ordered forward as they were the best shots. Will gave them instructions to dismount before firing, so their aim would be more certain. Will followed behind the marines, leaving them about a hundred yards ahead, so as not to interfere.

Through the snow Will just saw the first of the

marines swing his leg over the rump of his pony and drop to the ground, quickly followed by the other marines. There were eight single shots, indicating that the marines had chosen their targets, but fired both of their rifles. Will pressed on and as he joined the marines, he dismounted and in the classic kneeling position aimed his rifle at a faint outline of a mounted soldier. He took careful aim and fired, quickly dropping his expended rifle and bringing the second up to the firing position. Beside him, Tucker fired, and gave a whoop of satisfaction.

The French caught in the narrow valley, could only try to out ride their pursuers. The marines were already catching their ponies and remounting to ride after the enemy. Tucker was faster than Will, and was up and away before Will had caught his pony. Henri rode past him grinning hugely.

Lying in their path were three dead French cavalrymen, their horses galloping after the fleeing colleagues. Hard on their heels the marines on ponies more suited to the terrain were fast catching up. Will was worried that in the adrenalin fuelled spirit of the chase that the marines would get too close to their adversaries. He was relieved to see that the Sergeant, leading the chase had slowed. When Will joined Tucker, he found that the Sergeant had wisely stopped his men, and all were dismounting.

"Got to reload!" Shouted the Sergeant for Will's benefit. Tucker, who still had one rifle fully loaded dropped from his pony and crept forward unbidden, to take up a position behind a rock in the lead. Henri, who had not fired his rifles dismounted to take up a position on the other side of the track. Because of the snow, they did not hear the French returning at the charge, sabres drawn. They came out of the curtain of snow straight into the sights of Tucker, Henri and Millward.

Millward had taken up an unusual position. He was still mounted, but had his pony right up alongside a bare tree with his rifle resting on a branch. Will busy reloading glanced up as the riders came through the curtain of snow. Sabres drawn, heads down, screaming at the top of their voices, the French were met with carefully aimed precision. The leading cavalryman fell from his horse, his reins pulling it across the narrow track. As a result, the second rider crashed into the horse, which screamed and kicked out crippling the second horse that went down with its rider underneath it. The track was blocked, but because they had been charging at the gallop, they were unable to stop and all piled into each other. Three veered off, and went plunging down the steep side of the valley, screaming, into the stream at the bottom. By now, the marines had reloaded and were picking off cavalrymen who were trying to get control of their mounts.

One Frenchman somehow produced a pistol and fired it, but the English were out of range. The French at the back, who were able to maintain their seats, turned their horses and cantered away. Cautiously Will led his men forward to administer to the wounded. There were three dead, two dying, and a further four seriously wounded. Amongst them was a moustachioed officer who handed his sabre to Henri as the later bent down to bind up the man's wounded shoulder. The marines remounted and trotted after the retreating cavalry to make sure there was not another futile charge.

Once the wounded had been seen to by Henri, and all their weapons confiscated, Will ordered his band to follow the Marines, taking the French horses, leaving the cavalrymen to make their own way on foot. There was no way of burying the dead in the frozen ground. A few loose horses joined their ponies as Will's group rode off. Totally unsuited to the steep and stony tracks that they were about to follow, they were allowed to drop off and feed on scraps of grass that showed through the deepening snow. It was easy to follow the tracks of the marines and their quarry. Antonio pulled up as they drew level with the marines.

"The Frenchies have gone that way!" Called the Sergeant of Marines.

Antonio consulted his rough map. "Not shown on my map. Probably a goat or sheep track. Too narrow to lead anywhere significant."

The snow was falling so heavily now, it was impossible to see further than a few yards.

"What we don't want is to have those fellows behind us. We probably wouldn't hear them in this weather." Explained Will. "So I think it prudent that we follow them to see where they are going. You ready to lead, Sergeant?"

"Aye Sir!" Replied the Sergeant; manoeuvring his pony into position to head up the narrow track. He pulled one rifle from its scabbard, and rested it across the pony's withers. He then urged his mount forwards up the steep gradient. The others fell in behind, rifles at the ready. The narrow track would have been difficult to follow, had it not been for the remains of the French horses' hoof prints in the snow. The path zigzagged backwards and forwards across the steep terrain. Bare trees, their branches beginning to feel the weight of the snow, grew sparser as they slowly climbed. Finally, the trees receded and they were in open ground, but unable to see beyond a few yards in either direction.

Then they heard voices raised in anger. There was a vicious argument going on somewhere beyond their vision, in French. The Sergeant held up his arm to bring the whole party to a halt. Will joined him and quietly ordered everybody to dismount. Millward was given the pony reins to hold, whilst the rest were dispersed in either direction, with strict instructions not to fire unless they could clearly see that their target was a Frenchman. Will gave his men about five minutes to get into position. Then he shouted in French. "You are surrounded. Throw down your weapons, let go of your horses and you will not be shot. If you try and escape, you are easy meat!"

The arguing ceased and all you could hear was muttering. The French must be well within range for it to be possible in the prevailing weather for them to be heard.

From somewhere; it was impossible to tell from whence, there was a single shot.

Then there was a shout, clearly in French to say that they surrendered. Will indicated with his arms that his men should move forward slowly. Only those either side could see him, but they repeated the signal. Inching forward until he could make out the French cavalrymen huddled together, their horses loosely held by their reins, he was finally able to see that they had stuck their sabres into the ground in front of them. Their arms were held above their heads.

Marines appeared from behind the fifteen Frenchmen, their rifles at the port. Will explained to the prisoners that they were in a very dangerous place. The snow was making it difficult to see where they had come from. They must descend immediately, following the tracks. They would be on foot.

Reluctantly the French set off, their riding boots totally unsuited for the damp snow. Will's party followed on their ponies, leading the shivering French horses. It seemed to take forever until Antonio reined in and inspected the ground closely.

"We are back on the original track. What do you want to do?"

"Does your map show of any settlement up ahead?" Asked Will; rubbing his hands together to try to warm them up.

"There is a river at the end of this track. If there is a river, there could be flatter ground, who knows? If there is flatter ground, then there might just be a farm."

This time Antonio rode in front, his pony probably

better at reasoning out where the track lay, than his human master. At last, the track started to descend, twisting this way and that down the steep side of the mountain. It did not bode well. Finally, they reached the bottom, and through the curtain of snow, they could make out a series of the classic round thatched barns that littered the region. They must be in a narrow valley, cut through the mountains by the fast flowing stream. The prisoners were asked to give their word that they would not try to escape. If they gave their word then they would be fed and given a hot drink. One of the barns was virtually empty. The horses and ponies were herded into this barn, where there was enough hay for them to keep them happy. The prisoners were put in a rather fuller barn, and the door wedged shut. Will's group made themselves comfortable in a third half-full barn.

On Millward's instructions, the marines carefully brushed any remaining hay from an area near the door, which luckily faced away from the wind. Here Millward carefully set about starting his spirit stove. On Will's insistence, the prisoners were the first to be taken hot drinks, and a piece of bread. Then it was the turn of Will's group. The wind had started to get up and was blowing the snow into drifts on the windward side of the barns. Will thought it extremely unlikely that the ordinary French soldier,

A Secret Assignment

without an officer in charge, would try to escape in this weather. Each member of the party drew hay straws to see who would take the various hourly watches. From the entrance to their barn, it was possible to make out the door to the barn in which the horses and ponies were stabled. It was therefore thought unnecessary for the guard on duty to be outside in the freezing cold. If the prisoners were to try and break out they would have to kick down the barn door, which was propped shut with a heavy branch of a fallen tree. If the branch were to fall down, then the cord attached to the top would be jerked alerting the sentry to a possible breakout. Wrapped in their blankets, covered in hay, it was still really too cold to sleep properly.

At first light, there was some relief that the wind of the night had died down. Snow was thick on the ground, but at least you could now see properly. Millward made another series of hot drinks, using the water from the stream. Everybody, including the prisoners was given bread and a piece of hardtack. Will reckoned that the prisoners, set free on foot to make their way back to their own lines, would take three days at least. His party could not be expected to give up all their provisions, but they scrapped together just enough to keep the prisoners going, so long as they eat wisely. Each prisoner was searched to make sure that they had not secreted any weapons, save for small knives. They were allowed to have a pistol and some powder, but no shot. This they would have to use sparingly to start a fire when necessary. Their horses were led out and arranged in pairs for Will's party to lead from their own ponies. The French saddle packs of blankets and clothes were handed over to the prisoners to help them keep warm on their route to freedom.

As the sun made a rare appearance, Antonio led off, followed by Will and then the rest of the party. The French prisoners stood and watched them as they crossed the stream and started up the steep track on the far side. They looked very dejected and uncertain.

When they reached the top of the track, Antonio turned his pony round to come alongside Will's.

"That was a very Christain thing, you did back there. Most soldiers would have shot them!"

"We are sailors – remember!"

"Still I think they will remember you with gratitude."

Chapter 28

Because it was difficult to follow the narrow mountain tracks in the deepening snow, Antonio suggested that they cut south to join up with the road to Lugo. Will studied the map and decided that if the English army were retreating, they would be doing so through Lugo. Although it would be more difficult and take longer, he chose the route through Meira and Vilalba. He hoped that only a few of the units would be directed north about.

As they were about to cross the road between Lugo and Meira, they were challenged in English. Will replied. "A party of English Marines!"

"Oh yer! Advance and be recognised, but no funny business!" Came the reply.

They edged forward, rifles across their pommels. The skirmishing party were standing behind trees, their muskets trained on the advancing riders.

"I am Commodore Calvert, His Majesty's Britannic Navy, returning from a special mission, behind enemy lines. Your Commander is ordered to show himself!" It was said in a commanding voice.

A Sergeant stepped out from behind his tree, his stripes just showing beneath the brown blanket that was wrapped around his body. Will smiled down at him. "We are glad to see a friendly face!"

"Yer, but how does I know if you are who you says you are?"

"A good point, my friend! Obviously I am not wearing uniform. However, this is a Navy sword for you to look at."

The Sergeant stepped forward to inspect the proffered blade. He examined it with care, then looked up at the bearded face of the man sitting on a pony, with two perfectly good horses on leading reins behind. He scratched his head. "Where are you headed for?"

"We are returning to our ship, which we hope is still waiting for us near Corunna. We aim to head for Vilalba, so as not to impede any of our retreating troops. I gather you are protecting their flank."

"Why have you got all those horses, yet you are riding ponies. It doesn't make sense!"

"These are captured French Cavalry horses. We left their riders to return to their units on foot. I don't think it could have been a very pleasant experience. The snow up in the mountains is already getting pretty thick. What is your unit, and if I write a note, could you make sure that it reaches your commanding officer?"

The Sergeant in charge of the Skirmishers nodded. Will pulled out his pad and scribbled a note to say that he and his party had successfully armed the Spanish guerrilla group under signor Ybarra. "What is the situation to the South?" He asked as he passed over the note.

"General Moore has ordered a retreat. We thought we would be making a stand at Lugo, but he has ordered the army to carry on to Corunna. Our orders are to make sure no Frenchies try and use this route to attack the flank."

Whilst Will had been talking to the Sergeant, Tucker, and the Marines had edged forward and started to engage the other skirmishers in conversation. It was obvious to the skirmishers that they had met up with a party of fellow Englishmen, even if they were marines and 'blue-jackets'. A sip of rum from the last of Will's party's stores, helped to seal the bond.

Will quizzed the Sergeant on the state of the English Army, which was bad news. Apparently, a large number of troops had suffered because of the terrible weather; whilst a number had managed to break into wine stores and get so drunk, they had to

A Secret Assignment

be left behind. From this, Will assumed that the moral of the English Army was well below par.

Now that they were on relatively flat terrain, their speed across the ground was much better than before. As a result, they were able to reach Antonio's farm just as the light was fading. They were given an ecstatic welcome by Antonio's wife. From seemingly nowhere she produced a filling meal, washed down by the local tipple. Antonio apologised for not being able to offer them beds to sleep in, but they were all used to hunkering down on straw in barns, which were far more open to the elements than those of Antonio.

The next morning, leaving the captured French horses to glean what they could from the lightly snow covered fields, they continued down to the shore where they had originally disembarked. It said something about the watch keeping aboard *Hound* when almost immediately two cutters were seen pulling away from the ship.

Back aboard *Hound,* they were given an enthusiastic welcome, with many questions asked. Antonio was paid in gold, and 'dined' by the officers. Oscar Cranfield had certainly kept the schooner in first-rate condition, despite the weather. The decks gleamed, the cordage was neatly stowed, and the crew smartly dressed. After Antonio had been put ashore, the anchor was raised and *Hound* sailed across the Ria de Betanos and turned to run towards the town of Corunna. Will was surprised to see that there were virtually no merchant ships anchored off the port. There were a few small Royal Navy vessels at anchor. He assumed that it must be because of the weather and the wind direction. He ordered Cranfield to anchor well into the Ria de Corunna, which would provide some protection from the remains of the swell from the Atlantic. Here they could clearly see what was happening ashore. Troops seemed to be making camp on the hills behind the town. Artillery pieces could occasionally be seen being driven along the road beside the bay. In the town, uniforms appeared to outnumber civilian dress.

Will had himself rowed across to the town, with Lieutenant Tucker in attendance. He wore his best Commodore's uniform. He first went to the English Agent's home, but found that he had left. Not wanting to get in the way, he decided to return to *Hound*. He noted in his diary;

11th January 1809. Anchored off Corunna where the first of the English regiments appear to be arriving. Town full of military, but virtually no merchant ships in the harbour. There seems a good supply of new muskets, as well as boots and other essentials for the English troops. Mayor was seen riding *around on a fine charger. I gather that he is trying to rally the inhabitants of Corunna to support the English military. Understand from questioning ashore that the Army is awaiting transports held up by the weather. I pray to God that the Navy can get here in sufficient strength before the French turn up.*

Hound stayed where she was anchored for the next three days. On the 14th January the bulk of the transports finally appeared escorted the Navy. Will had watched the way the English had arranged their defences. Bent over the chart, he carefully measured out the range of his long barrelled cannons and decided he might be able to give some covering fire if needed to the far bank of the river Mero. He did not want to get into an artillery duel with the French, if they were able to bring up heavy artillery. He ordered that kedge anchors should be laid, so that the stern could be swung either way, so aligning his cannons on possible targets. Instead of their precious heavy main anchor cable, *Hound's* crew laid out two light lines to secondary anchors, which would also help in aligning the cannons. It meant that if necessary, the lines could be chopped clear and the stern kedges used to haul *Hound* out of range of any enemy fire.

Now that there were senior Royal Navy officers in the bay, Will was supposed to be rowed over to report to them. He decided to forgo such a meeting. He reasoned the Senior Officers would have enough to worry about. It was a painful wait, watching the English prepare their defences, whilst boats toiled between the town and the ships anchored off, transporting the sick, artillery, and various non-essential elements of the army. On the 15th the crew witnessed the terrible sight of horses being slaughtered on the cliff top and on the beach. Then the guns opened up, and battle commenced. Because of the smoke from the guns, it was almost impossible to see what was happening ashore. Will ordered one of the cutters under the command of Lieutenant Kemp to be rowed up the entrance to the river Mero, to try to ascertain exactly what was happening.

It was a short trip, as Kemp reported that they had been fired upon by French troops about a mile up the estuary. Lookouts up the foremast kept a running commentary on what they could see. When it became clear that the French were advancing along the shore of the river, *Hound's* forward long barrelled 18 pounders opened up, firing grape at extreme range. The lookouts reported that at first the French withdrew, but that they were concentrating their advance further inland towards the English on the high ground facing them.

Realising that there was little that they could do to

help proceedings, they could not be expected to carry any number of troops, as the schooner would have been unmanageable. They cut the forward anchor cables and using both the stern kedge anchors and the cutters worked *Hound* to a position from which she could set her sails, and use the wind.

On the morning of 16th January, there seemed to be a stalemate. The French did not attack as expected. Aboard *Hound,* they observed a continuous procession of ships boats plying backwards and forwards between the town quay and the various ships anchored in the harbour. Obviously, the evacuation was underway.

Then in the early afternoon, it appeared that the French were attacking the English positions. Throughout the rest of the day, the sound of fighting and heavy guns carried clearly across the water to where *Hound* was anchored. When night fell, the battle seemed to peter out. From the sound of oars splashing in the water, it seemed that the number of boats hurrying backwards and forwards between the shore and the ships in the harbour had increased markedly. The fires on the high ground outside the town continued to burn, which seemed to imply that the English regiments were still in place.

Will sent the jolly boat to investigate. It returned

with the sad news that the British General Moore had been killed and that General Hope was now in command. Apparently, the English were embarking all their troops. The fires were a ruse.

Will ordered *Hound* to be towed nearer the shore, and once again light anchor lines were laid out. As dawn came up, it was clear that the English had forsaken the heights and the last of the troops were embarking. The lookout reported that the French were now on the heights where the English had been the day before. Will had to decide what to do. He was just about to order the ship to sea, when the report came down that the French were hauling heavy artillery up to the top of the heights. If the French could turn their guns on the British ships clustered close to the town, they could wreak terrible damage. He realised that *Hound* was probably the only ship with the firepower to reach the French positions. There would only be a short period, in which *Hound* could interfere with the French positioning of their guns; before their heavy artillery sought out *Hound* in revenge.

The long barrelled cannons in the bows were elevated as far as was possible. They were double charged. Then they started to lob their heavy balls at the French. Then Will ordered that grape should be used, as it would have a better chance of upsetting the repositioning of the French artillery. Once the

French started to fire, the anchor lines were cut and *Hound* swept round and headed for the sea.

Chapter 29

After a fast crossing of the Bay of Biscay, in moderate seas, but biting cold winds, *Hound* finally anchored in the Dart. Will was rowed ashore, where he was greeted with great relief by Lady Calvert and the rest of the family. Pausing for only a day, he then set out for London on horseback. Used to the saddle, but not the gait, he arrived after one night's stop halfway.

He reported to the Aliens Office, rather than the Admiralty. Here he handed over his secret journal. Next, he went to the building alongside, to be greeted with great friendliness by the well-tipped Porter. He was swiftly shown to the office of Lord Mulgrave, the First Lord of the Admiralty, to whom he presented a copy of the same journal. He was then asked to give a verbal description of the battle of Corunna, which was limited as he had been unable to see what had gone on. He was able to report that he thought that the embarkation of the English Army appeared to have been completed successfully. Lord Mulgrave, realising that *Hound* had not been there on 'official business', was happy to accept the journal for his own reading, rather than as official log of the ship. Mulgrave confirmed that as far as the Admiralty was concerned, Will was still on loan to the Aliens Office. He confirmed that he had not been given any indication of what the Aliens Office required of Will.

After leaving the Admiralty, Will returned to the Aliens Office to see Mr. Granger. Granger had yet to read Will's report, but confirmed that with the withdrawal of British troops from the Spanish peninsular there had to be a policy review. He suggested that Will confer with Lord Castlereagh.

Unfortunately, for Will, his Lordship was at the House of Commons. His secretary confided to Will that Castlereagh had to carry more and more of the burdens in the House of Commons, because Lord Portland, the Prime Minister was not well. Will decided to make his way to the House to meet with Castlereagh when he was free.

Because Castlereagh's private secretary knew that Will was a close friend of his Lordship, Will was allowed to wait for the Minister of War in his rooms.

Two hours later, a haggard Castlereagh burst

through the door swearing under his breath. When he spied Will, he stopped in his tracks.

"Will, what a pleasure! Sorry I have been having rather a hard time of it. I think there may be a plot against me. I know it sounds farfetched, but I have been having a lot of trouble with Canning, the Foreign Secretary. He is Portland's son-in-law, you know. What with Portland not being in the best of health, I believe that George Canning is manoeuvring. Such relentless desire for high office is dangerous!"

He gestured for Will to sit back down, as he threw himself into the chair behind his desk.

"Very sad about Moore! Were you at Corunna?"

Will nodded.

"Was it terrible?"

Will then gave a full account of his time in northern Spain, and witnessing the final battle.

"So you actually came face to face with the French military! By God, I shall have to tell Sir Arthur about this. He was singing your praises the other day. Said your reports were succinct and to the point."

They were interrupted by a Commons official.

Castlereagh had to return to the House.

"You go and see that lovely wife of yours. We have a lot to consider this end. I am sure we shall need your talents in the very near future. Have to keep you out of the clutches of the Admiralty; otherwise they will have you wasting your talents commanding a ship of the line going nowhere!"

With that, he was gone. Will hired a mount and set off for Devon and his family.

A Secret Assignment

Boston Harbour

A Secret Assignment

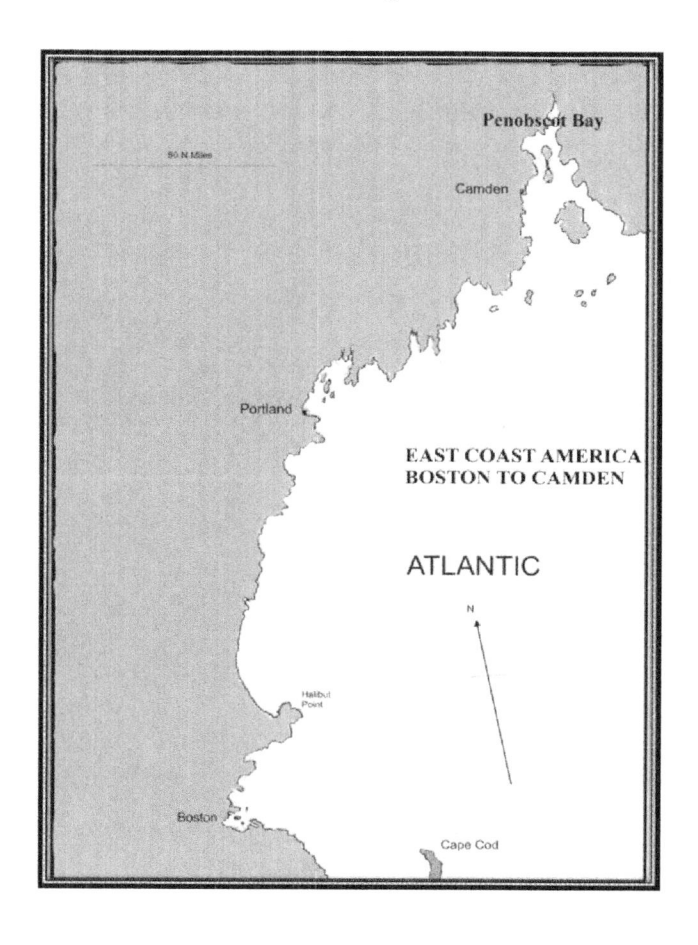

EAST COAST AMERICA
BOSTON TO CAMDEN

ATLANTIC

Penobscot Bay
Camden
Portland
Halibut Point
Boston
Cape Cod

A Secret Assignment

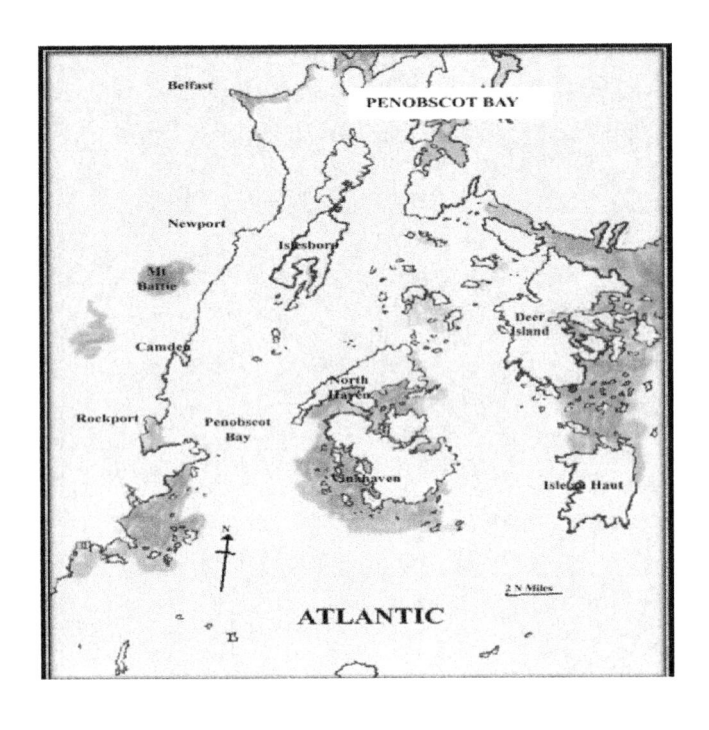

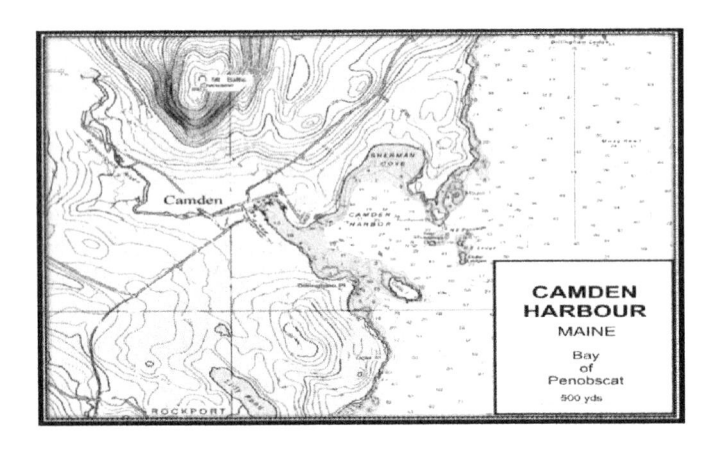

A Secret Assignment

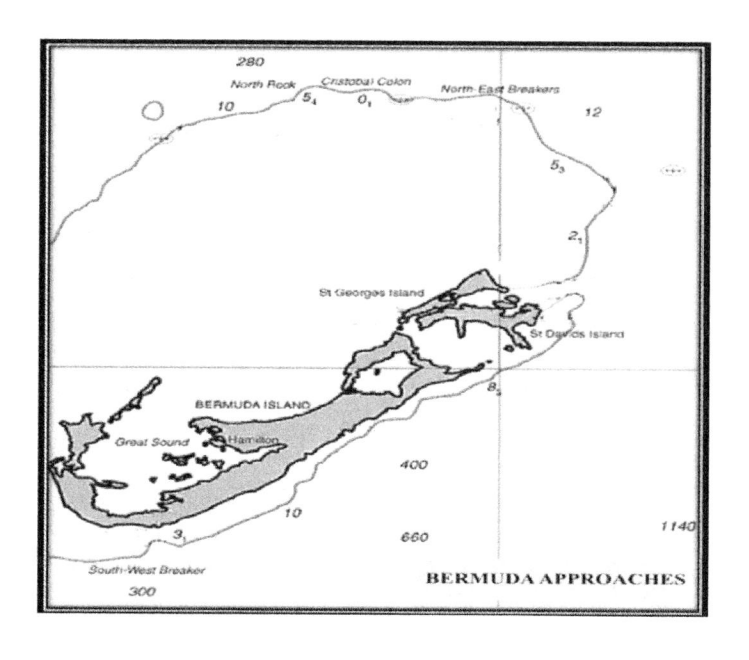

A Secret Assignment

Northern Spain

Map labels: Corunna, Lugo, Cantabrian Mountains, Gijon, Leon, SPAIN, Burgos, Santander, Santona, Sonabia, Bibao, Doniblane, FRANCE, ATLANTIC, N

A Secret Assignment

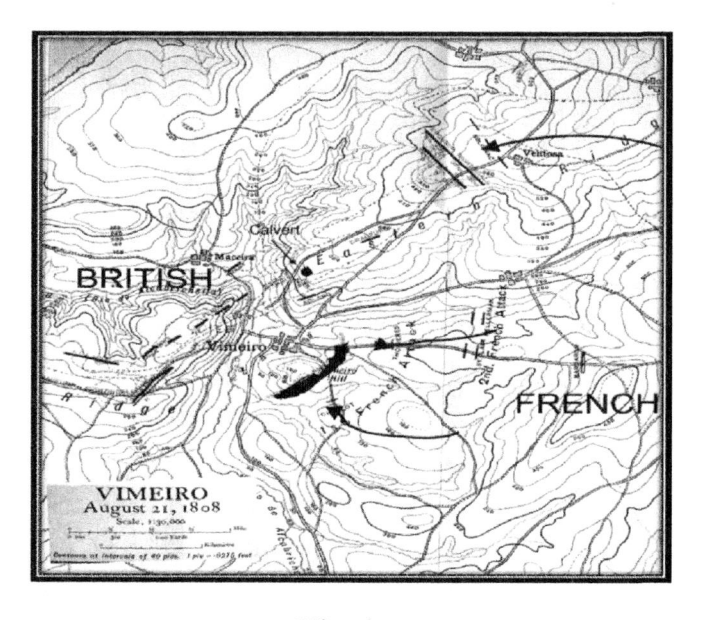

Vimeiro

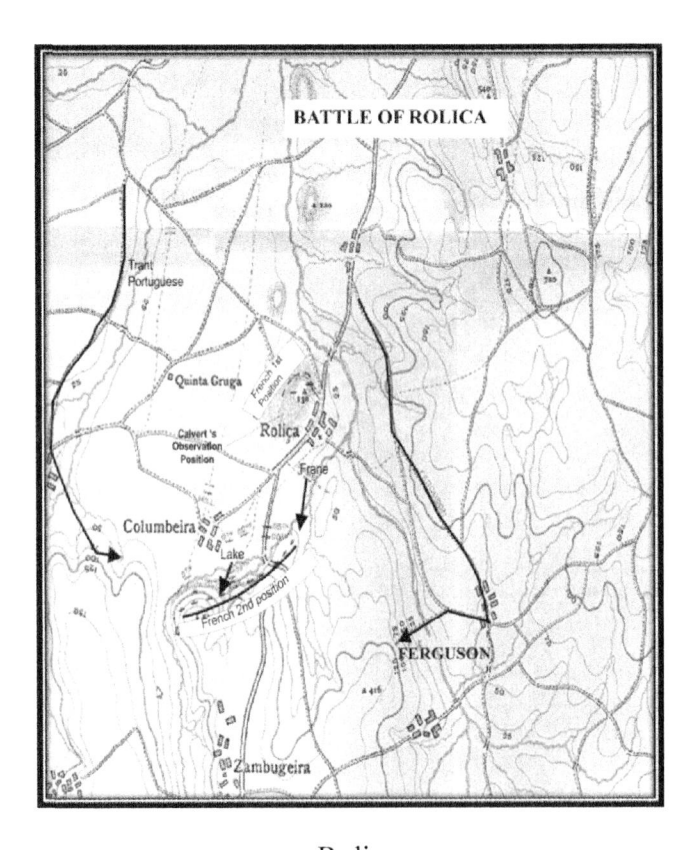

Rolica

Printed in Great Britain
by Amazon